# ACUTE LEFT TURN

## TWO FRIENDS ON A BREATHTAKING JOURNEY TO REDEMPTION

# ACUTE LEFT TURN

## TWO FRIENDS ON A BREATHTAKING JOURNEY TO REDEMPTION

## ROBERT COX

ISBN: 978-0-6453347-8-4

*I dedicate this book to my parents, sisters Gwen and Jude, brothers-in-law Geof and Twig, my sons and darling wife, and to my nieces, nephews, cousins and my entire extended family.*

## About the Author

Robert Cox was born in 1936 and grew up in Rhodesia. He experienced a very happy family life with much travel and adventure. After completing secondary and tertiary education and Army National Service, he took a 'gap' year to Australia and New Zealand – which turned out to be two years! Later, after marrying, he returned to Australia with his wife and two sons, and travelled the entire continent. This life eventually set him into 'writing mode', covering experiences and research from throughout his life.

# Acknowledgments

I would like to thank my parents for their close and loving attention to us 'kids'. Thanks, Mom, for guiding Gwen and Jude through their degrees in music and careers as music teachers, and for always being there when needed by me. From the time I commenced travelling, thank you to writing to me every week no matter where I was in the world!

Thanks, Dad, for always guiding me towards a career in Business Administration and to earning my MBA. Before that, however, in teaching me woodwork and simple building techniques. Congratulations for your eminence in the community and for your award of the BEM (British Empire Medal).

I would also like to acknowledge my wife's family — who were well known to my parents — for their love of their daughter, grandchildren and myself.

# *Prologue*

R od Cochrane was born and raised in the small Central African 'railway hub' town of Aberfoyle: a very progressive town, which was also the Administrative Centre for that Province. Son of a well-known family with business interests in the town, he also had two sisters, one older named Jacqueline (Jacky), and the other younger, named Caroline (Carry).

Right from the start, and certainly from year two, he had his eldest sister and parents on the run. Slightly but athletically built, he was everywhere but where he should be! At the age of four Jacky taught him to ride a bicycle, in an amusing sequence that has never left his mind.

She had him out on the front pavement of their property, which was situated opposite the Municipal buildings with their curved, sealed drive-in to the protected entrance and beautiful neatly hedged gardens with elaborate pond.

1

Actually, the property had streets around three sides. She coached him with the following instructions, "Okay Rod, your turn to learn to ride. These are the handlebars for steering, and these are the pedals to push around — to get going, and these are the brakes — squeeze them to stop."

"Okay, I'll hold the 'bike' upright: you get on. Are your feet on the pedals? Right!" … and running forward she gave him a mighty push, shouting, "Pedal Rod!" That was instruction over, and he was riding hell for leather towards the corner which, when he reached it, was un-navigable at speed. Bit of a crash? But so what …! That was neither here nor there for those kids, and he was now able to ride a bike.

A short time after the learning spell, aged five, he was wheeling his bike out to the side street and planning a fast ride around the block. He whooped loudly, "Let's go!" and he was soon racing down the pavement of the side road. He was very aware of all the small trees on the edge, flying in the opposite direction and got caught-up in the excitement of this bike riding, when suddenly he saw a car reversing out through a thick hedge and across the pavement.

His senses screamed, "Brake hard!" But they were too late and his speed was too fast and he crashed into the back wheel of the Town Mayor's car and was thrown backwards onto the pavement. Fortunately, being extremely light-weight he was not hurt.

Before he could stop himself he called out, "Why don't you look where you're going?" Clearly the Mayor was most shocked and distressed to be involved in an accident with a kid, but Rod was most indignant because the front wheel and supports had broken off the bicycle.

He received an "I'm sorry," from that worthy gentleman, who then in decency added, "Well, at least we can load you and the pieces of your bike into the car and take all of you to your home." On arrival and after unloading, the Mayor carried the pieces and made sure that Rod was wheeling the bike. They progressed down through the garden, and on arriving at the verandah the mayor put down the pieces and knocked on the door.

It was Rod's Mum who opened the door and greeted the mayor, whom she knew. He replied, "Hello Mrs. Cochrane, I've brought Rod back: he's had an accident against my car. Unfortunately he didn't see me coming through the hedge and because of its thickness, neither did I see him."

By this time Rod's Dad had also come to the door and replied, "Thank you Sir, we really appreciate it and hope that neither of you have been hurt?" Once they had ascertained this, the three adults realised that it was an amusing event that they would always be able to recall amongst the two families.

Jacky, Rod and Carry all attended the local Pre-School, Kindergarten and Primary School in their successive years. While progressing through 'Pre-School' and 'Kinder' grades, Rod had no problems: essentially because the buildings were close together and all the kids were confined within a small yard. From the time that he entered Primary School however, things changed, as there were now 'Borders' and Dayskies' in the school. He did not enjoy those years, for he suffered minor bouts of both physical and psychological bullying. This could have been due to his slight stature and the fact that he was young for his class.

His escapism from this was to mount his bike — or later his horse — and to ride all around the outskirts of the town: the hills, the dales, the Industrial areas and the Railtown. It was during these excursions that he got to know the extent of the town so well that he repeatedly confounded people with this knowledge. For instance he knew the exact path of a very old 'Mining' rail route from the beginning of the century, before the town started to grow. He was able to explain, and prove the exact route that it used to follow through the town. Sometimes he took friends or members of the family out and actually showed them bits of ancient rail, sleepers and track nails.

On one occasion his claims were ridiculed. So he asked the 'offender' to point in the direction of the close mining town, and then said, "Okay follow me." They rode their bikes in that direction and at the end of a 'No through Road' in one of the town's new elite suburbs, and in thick bush on the far side, was the continuation of this old rail route to the Mine.

In much the same vein, very few of the inhabitants knew anything about the town's river of the same name. Where it rose or where it went after it passed the town. Again, Rod could give a very clear answer to any such questions.

# CHAPTER 1

When he was about five years of age his parents employed an experienced African Maintenance man, Jonno Filagwa, who had a young son by the name of Mukwe. He was much the same age as Rod. They immediately became firm friends and as it turned out, the friendship was to last a lifetime.

Soon after they started playing with one another, a couple of incidents occurred that totally bonded them as friends. Early one morning just after breakfast and the departure of Rod's Dad to his workplace, Rod headed out into the back garden of the property. Because it was so early it didn't occur to him to rouse Mukwe, who was probably having breakfast with his family anyway. He ventured past the banana tree and the orchard to a serene area of short-cut grass and mature trees. One of medium height was an indigenous Msasa; then there was a tall mature

'Kenyan Koffee' tree. There was also a sprinkling of Gum trees — all of which made an impressive clump. With the sun having only just risen, the gums were throwing deep shadow on the rest; but the 'Koffee Shade' tree stood boldly and shimmering above all the others. Walking towards them he acknowledged in his mind that he had already climbed the Msasa, so decided that he would have to climb one of the higher trees.

While viewing them and the job at hand, many other thoughts and recollections were running through Rod's mind, and he expressed these, "Why do most of the boys at school scorn and ignore me to the extent that they do? It's not as if they live better or more exciting lives than I do — in fact they don't explore or discover, to anything like the extent that I do, or that Mukwe and I do. Maybe that's it. They are casting a racist view on me and Mukwe, even though he goes to a separate African school. Or maybe they just get together and kick a footy or hit out with cricket bats. If that's what they do, it's pretty disappointing that they don't invite us to join them." "Ugh! to hell with them — I've got a 'Kenya Koffee' tree to climb."

So Rod pulled off his runners ('tackies' — locally ) and started climbing. The lower part of the trunk was fairly easy with plenty of branches to grab hold of, and clamber onto. However, the higher he got the harder it became and he had to do some monkey-like creeping-up with legs and arms around the trunk to get to the next branch. After a couple of these ascents, he noticed that the big branch that he had clambered onto stretched straight out to the side. He exclaimed loudly, "Wow! that'll be beaut. I'll bum my way out along it, then turn around and come back."

What he didn't realise was that the further he went along it — at about eight to nine metres above ground — his weight would cause it to sag. When this happened he was lucky, in that there was the branch of a neighbouring tree immediately below him, so he opted for the lower one — Oops!. The branch that he had vacated shot up and out of reach. Calamity ...! the branch that he was now sitting on was too difficult to work his way along. A loud bellow followed — "Mom, Mukwe, any passer-by! help"

Mukwe was the first to hear, and came tearing out from his breakfast followed by his father. He quickly noticed that his mate was high up in the branches, and exclaimed "Hey Rod!" what ya doing way up there — ya punce? Only birds are supposed to be up there: come-on fly down."

Rod's Mother was the next on the scene. The two adults made a quick assessment and decided that they could rescue the situation. Meanwhile Mukwe climbed a little way up this 'new' tree, saying, "Okay cool it, we'll get you out of this." Mukwe's father raced off to get a long length of tow rope, while Rod's mother called-up that they would concentrate on the tree that Rod was currently clinging to. Having been given the rope Mukwe shunned further up the tree, this time to Rod's branch, and worked his way along it with legs hanging down but could only get to within three metres of Rod.

Viewing it from way below, the adults worked out that Mukwe had to tie the rope very securely to the branch in front of his position. This he did, then said, "No problems Rod, you'll be out of this in a few minutes." Then Jonno instructed: "Mukwe throw the rest of the rope across to Rod." "Now Rod take up the slack. Pass it all over your right shoulder and under your left arm. Now pass the rest of the rope around your waist from the left, and back to the front." He then checked if there was still slack, and continued his instructions to Rod, "next you must tie the slack in a knot to the rope coming from Mukwe." Rod tied a double-knot to make sure.

The adults then consulted again and Rod's Mum said, "Rod you're okay, because even if it does slip you will only drop a little way and will be hanging from your chest." Mukwe was then advised to start gently pulling on the rope, and Rod to lie forward and go with it. The rescue then commenced and with slow progress and some tears, Rod reached safety and was helped by Mukwe, first to the trunk and then down to the ground. He vowed and promised (albeit with his fingers crossed behind his back) that he would not attempt such a crazy stunt again.

* * *

It was in this vein that things proceeded for the next year or so. Both Rod and Mukwe were fully into Primary schooling by then, even though they were at different schools. There were three semesters in each year, and their respective parents expected appropriate application by each of them, to the schooling and homework that had to be done in each semester.

The holidays were something else though: and the children of each family made the most of them. Usually rising soon after the sun, 'burning it' all day and getting back just before dinner — or just after — to the annoyance of Mothers. The Cochranes' often visited greater family in the district to join up with cousins. Rod's sisters were seriously into music lessons by then, which took up much of their time, but much to his regret later in life, Rod showed no such inclination. This gave him and Mukwe the opportunity to venture out around the town and district, either on bikes or horses, and to further extend their geographic knowledge of the district.

It was during this period also that they both experienced a desperate and exciting event whilst out in the bush with Rod's two uncles. A friend and associate of the two men had invited the group to come out to his ranch for a short hunting trip. On arrival, and after a quick lunch, the group headed out into the thick bush on foot, following game trails. It was wild country, with heavily forested hills and steep ridges disappearing northwards, alternated with wide grasslands. The broad spectrum incorporating every shade of green and gold imaginable, impressed and livened the senses of the two boys.

Walking behind the adults, the two boys chatted excitedly with Mukwe suddenly expressing, "Chee...z! Look at those hills disappearing away into the distance — starting off green with the bush, then light blue and finally dark blue. I've never seen anything like that before."

Rod totally agreed saying, "Yes, and the sky is also much bluer out here than in town." He had also observed a couple of eagles flying high up in the clear atmosphere and added, "I wonder how far away the nest is, belonging to those eagles. Wouldn't it be great if we came across it?" They all walked through this savannah for miles, and although they saw much game out in the distance, on this occasion none were sighted close enough to shoot. Neither did they discover the eagle's nest, which was a great disappointment.

Eventually the owner: looking at his watch said. "I'm afraid the hunt is not going to work-out today, but I'm sure there will be many more opportunities in the future." Having walked a broad loop, they arrived back at the ranch centre, empty handed.

Soon after their return a very heavy summer storm threatened and they were all amazed at the clamour, as it ravaged over the ranch. This fact however imposed somewhat of a predicament on the Uncles, and the host. How to navigate off the ranch and back to the main road

— in their little Ford Model A vehicle?!

Sure enough when they reached the stream it had almost become a river over the concrete drift, flooding strongly at about knee depth of an adult. The ranch owner had a much newer 'pick-up' truck and said, "My pick-up is diesel, so I think I'll test out the causeway crossing. I don't think I'll have any problems." He was quite right in his assessment and reached the other side without any form of mishap.

A loud and animated discussion between the three men flowed across the flood, mainly focused on the risk to the two kids, but also because the river was still rising. Rod ventured, "If I went further up-stream, I could swim across." None of the adults would have a bar of this, and he apologized to all — principally because he realised that he had not been thinking of Mukwe, when he talked-up.

Fortunately Rod's uncles were mechanics, and they all concurred that a long rush at the water, with doors open and kids clutched high, would be successful. It was thus that Rod's Uncle Fred shouted over the noise of the floodwaters, "Okay! Into the car we jump, and you boys climb on top of Cecil and I but leave the doors wide open." The car plunged into the river on the track of the concrete drift; made good progress — notwithstanding the water raging through it — and spluttered out of the other side, then stalled!

There was much loud and congratulatory back slapping, followed by emptying of the seat wells in the car, and the drying of the spark plugs. Once the parties had seen the rancher safely back on his side, they headed back to town feeling well satisfied (and relieved!) over the great day out.

It was a day that Rod and Mukwe would revel about to their friends, for months to come.

# *CHAPTER 2*

About a year later, a particular event occurred that caused quite a stir — as well as reprimands for each of the boys. What took place however gave Rod the opportunity to repay his debt to Mukwe in full, for the tree climbing episode. Rod was returning from a day out at his cousin's family farm which was about eleven kilometres from the town. Having ridden out on his bike that morning and having spent a great day with Rick, Ed and Kathy, Rod had left the farm at about 4.00pm so that he would get back in daylight. A bit tight on timing, but in his mind he felt confident because it was a sealed road. Also he was pretty fast on the bike, and he would take the little-known shortcut back home.

When he reached the point along the road where the shortcut turned off, he turned into it but felt a strong premonition of trouble. "What could it possibly be?" he exclaimed out loud, "I can't remember hearing anything bad about the track, or the river-crossing." He watched the surface of the twisting track for bad erosion or man-made obstructions, as well as the grasslands on each side in case of snakes or other pests. What he didn't expect was to meet Mukwe down in the 'muddy doldrums' of the track — just as it crossed the river.

The latter was on a mission by bike to the outskirts of the town, arranged by his father. He was about to explain when Rod in a fit of excitement said, "Gee Wizz! Muk, what's so important as to send you out alone to the outskirts of town? It's quite a long way out there, you know?"

When Mukwe gave the name of the people, Rod was more than surprised because they had a very torrid reputation in the town. Having joined him, off they went in that direction. While riding along, Rod said " Hey! Mukwe what exactly did your Dad ask you to do, because it seems a little strange to me?"

"Why do you say that? I think it's got something to do with picking up an envelope for my Dad."

That deepened the suspicion in Rod's mind. So he said, "You told me last week that you had witnessed a bad fight in town, from quite a distance away, and you had noticed a guy being knocked down and out." Mukwe agreed that he had. "Well, said Rod, my Dad read out to us from the newspaper, that that person had been admitted to hospital because of the terrible 'bashing' he had received. Do you think that the sons of these people that you're going to see, could have been responsible? It wouldn't surprise me."

"Hells teeth," said Mukwe, "it didn't even enter my head that it would have anything to do with that fight. S__t! Do you think we should carry on?"

They talked about it and eventually Rod said, "Yeh ...! I'll just keep in the background."

The direct route that they followed enabled them to avoid the many Left turns, Right turns of the suburbs. It was passable only on bikes (or horses) and took them between the beautiful green Racecourse and the stables, before it got them onto the outer town road. Mukwe with head down and a feeling of impending doom, noted that a lot of the properties along the road were in pretty bad shape. He pondered again as to whether he and Rod should pursue this venture, and just what sort of people could allow this sort of deterioration. This increased his dread.

Some twenty minutes later they arrived at the last property which was on the corner. It was quite large, heavily treed and with a big heavy gate — that was open. They got off their bikes and walked them in until they got near to the house.

As Mukwe started to walk towards the door it opened and two tough looking individuals came out: one in his early twenties and the other a 'late teen'. "What do you want?" they challenged. Mukwe advised that he had come to get some 'paper' thing for his dad, and gave the name. "Who's that with you? — you were supposed to come alone." came the retort.

He merely said, "It's my new friend Rod. I met him on the road while I was coming here."

"Rod who?" the elder one interjected. Mukwe replied that he didn't know. because they had only just met. Rod was not prepared to add anything — coming from the well-known family.

"Bullshit!" said the older one, "We want to know who you've told about the fight that you saw." Mukwe told them that he had only told his Dad about it. This didn't satisfy them and the younger one threatened that if they talked to anyone else, they would get beaten-up. "You've screwed up." said the older brother "We'll give you a lot more than the paperwork for your Old Man." With that he turned to go back into the house, adding to the younger one as he went, "Bant, go and lock the gate."

Luckily there was a high hedge and tree between them and the gate, so as soon as Bant was out of sight and with the older one still inside, Rod grabbed Mukwe and said — "I know where we are; quick, pick up your bike and follow me over that low wall on the side fence line." They raced across like a flash, with Rod piling over and taking both bikes from Mukwe, who was following.

However, no sooner were they over than the brothers got back into view. All hell broke loose amongst the brothers — the older one armed with a whip shouted, "You can't get away from us. We'll chase you in the pick-up and bloody shoot you when we catch you." Obviously they thought that the boys would ride hell for leather down the suburban road, to try and get away.

Rod had other plans, for he knew of a shortcut down an unused narrow wooded lane towards town. They reached it within thirty seconds and were making their getaway when Rod suddenly said, "We've got to hide for a short spell, Muk, until their car goes down the street. Get in behind here, now!" and he pointed behind a dense head-height bush.

Once the brother's car shot past the opening they continued down the series of tight, bendy lanes and across the Racecourse towards the forbidden river crossing, where they had met that afternoon. En-route Rod muttered to himself, "Those brothers were probably going to 'buy' Mukwe's silence, and thereby cover their guilt." On putting this supposition to Mukwe, the latter agreed, and apologized for getting Rod into such a fracas. Meantime they were going to have to hurry as the sun had already set.

On arrival home, at about 7.00pm — trouble, with a capital 'T'! The police had been called out, as a result of Rod's absence. Rick's family on the farm, had advised that he had left there at just before 4.00pm. Although there was terrific relief at seeing both boys, they got severe reprimands, and each learnt a lot from such a foolhardy escapade. Mukwe's parting comment was "Now we are even."

The day was also significant for the fact that the 'bashing' victim, had been able to accuse the two brothers, from whom Mukwe and Rod had nearly 'met their Waterloo'. The brothers were arrested a couple of days later and ultimately jailed. The family of the jailed men faced such disgrace in the town due to the nature of the case, that they fled from the town, whilst the sons were still in jail.

# CHAPTER 3

The next few years passed much as before, with all the kids being extremely active. A particular process between the two boys was that Mukwe was teaching Rod to speak his African language. There was no real political progress towards racial integration so Rod and Mukwe remained at separate schools. Jacky and Carry continued with their music, whilst Rod added swimming training (whites only) to his programme. Mukwe's school were promoting soccer as their principal 'out of school' activity for their boys, and he became dedicated to that sport.

All of them tested a bit of casual romance during this period, but analyzing it later the general consensus was not brilliant: none got to the hugging and kissing stage!

When Rod had just turned nine, with sister Jacky well into her tenth year and Carry just seven the family took over the small farm by the name of Fairhill, which had previously been held by the Parents and a Sister of Rod's mother. This was the same little farm, eleven kilometres out of town, which was previously mentioned. Mukwe's family (with his Dad being Maintenance man) also combined in the move, as they would all be critically required to assist in getting the project 'under way'.

Rod's Mom and Dad and family, just loved the fact that they had been able to purchase Fairhill. It was situated up fairly high, and had a glorious view back over the town and the range of hills. The property was 100acres in size, with about half of it being beautiful Msasa forest and the other half open savannah. At that early stage it was not fenced — nor were any of the properties still further from the town. The buildings on Fairhill were adequate, other than the Homestead — which was exceptional. It was a large double-brick, three-bedroom home with separate dining and lounge areas and all the necessary support rooms, but its principal features were the high fully thatched roof, and all stable-type doors. It had no ceilings, because the inside of the high thatched roof lay on wire netting and exceptional treated gum poles. These provided a unique supporting feature.

Much immediate work had to be done to the house and to external buildings: It was also vital to provide an access port for the kitchen's new Esse wood/coal burning stove, through the necessary high external chimney. The main Carport was also significantly enlarged to provide additional parking and to incorporate a Workshop.

The kids all continued in the same Primary Schools, and activities remained as before. Jacky and Carry were fortunate in that they befriended two sisters, Florina and Anne, who lived a couple of kilometres down the road of the same outer suburb. Transport into town each day and return each evening, was of course extra. To Rod and Mukwe this move opened up new horizons — when not swimming or playing soccer with the other town kids. Their horses were now stabled much closer and they were able to explore further and further afield.

In retrospect, a factor that inhibited much of the initial free-range thinking of the kids, as well as gardening and crop farming by the parents, was a distinct water shortage on the property. It was situated on an ancient volcanic ridge, and as such the water was extremely difficult to access — either by well, or borehole. For this reason alone, they all started out by having to collect extra water from a neighbouring farm by... 'Donkey Power'!. Initially, not even a water cart was used — that was stage Two! To start off with the donkeys carried shaped leather containers, on each side of a saddle arrangement, and these were filled three or four times a day and transported back by the donkeys,. When they arrived, the water was poured out into 'cooking', 'washing/showering' and 'laundry' mini-tanks.

Rod's Mother and Father as well as Mukwe's Dad quickly realised that this was not sustainable. So his Dad (who was very mechanically minded), worked away at designing a self-made Boring Machine. Fortunately all components (and extra advice) were obtainable at the Motor Vehicle workshops, of which he was an Executive.

In quick order heavy steel framing up to a length of five metres / plus cross supports, as well as a five tonne truck chassis, diesel engine and gearbox were procured. The first stage was to fill four forty-four gallon drums with concrete. The next to secure the truck chassis with gearbox, engine and drive mounted in-line, on top of them. The final stage for the operation was to align all this with the five metre "Drop-Tower". Mr Cochrane then designed and fitted an elliptical drive wheel with a V edge, to take the heavy steel cable. This was attached to the sharpened and hardened steel Drop Bar for the actual boring process. This drive wheel gave the drop bar about 60 centimetres lift, for each drop. The Drop Bar attendant would then twist the bar half a turn on each lift, before the next drop.

Many holes were bored over a six month period, but it was only in the last month or so that two of the bores struck water. The reason for the failures was due to the drop bar striking the volcanic rocks on a downward edge, and just slipping down the edge of the ultra-hard rock. In some of these cases the heavy bar jammed and had to be very carefully winched out.

After this had occurred a few times, Mr. Cochrane was deeply concerned and he ventured out to the corrupted bores, accompanied by Rod. It was here that he noted just how downcast his Dad was; but that he was also deep in thought and obviously planning varied solutions. On one occasion Rod remembers his Dad speaking, "If we poured down a large bucket-full of strong concrete into each of these affected shafts, would that solve the problem?"

When Rod was about to answer the question, his Dad suddenly said, "Oh! I'm sorry Rod — I was just voicing what was flowing through my mind."

Because Rod had liked the idea his reply was, "Sounds good to me."

Much consultation took place with the hands-on Operators; with the senior one pointing down and adding, "When the concrete has dried hard, we will break into it using the 'drop-bar' at ninety degrees to the slope of the ledge down there." They used this technique and succeeded with the two shafts — although the second one took a couple more applications.

It was during this period that Rod was given his first puppy, Monty, an Alsatian/Collie cross. It was delivered to the property, and in no time skedaddled down to where many of the abandoned bores existed. In typical puppy trait, racing around chased by Rod and Mukwe, he fell into one of the abandoned holes that had been filled with soil, but which had turned to soft, soft mud. Fortunately the particular hole was only a metre deep, and Rod pulled the puppy out by its tail, within a second. Much quick washing of head and nose followed, and Monty was fine. As soon as he was able to see, and had had a good splattering to get the mud out of his mouth, he eyeballed Rod and with happy lolling tongue, licked his face: unmistakably passing a message between them saying, "Okay so you're the one; you'll look after me, and I'll look after you!" It goes without saying that from then onwards every abandoned hole was covered with a strong lid.

In conclusion, The Cochrane family got its water supply, but in the early days, never enough for irrigation purposes. And on the connection that Monty had with the water search, in later years the close and loving bond that that existed between them, would re-shape Rod's and Mukwe's lives forever.

# CHAPTER 4

O ver the next two to three years life continued peace-fully and happily on the Fairhill property, for the Co-chrane family and for Mukwe and his family. All the kids progressed through Primary School, and for the Par-ents much progress was made towards sustainable garden-ing and cropping. Jacky and Carry advanced their musical prowess, whilst Rod and Mukwe continued with their sport.

During the Christmas holidays after completing Primary School, Rod and Mukwe were walking through the bush with Monty, when 'out of the blue' Mukwe asked, "Rod, what do you remember most clearly since we have all been out here, at Fairhill?"

Rod thought about it for a few moments — "The trip that the family made — accompanied by our cousin — when we were on our way to Lake Fairy. Mum and Dad were in the front of the car with Carry, whilst Jacky and I were in the back with Laurie. Suddenly there was a 'whoosh' and Jacky was no longer there."

"Holy mackerel!" said Mukwe, "How could that happen: surely she must have been badly hurt?"

"Well it was the inward facing door in the old 1937 Chevvie. It just flew open with the wind force, and she went with it. No, she wasn't badly hurt — probably because it was a dirt road and Dad wasn't travelling too fast. I looked out the back window and she was already getting up and beginning to run after us."

"No more picnicking at the lake, hey!?" said Mukwe.

"You're right," countered Rod, "my parents had to take her straight to the hospital, for a check-up. Amazingly enough she was okay, except for a couple of minor scratches. So much for that though, what really stands out most in your memory Muk?"

He was ready for that and said "Apart from building extra houses, kitchens and sculleries for all of us, that experience when I nearly trod on that massive Black Cobra snake, whilst you and I were walking down by that little dam, on the next property."

"Hell yes! I remember that countered Rod, "by the time I saw it you were right up to it, and for sure I thought you were going to tread straight onto it. As you say, it would have been well over two metres in length, and about as thick as your forearm. As things turned out, it just slid quietly away into the longer grass."

"Man we've been lucky with snakes on so many occasions, haven't we?" said Mukwe. "Remember you had a close shave with a Rinkals, didn't you?"

"Yes!" "And remember that big Puff Adder on the verandah, that got right under the chair that Mrs. Frost was sitting in. If it hadn't been for Uncle Stan convincing her to walk straight towards him, without asking questions, who knows what might have happened."

Many more memories and recollections were brought up by each. Suddenly Mukwe started laughing, and couldn't stop until he was able to retell the funny event that happened when their mutual friend Will was visiting. "We were all there playing 'quickest on the draw', with toy pistols. Us boys had established a 'one-two-three, draw and fire', to establish the fastest pistol drawer."

"Just when we were getting close to recognizing an eventual winner, Jacky joined us and was fascinated by the contest. She asked to be given 'a go', and was matched against Will (who, in retrospect, we have always felt could see a humorous end to the matching). The exact rules were explained to her, and the pair got into position to 'fight it out'. The flag was dropped (figuratively) and the count started." Except that for Jacky it was "One, two, BANG! Three." "True to form, Will dropped as if 'shot dead', and everyone just collapsed laughing, including Jacky, who said that she had not meant to corrupt the game!"

With vivid memories tumbling through minds, Rod said,

"On not such an amusing note, at the time; remember that night a couple of years ago when that grass fire whipped through, and you and I were posted to the side of the fire — after the front had passed — to extinguish the flames there?"

"Yeh!, I do," said Mukwe, "

all the properties around here were very lucky to escape serious losses."

Rod replied, "For sure, as well as every person involved. You may recall however that in my case it was a different 'let-off'. We had succeeded in putting out the fire on a certain stretch and were walking further back through heavy bush, to an area that was still alight. In the total darkness I stepped into an old abandoned mine shaft, which, thank God was only about two metres deep on the side that I fell into."

"Bloody hell!" do I remember that? "I suddenly realised that I was talking to myself. Two metres, or more, wouldn't have mattered. You were jolly lucky that I was with you and able to help you get out of that hole."

After that particular day of recounting memories, there were many more when they were all together, or when Rod and Mukwe were out riding or hunting, with Monty. Jacky and Carry were always occupied with their music, and with their friends the Frosts, down the road. At the weekends the boys would go into town to watch sport and catch-up with their friends. Looking back, time just flew and the next thing that they knew was that the first term of Secondary

School was upon them. The boys were off to Boarding Schools down in another Province, whilst the girls attended the local High School.

# CHAPTER 5

The start of High School for the two boys was pretty exciting, in that they had to get there by train. The journey took a day and a bit, and there were two changes of trains. They also agreed that it was interesting meeting up with so many other lads from surrounding towns. If nothing else, they would be able to look forward to the return train-journey!.

Rod and Mukwe, as well as Rod's cousin Rick, were sent to particular Male 'bush' Boarding Schools because the School's had excellent reputations for academic and sporting results. No doubt due to the fact that they were confined, and had many dedicated staff both teaching, and looking after the boys. Mukwe was enrolled at a separate all African, Anglican School. It was not far however, from Rod's school: about fifteen kilometres away, with the Undwani River separating the two schools.

Within two weeks they had arranged to meet at the river, on the Sunday. The scheme was to fish for Black Bass, and they found it well stocked — giving each of them some success. Over the ensuing years they often met at the river to continue their addiction for the bass. It was also great to meet the other kids, and to join in sporting activities and games with them.

The first month of the first term was pretty intense for each of them, with everything being strange, and the schools being so big and spread out compared to what they knew. Initiation ceremonies were still practiced against the new boys. As each 'newby' was brought before the loud and taunting audience of third and fourth 'Middles', he was expected to tell jokes; recite nonsense the middles had dreamt-up — to belittle the teller, or to sing appropriate songs. If the audience were not satisfied the atmosphere descended to a state of psychological bullying. Somehow Rod felt that he had got off fairly lightly in this fiasco, and could only attribute it to elder cousin Rick's reputation: summarized in a few words it would have been a threat of, "You beat-up my little cousin, and I'll beat the hell out of you!"

Amazingly this was all halted permanently by Government decree, during that first term.

Neither of the boys shone at cricket, unlike the many who had been playing the sport for years. Both dropped out and took up tennis in the summer terms. However, Mukwe's school practised soccer in every term and he made the first team of his age group. In the winter term Rod played rugby, but due to his extra light build he didn't make first team of his year. He continued playing it though, throughout his high school years because he rated it a wonderful game.

One area of the school's sports in which he was right up among the best, was swimming and he got plenty of opportunities to compete. Strangely enough, although he personally felt that freestyle was his strength, it was breaststroke in which he was champion. Throughout his years in Grey House at the school, they won the Inter-House swimming against the other four houses.

Both Rod and Mukwe enjoyed Sunday of every week, because they could book out (officially) and go bush for the day — if they weren't away playing sport. These outings were often with other kids of like mind, and they could obtain a lunch pack from their respective school kitchens. Add coffee and condensed milk to that lunch pack, and they were set for the day out!.

As mentioned, they would meet at the Undwani River but could go to many other places from there. There were many streams and little dams in every direction from the schools; all of which they very soon became acquainted. The main 'culprit' leading to this, was Rod's cousin Rick who was a year ahead of them in school. It was not surprising that he had the 'go-bush' urge, in that his family were farmers, on extensive acreage. He was effectively the leader of any group that included Rod and Mukwe, and as a large and respected member of the school, imposed strict rules for the outings and put up with no 'bullshit'.

The academic side progressed well for each of them: once they had settled down the teachers in their respective schools, ensured that the boys applied themselves to their studies. Quite naturally Rod and Mukwe helped one another, and if either were 'stumped' cousin Rick would also help-out. At the end of every Term exams were held, and by the end of the year both had frequently managed 'top-three' positions.

All of them really looked forward to school holidays, and getting home to catch-up with sisters and family. There was always plenty of work to do on the property, but also plenty of time to go riding on their favorite routes. Both of them would head into Aberfoyle each Saturday, to watch their local teams play sport — some of the members of which, were their heroes from the past.

Whilst helping Rod's Mom with grape-vine pruning during the Christmas Holidays, at the end of their first year of schooling away from home, Rod and Mukwe were recalling some of their experiences, about their respective Boarding Schools. Rod asked, "Muk, what were some of the things that most struck you, or that you will never forget about your School?"

Mukwe thought about it then said, "Our weekend 'away' journeys with the soccer team, were amazing in that they were so well planned. Apart from the game venue, we always had good accommodation and meals. The train trips were also great, as you can imagine — something about the noise of the wheels on the track!! I was also surprised at how clean and well organized the school was, plus the strong emphasis on the Bible, and attendances at church. How about you Rod? What lifted you most — compared with here at home?"

Rod had already worked out his strongest impressions. "Yeh! Like you Muk, the Chapel at our school with its magnificent 'belltower', always sticks in my memory. Early on Sunday mornings the Chapel bell wakes up the school, instead of the one behind the Prefects Centre. As you know, we have to go to church on Sunday mornings only: ah! except for special occasions. The sound effects are so good in the chapel, and all the students sing at the top of their voices. Incredible! I'll never forget it."

"Other really good memories are the fact that one of my subjects is Woodwork, and thanks to Dad I'm well ahead in that."

"I also clearly remember the number of Black Eagles that we used to watch preying on the 'dassies' in the granite hills, near Railway dam. Do you remember those ...?" Muk signalled that he did. "The last memory is not one of joy and celebration. I was dead scared of the house prefects, as they were permitted to cane us junior students for any minor mistake. That was something very new, and painful!! Even Dad didn't whack me like that!".

The second year continued much the same as the first,

including the enjoyment of the return train trips. Both Rod and Mukwe were very pleased that they were no longer 'newbies'. They were able to get on with sport and 'what it was all about'. Rod got seriously into tennis — practicing daily and competing. Mukwe, predictably, carried on with his excellent soccer achievements. The same effort was required towards their studies, even though they both had new class teachers.

Rod particularly remembered his, as he was an absolute character within his profession. Not only was he an extremely competent teacher, but heavily involved in the physics of Telegraphy in the country. Add to that, the fact that he was about six feet four tall, and very strong. A true story goes that he was handed a senior 'shot-put' steel ball, at his house, and he asked, "What is this?" When told what it was and how it launched, he asked, "Can I give it a go?" He then did so, and apparently, broke the country's senior record.

A further memory of Rod's was that this teacher would come into the class of a morning, having marked all the homework during the previous evening, and very cleverly swish each student's book to them. Ninety five percent of the time he would be dead accurate. On one occasion he did same to the naughtiest boy of the class, who was sitting in the back row near the open window: the book flew straight out of the window. He exclaimed, "Agh! Sorry: go and get it." Pariah Dog, as the student was affectionately called, climbed straight out after it, to the delight of the class. On another occasion, this same teacher was near the triangle in the centre of the school, when his dog and another (intruder) dog got into a fight in the triangle. He ran out and grabbed each — mid fight — by the scruff of the neck, and whilst still holding them, immersed them in the pond and then dumped the intruder outside, and gave his a' 'whack'. As one can imagine, the whole school was in hysterics.

Their 'mob' or group of friends also continued going bush on Sundays whenever an exit could be arranged, There was a particular site, West of the school and about two kilometres down the stream that flowed out of the School Dam, which they really got to like. The stream had created a distinctive double bend which made for many very pleasant camping sites. On one weekend there was a storm upstream and it came down in high flood. They all had a ball diving into the streaming flood waters and allowing it to pummel them downstream and around this double-bend. They would then run back through the bush — sometimes accompanied by antelope — to the start point, and dive in again. Much shouting and mirth, throughout the whole episode.

After a month or two of regular visits to this site, the boys decided that a large defunct anthill close to the river, had potential as a den. It was necessary for the boys to bring in picks and shovels for the remainder of the term, and in that time, they cut a broad tunnel into the anthill, and finally cut out a large room (den), from the surface — down to the level of the tunnel. The last Structural effort was to build a timber and thatch roof for the den. This site became their all-time favorite Sunday destination.

However, they were always eager to extend their search further and further afield. On one such occasion they were riding along a known track from one camping area towards another, newer one, when Rod exclaimed, in disgust. "Agh enough! This is a long way round, and will take forever. I know a short cut straight through the bush."

So off they turned and were riding their bikes through the dry long grass; down the dongas of streams, and through the water; round large rocks etcetera, headed by Rod. Suddenly he remembers riding into a mass of spider webs that were so heavily inter-twined that he stopped 'mid-air' whilst his bike carried on. As one could imagine, the friends in the group thought that it was the funniest thing they had seen in ages. A stop was called for coffee and bikkies, while Rod untangled himself — much to the glee of all.

During that year there was one set-back, relating to bullying of the boys in the two junior years. It would seem that the third and fourth-year guys were getting the 'hell-in' with some cheeky juniors. One night, these Grey House juniors were unexpectedly paraded outside the back fence of the house, and made to run a gauntlet — in their pyjamas — between two rows of the 'middles', who were armed with belts, thin bamboo canes, with others throwing green fruit at the running juniors. Rod remembered being hit in the body by a green plum or peach, as well as being whacked with the belts etc. As a second-year kid he considered the event fairly minor, but a couple of 'newbies' were actually hit on the head — one of them front on.

The stupid organizers of this 'late initiation', must have thought that the very strict Housemaster was away. But he wasn't, and caught them red-handed. Serious consequences: with a couple of them very nearly being expelled.

Recollections of years three and four were much the same as for the previous years, whether it was in class, on the sports field/swimming pool, or out bush. It was also during year four that Rod first became an Army cadet. Most of the Secondary schools in the State had cadet forces with — even more importantly, Brass Bands! For Rod though, and for Rick his cousin, it was the first time that they were permitted to shoot on the School's weapons range. Both became very good range shooters, thanks to Rod's Dad being a Bisley shooter and able to give them first class tuition, as well as 'on-range' practice during school holidays.

An event during year four that was quite different from anything in the previous three years, for both boys, was the Flu Epidemic. They were each very lucky not to be seriously infected. Rod was one of the earliest in his House and School to be admitted to the school hospital, and to be treated against the infection, but from then onwards the epidemic just took over the school. He well remembered the quick cure that the medical staff effected in him — except that on the last day before leaving the hospital, he felt pressure in his nose –raced to the toilet, and had the largest nose-bleed that he had ever experienced. When it finished, he felt one hundred percent and never had a repeat of it.

By the end of the first week, neither the School's, nor the Town's hospital could cope, and a dormitory in each house was set aside for the doctors and nurses to treat boys going down with the 'flu'. Within three weeks, two thirds of the school students were infected, and the Education Department closed the school.

Mukwe's school was also closed, due its close proximity and the fact that they had also been affected, but to a lesser extent.

"You beaut! Off home early for the holidays *and* already cured," exclaimed Rod.

For the majority of the fourth year at secondary school, Rod was fifteen years of age, and he maintains that it was over this period that he lost his first two, of 'the Black Cat's Nine Lives'. During one of the terms, the usual group had been out into the bush and were returning to the school on the Sunday evening: they were spread out along a fairly broad track with Rod ahead of Rick. The latter was carrying the small axe (or adze) that they used to cut dead wood for their camp fire. Only he wasn't just carrying it — he was spinning it over to catch it by the handle each time. Being Rick, he got bored of that, and started to flick it such that it spun twice, before he caught it by the handle. That achieved a couple of times, he had to give it a bigger spin ... Rod suddenly heard a shout of panic from Rick, "Look out Rod, the axe is in the air and coming your way." What could Rod do but cover his head with his hands. The axe landed a metre directly behind him — coming down from probably four metres in the air. Phew!! Gasps of relief from everyone: especially Rick!

The second occasion was during one of the holidays, spent with a school pal about two hundred kilometres from the school. They were riding into the town on the sealed road and approaching a tight "S" bend. It was downhill and they were going 'full-bore' on their bikes.

There were already many cars coming out of the town and traversing the "S" bend, when Rod, who was riding behind his pal, misjudged a brick that had fallen onto the road. His front wheel struck the brick and he flew ... and flew, and he can remember saying to himself, "Fall onto the road on your shoulder", and heard the screech of vehicle brakes being applied. Amazingly enough he did land on his shoulder, and was not hit by a car. His crash however, did cause all vehicles to stop, and many drivers to rush across to him. After checking that he was quite OK he was embarrassingly, rebuked by some of them, for recklessness. He silently ticked-off — the 'Second Life of the 'Black Cat's Nine'!

Soon after this 'pile-up' and back at School again, Rod was interrupted by cousin Rick, who tore into the Prep room, and told him that his (Rod's) Dad had been involved in the daring rescue of a crashed aircraft pilot. Once Rod had phoned home his Dad gave him the details: he had been in the process of going to bed, with the constant din of Trainer pilots doing 'circuits and bumps' in their Harvard aircraft, when there was a mighty crash. He was able to place it as having occurred on the next-door neighbour's small rural property. He had quickly jumped back into his trousers and windcheater; leapt into the car and raced down to where he expected it to be.

Sure enough it had crashed down through the upper branches of a Gumtree plantation and was starting to burn, at the base. It was a case of 'through the barbed wire fence, and off at a run to the burning plane'. The moment he reached it' he was able to see that although the pilot had managed to open the cockpit, he was still strapped into the pilot's seat, and was not moving. He climbed up the back of the wing, away from the side that was burning, and got to the cockpit. The trapped pilot could not answer him, which was very disturbing. Just at that point a neighbour from the side — nearer to the Air Station arrived and after a quick assessment, he was able to reassure Rod's Dad that he had phoned the 'Station" and reported the crash. A rescue vehicle and ambulance were on the way.

In the meantime Rod's Dad had started to cut the seatbelts holding the pilot in. They were very tough and it was taking valuable minutes, with the fire getting closer and closer to the cabin. Over what seemed like an age, he finally cut through the last belt and hoisted himself into the cabin to get his arms around the pilot: he then started to drag him towards the edge of the cockpit. Fortunately the rescue vehicle and staff arrived just then, and were able to assist in getting him out. Seconds later the cabin also caught alight. With three of them carrying/shifting him down the wing, they managed to get him away from his burning plane and to a clearing where the Paramedics could get him onto their stretcher; out to the ambulance and off to the local hospital.

On complimenting his Dad, and enquiring as to the pilot's state, his Dad could only report that he was still in a critical condition. One last pointer from his Dad though — always carry a sharp penknife!!

Some months later, Rod's Dad was awarded the British Empire Medal, (BEM) and the whole family joined him for the Presentation, at the Colony's Government House.

During this school year, Mukwe's Undwani School soccer team also had a close call. They had played a game of soccer in the city, against a predominantly 'white' team, whom they beat. Parents of the city team were furious with the result, and started to attack them. The police had to be urgently called to break up the fight. Notwithstanding this, Mukwe continued his love for the game of soccer which he was now playing with a high degree of skill.

Although Rod's academic work took top priority during his final year, and to which he applied himself diligently, he always remembered two sporting events with delight and pride. Sports Day for Athletics was held towards the end of the first term, and not only were his parents attending, but sister Jacky as well. A friend Mel — one of the gang — had met her the previous Christmas holidays, when he had come to spend some time with Rod and Mukwe, and it turned out that Jacky and Mel had been writing to one another. Great! And as the weekend progressed, so did their romance. Mel did himself proud in the sports by winning the 800m race, with terrific admiration from Jacky. Rod's 800m Relay team excelled themselves as well — although they were unable to beat Mel's House team.

Mel and Jacky eventually married some years later, after they had each earned Tertiary Qualifications. Jacky achieved a Diploma from the London School of Music, while Mel got a Bachelor of Forestry from Edinburgh University — much to Rod's pride.

There was one last event, apart from Rod achieving Matriculation and University entrance: It occurred at the beginning of the final term of the year, and of his High School career. The seniors in each House, i.e Cadet Age, took part in the Inter-House Range Shooting competition using .303 Rifles. There were five Houses competing, with four members in each team, and they had to shoot it out over the 200m, 300m and 500m ranges — with each member having seven shots at each range. The final competition was 'Falling Plates' of which there were five plates. The members of each team had three shots each, to knock down their five plates within one minute!

43

At the end of the longer ranges (and before the plates competition) Rod's and Rick's house — 'Grey,' had tied with 'Gaul House', so those two houses qualified to continue into the 'plates' event, to decide the winner.

Right! — "Get ready you eight shooters; sixty seconds to elapse; Go!" All of them went absolutely mad with frantic bolt and trigger action, until seven out of the eight shooters had expended all their rounds — except Rod. At this point each team had managed to knock down four of the team's five plates. Unbeknown to Rod, in his deep concentration, he had about three seconds left ... Steady, aim, and fire at the fifth plate. Wham! Down it went, and so Grey House was the winner, and Rod a bit of a hero, there on the range.

One final and dramatic occurrence to finish off school days, the memory of which has stuck in the minds of Rick, Mukwe and particularly Rod, was the long cycle ride home from the train interchange. It was a distance of about 200kilometres — which turned out to be about three hundred, in the end. The stage1 train had pulled into the interchange station at about mid-afternoon. After getting their bikes and gear off, and having a meal, they commenced the ride just before sunset.

They did not bother about cycle-headlights for their bikes — believing that they would be perfectly able to see their way from starlight, and later the moon as well. They had progressed fifteen kilometres or so, and contrary to their beliefs, it was as black as pitch on the road. They were riding slightly uphill; three abreast, with Rod riding on the inside (towards the middle) of the sealed road when, suddenly, he caught sight of a 'head with hat on', bearing down on him. 'Flick right and vacate bike'. The next instant there was a resounding crash as the front wheel of the approaching cyclist (also without lights) rammed into the front wheel of his bike. Rick was horrified and shouted, "Jesus! Rod are you okay?" The opposing cyclist had a mighty fall, but after helping him up it turned out that he wasn't badly injured. The only thing injured was the front wheel of Rod's bike, which had suffered totally broken spokes on the one side, and the curves of the wheel were at ninety degrees to each other. Further progress towards home was out of the question. Fortunately there was a Military base about five kilometres further on, so they progressed to there with Rod on the bar of Rick's bike, trundling his along on the back wheel, and with Mukwe carrying the damaged wheel.

At one stage Mukwe expressed concern saying, "Are you two getting along alright? Your progress seems to be pretty windy. Can you see where you are going?" Rick assured him that although it was difficult in the dark, they were making ground.

Finally they arrived at the Guardhouse and gate of the Military base, to the astonishment and consternation of the Guard on duty. He halted them and ordered, "Stay right there and don't move. He went into the guardhouse and phoned his superior, then came out — wait where you are; my Boss is coming down." That 'worthy' got great amusement from the development and put them up in a cell behind the guardhouse, but accompanied by pillows and blankets! The boys got the impression that this diversion added to the soldier's quality of life on the base!

The Officer in charge at the Military base phoned the parents to advise of the events and inform them that the three would be running a day late. The next day, the militia ran them back into the town, and they were able to have the wheel repaired at a Cycle shop. It was a pretty quick job and this time they were on their way by mid-morning.

Much better progress, and by nightfall they had covered about 110kilometrs. Unfortunately for them though, there was a thunderstorm heading their way. They had passed over a well known river, that also eventually ran into the same major river as their hometown river. Cycling uphill through very open country, they were better able to see the thunderstorm heading their way, and which was obviously more than 'just the usual'. The lightning and thunder crashes seemed to be almost continuous. Progress was being made however, even into the forward part of the storm. Suddenly a massive bolt of lightning struck so close to them, followed instantaneously by a deafening crash of thunder, to the effect that they all thought that they had been hit. Rod and Mukwe were thrown off their bikes with Rick — being taller- just managing to stay on his. None of them were hurt and they just had carry-on, and hope for the best.

After about five further tempestuous kilometres, they espied a light up ahead, off to the side of the road. When they were abreast, they could make out a farmhouse, and decided to see whether the farmer could give them shelter in a shed or barn. They rode up to the house, dismounted and knocked on the front door. As it turned out, the owner was a widow farmer and she was appalled that three boys on bikes could be out at night, in such a storm. She immediately let them in; gave them dry clothes and a hot meal, and put them into beds in her son's bedroom. What a let-off from their experiences.

An amusing culmination to their hectic day occurred during the night. Rod had the bed by the window and had been fast asleep, when he was awakened by strange noises outside, but close to his head. The next thing a hand appeared just above him. He called out: "Who are you?; what are you trying to do?"

The reply from outside was "What are you doing in my bed?" Rod explained that he and friends had been caught in the storm, on bicycles, and that the lady had taken them in and given them the beds for the night. His retort was "Oh! I'm the son, but don't worry, I'll go back to town with my friends, and come back tomorrow."

Next morning they were given breakfast, and their clothes back, which had been dried off and re-ironed. One couldn't get better than that, for hospitality. As it turned out, she was a customer of Rod's Father's motor dealership. The three finally reached Aberfoyle by lunchtime — twenty four hours late!! One of the first things that the boys did was to purchase flowers and other gifts for the widow farmer. Then on the first appropriate occasion, to run out to her farm again, accompanied by their parents, to present the well-earned gifts just before Christmas!

# CHAPTER 6

After celebrating Christmas in that completion year of secondary school and seeing the New Year in, Rod commenced work as an Articled Clerk to Chartered Accountants in Aberfoyle. Mukwe took a different path and entered the two-year Agricultural College Diploma Course. Both still played a lot of sport, and they therefore caught-up with one another frequently. Total application to their new careers however, had to be their prime focus and they each made great strides. Rod's employers and Mukwe's lecturers' were well pleased with their progress.

During one period of study leave Rod had a close encounter — in fact a very close encounter: He was studying for the next exam. His future was on the line, but he was having trouble swotting inside the family farmhouse. His mum and dad were arguing and he didn't want to make things worse by asking them to be quiet. So, Rod took his textbook on

Business Administration — the course he hoped to study the following year at University — to the sheds out the back of the house.

The sheds included a workshop with an array of tools, welding equipment and old engine parts, as well as a couple of storage rooms. The first of these had been fitted-out with shelving and fuel storage on the far side. In the second there were even a few pens for sick animals, but fortunately they were not being used that afternoon. Rod opened the window over the leafy back garden and couldn't help exclaiming, "Ah! I love this view across to the dense bush." The open window also let in a fragrant breeze to help dispel some of the odours. One of the smaller workbenches became his desk and he found an old vinyl-covered chair to complete his makeshift study.

Rod resumed his swotting, but after a while he realised something was disturbing him and he noted that there were a few bees flying around — some of them were actually connecting with him. Whilst wondering if he should just go back to studying many more bees came in, all of which took not the slightest notice of him. He then detected a distinct hum coming from the first storage room.

His mind suddenly changed gear into action. He stood up, moved across and opened the top half of the stable door into the storage room and realised why the hum was so loud: there were thousands more bees in this space. Looking around, he noticed that the reason for this was that the room's small window was open.

With his mind still racing full bore, he recollected information that he had learnt from his school friend Gus, and the books lent by him. Gus's Dad kept bees for the purposes of collecting their honey. The first important fact that jolted Rod's mind was that African Bees had the reputation for being the most dangerous species in the world. This was probably due to the fact that they had been forced through the ages to co-exist with Africa's wide variety of other insects, mammals, birds and human honey-gatherers.

In the absence of anyone else Rod said, "Hopefully the new Queen is cunningly and excitedly inspecting this room to see whether it will meet her regal needs, after she has done her mating flight." He knew however, that they were deadly. How could he get rid of them? The window through which they had entered was fairly small — if he went and opened the door, which was a much larger opening, they might all fly out. So, he entered the storeroom and opened the door to outside. Stepping out in a state of suspense, he waited to see what would really happen. After an anxious minute, they all flew out in 'busy' mode.

Rod was amazed as he followed them into the yard area and witnessed them suddenly flying vertically into the sky. He recalled from part of the Bee book he had read, that the new Queen will continue to fly straight upwards until only a principal male and some close male suitors are with her. Initially, Rod saw them very clearly, but then they became a grey blur. He mused to himself, "Will they become a less visible, grey smudge and fly out of sight? Or will they return? Is the book right or wrong?"

Suddenly, the light-grey smudge came plummeting down towards him, so he ran inside and closed the door, shouting to himself, "But the same damn window is still open!" Rod was petrified, because the bees — sure enough — swarmed back into the room through the open window. Mercifully, they still showed no interest in him at all. But where were they going?

As he moved further into the room to observe them, he spotted the Queen landing in a boxed part of one of the shelves. Rod courageously and carefully approached the shelving. The bees of the hive were now all flying thickly around him, emitting a dense hum, and as he moved forward, they started settling on him but were not stinging him. They were crawling all over his arms, legs, shirt and pants, and every now and then he had to wipe them gently off his face. He soon realised that they were only interested in their Queen. He believed that if he could pick her up and take her outside to release her, all the other bees should follow her. However, if something went wrong, he whispered to himself, "Hell it will be a death wish. They would sting me for messing with her."

When Rod put his hand down gently to pick the Queen bee up, he appreciated just how lucky he had been to actually see her, before the hive swarmed over and covered her. Up close the sight of her was amazing because she was so much bigger than normal bees, with her body being elongated into two distinct dark brown slender body pods. She also had longer wings that were neatly folded back, and of much lighter colour than ordinary bees. Her eyes were dark orbs and were fortunately looking away from Rod as he checked her out. He noticed that her movements were strong, she made no sound and had a pleasing, sweet odour. As his hand moved closer, he was engulfed by the tension of knowing this move on the Queen was potentially fatal. He just prayed that his touch would not change the intense and peaceful hum surrounding him. He wondered — if the Queen stung him whether this would create such alarm that her many followers would immediately sting him too.

Nevertheless, his hand moved forward and he gently clasped her between his thumb and first two fingers, sensing what she felt like. Both parts of her body were dry and very smooth and she made no effort to wriggle free — almost as if being picked up was the 'Neat and Tidy' end result of her search. Rod suddenly realised he was breathless and his heart was pumping like a diesel engine. He had to take a quiet and deep breath to control his emotions. He could visualise the climax of himself being dead on the floor with thousands of dying bees swarming all over him. He prayed to God that no one, especially not Monty the dog or Kitty the cat, would come into the shed now or the whole situation would erupt, and the bees would start stinging him.

What actually happened was that the hive started settling on him. Initially, onto his right hand where he held the Queen, and then tickling and wriggling up his whole arm to the shoulder — quickly covering most of his body. As he turned to exit the storage room, he had to gently wipe many strays off his face in case they crept into his eyes or ears or nose. In the midst of this, he was surprised to smell the sweet scent of nectar and honey. He padded slowly towards the door, opened it and stepped outside hoping that no humans or animals would confront him and interfere with his careful progress towards a nearby tree with its convenient fork.

On reaching the tree, he gently placed the Queen into the fork, then very slowly withdrew his arm. He estimated that it took several minutes for the entire hive to creep off his arm and body and onto their new hive.

Rod immediately went back into the storeroom — the way he had come out, to make sure that there were no bees still flying around inside. There weren't any, but after a careful search he was able to pick up a few that were lying down in total exhaustion. Whilst taking them out to the hive, he was amazed that they did not sting him.

Finally, he went back in and whilst closing all windows and doors that could offer re-entry, his mother came in through the main door and said, "Oh hi Rod!" I expected to see you swotting."

Rod was somewhat surprised to see her and exclaimed,

"Swatting!" "Mum if I had done that, then you wouldn't have found me here, but flat on the earth outside screaming and covered by bees!"

# *CHAPTER 7*

After two years in their respective career paths, both Rod and Mukwe were called-up to do their stint of National Service army training. This certainly was something new for each of them, and the first six weeks or so were hard physical slog. By the end of that time, the permanent army Training and Disciplining staff knew who was who, and what was what, in terms of tactical ability. The fact that both Rod and Mukwe had experience with the use of sporting rifles, made a big difference. Over the following three to four months they had many memorable experiences within their Battalion.

The event that Rod remembers most vividly, was being involved with the Army 'defence truck' convoy. The convoy involved about eighty trucks, which the Battalion had ordered to hasten down some 1200kilometres, into the far Southern reaches of the Republic. Not only did it have to cover that vast distance — with much of it on unsealed 'dirt' roads, but it also had to cross the mighty Zambezi River en-route, by ... 'wait for it' ... Ferry! Rod well remembers being one of the leading drivers and coming round the last bend and seeing the surging brown flood, and witnessing the Commander and Senior Officers getting out of their vehicles: gaping at this dynamic spectacle, and the Commander saying, "How the hell are we going to get the convoy across this dangerous expanse of water?"

Then the Ferry staff came across — wondering 'what in the hell' was happening, only to be told that the entire convoy had to get across quick. Due to the three-kilometre crossing, and the fact that the ferry had to be shared with domestic traffic, one can imagine the dismay of the Operators. In the end it took approximately 60 hours for all the trucks to clear the river.

While that was progressing, the personnel attached to the convoy spent many hours swimming and playing in the river. The whole deployment south, including the many soldiers who had been flown down was very successful, but then of course the convoy had to return to base. As it turned out the Army decided that a longer route back — that didn't involve a ferry — was the better option! One thing gained from the truck convoy, was that Rod secured his Heavy Vehicle license.

Mukwe had a different experience over this time, in that his Battalion with its three Companies, were flown to the 'engagement' area on an Immediate Active Call-up summons. The Battalion went on the offensive right away, and over the course of the three weeks was engaged in a number of sorties.

Mukwe particularly recalled one, "Our Company had to split up into Platoons, and each had to make a circuitous advance against the waiting enemy, whilst being covered by the other two. It was a very aggressive series of advances against the well dug-in opposition, but we succeeded in routing them into wild retreat. Both sides suffered some casualties, although our Battalion only had some wounded — one of which was to my immediate right, as we were firing at the enemy."

Their joint Battalions were also involved in many actions against external insurgents.

Due to the fact that they were still doing their National Service, their Battalion was utilized in mainly defensive actions. One of these was when Rod was receiving instruction on radio communications — part of which was to keep the land forces in touch with the Airforce. They were frequently positioned on very high hills — to simplify these radio communications, and in such events these hills became 'warzones, where any opposing force were considered enemy, and fired upon.

One day when Rod had handed over radio duties to another squad member and had taken a stroll outside, he espied a lone figure coming up the very steep access road, towards their Radio Station. He gathered a couple of other operatives, and fully armed they went out and arrested the intruder. Under interrogation, he advised that he was the Minister of the local church. The "mountain men" radioed this information down to the Battalion HQ, and were told to keep him under arrest, whilst they investigated. Some fifteen minutes later, they were contacted and told to release him, as he had only come up, to 'Get Closer to God'!

Once our worthies had completed their National Service, they were drafted into the Reserve; known colloquially as the 'Territorials'. These Army Companies met monthly for full-on training, and annually for six-week camps, from which they could be drafted to active Units, as fully trained soldiers.

# CHAPTER 8

With his military service behind him Rod joined the Company, of which his father was Manager and a Director on the Board. He took up the position of Assistant Accountant, for which his father recognized that he was well trained. Mukwe furthered his career in the government Agricultural Conservation Department. He already had his 'two-year Diploma and was therefore given a good level of promotion. It meant however, that he was transferred to Culanci, a town seventy kilometres 'up the drag'. Rod on the other hand, still had to complete two extra years of study to obtain his external Degree in Business and Accounting. Notwithstanding the separation of employment, they kept in constant touch and often met at sports fixtures over the weekends.

Back in the-mix for each of them, and therefore able to consider a girlfriend here and there! None of these relationships lasted, due probably, to the fact that each of them had a desire to travel before settling down to married life.

There was one girl however whom Rod had met during this period, by the name of Kimberley (Kim for short) and with whom he spent a fair bit of time, and for whom he was seriously considering changing this 'rule'. He pondered, "How can I have such very close encounters with such a beautiful creature, without beginning to waver?" She worked for the Immigration Department and like him displayed a real professional personality. They each visited the other's family and were, quite rightly, well accepted.

One professional service that raised Rod's shares in her eyes, was help that he gave to her father. He ran his own business as a Sole Trader, and had encountered a serious 'run-in' with the country's Taxation Office.

Rod offered to help, and on an initial investigation realised that it was not an issue of error or dishonesty, but of being years in arrear with his Tax returns. Notwithstanding this, the Department had threatened a 20% surcharge, plus full payment of all past year's returns, as well as the current year's return. Kim's Dad accepted Rod to act as his Consultant with the Tax Department.

Rod negotiated with the Department and undertook to urgently bring all the returns up to-date, provided that they dropped all surcharges. This was done as quickly as possible with a lot of assistance from Kim –when they weren't in one another's arms — to complete all the books and returns for each year, and submit them. The Department upheld their side of the agreement as soon as they had received all the back payments. In providing this free service to Kim's Dad, Rod saved his Business.

Their relationship continued for a while on a loving Boy-friend/ Girl-friend basis, but a year or so later she was transferred to the Capital city, and from then onwards it was purely by correspondence — with only an occasional trip by each of them, either way. He continued to drop in on her parents, to ensure that all was well with the whole family.

In his second last year of accounting studies, an extraordinary event occurred that changed everything — initially for Rod and Monty — but because of their close friendship and bond, for Mukwe as well. It also brought a third acquaintance into focus, whom they had both known during their school years, and with whom they had each played sport. A loner by the name of Eden, who was currently serving a jail sentence based on a trumped-up charge laid by his mother's second husband, who was unequivocally hated in the town. At the time that Rod was enduring this difficult malaise, Eden's sentence had been increased, due to his having escaped from the jail.

The period covered by the event mentioned above, was unique in that part of Africa at the time. Rabies, which is a dangerous animal borne disease, was said to have become widespread and evolving. As a precaution, the Authorities had ruled that all dogs had to be chained up at all times. Rod, who was at home on the farm on study leave with his pal Monty at his feet, had not complied with this ruling. Both he, and Mukwe as it turned out, were unaware that someone (a disgruntled worker, or a passer-by) had reported a dog being untied at the address of the farm.

Rod was disturbed by the arrival of a LandRover type vehicle, which had sped up the drive. He went out of the house, accompanied by Monty, to see whom it could be. Walking out towards the 'drive' they were confronted by a policeman getting out of the vehicle, armed with a gun. This worthy demanded loudly and aggressively, "Are you Mr Cochrane?" "I have come to shoot your dog because it is not chained up."

Rod replied "Yes, I am Rod Cochrane, but you are not shooting my dog because he is good and obeys my orders, and when I am not here he is closed-up in the house." That had no effect on the policeman, who raised his rifle towards the dog. Rod jumped across to protect Monty shouting, "No! You can't do that". Too late — the policeman fired, but Rod was right in the way and he took the shot high in his left thigh. Fortunately it had been a high powered rifle, and although it spun him around and threw him to the ground, it did not cause a terrible exit wound.

The policeman was so shocked by the fact that he had hit a person with the shot, that he completely forgot about his original target; ran back and leaped into the LandRover and drove hurriedly away.

Rod realised that he was bleeding profusely and managed to tremulously utter, "Come-on Monty we have got to get inside and bandage this." On the way in Monty was licking his leg and kept looking up at his face, and whining his heartfelt concern. Rod knew where the wound plasters were — scrabbled amongst them until he found pads and bandages — and applied them, with haste and probably very little finesse!

Whilst looking for, and then tying the bandage, some urgent and disturbing thoughts were tumbling through his mind. He realised that the Police would be back very quickly to correct their 'stuff-up' and complete the job of shooting the dog, so he silently listed his thoughts and processed them.

"How am I going to inform Mum and Dad?" After all, this is their home and not only will they be extremely worried but possibly alarmed that I have done something bad.

He decided to defer that, and immediately phoned Mukwe at his workplace in Culanci saying, "I need your help Muk, as there has been a bit of a calamity here. Please could you meet me straight away at our secret 'picnic' spot off Hegarty Lane, due North of here. Do you remember it?"

Mukwe confirmed that he did, and added, "But is there anything that I should bring?" There was no reply!

* * *

Rod mused, "What would be the best way for Monty and I to disappear? I can't drive away as I would definitely be seen — so it will have to be my bicycle."

"I'll need stuff to take with me; what?" he said, "warm clothes; a blanket; food for Monty and I; more bandages and of course my gun and ammunition." All of these he immediately packed into his rucksack.

"Ready to go?" Yes!

"I'll ride off in the direction of Town with Monty on his lead. This he did, but — and a very important But! — the house is now out-of-sight so, I must do a one hundred and eighty degree turn and head off the other way through the bush on this known track." A cause for worry was that the path exited the heavy bush and entered open savannah. What if he came across farm vehicles or workers?

Getting to the 'picnic spot' was tricky because the track eventually ran out onto a farm road. Rod and Monty weren't seen by anyone but on a couple of occasions they heard vehicles and had to disappear into the thick bush. They finally made it to the designated spot.

\* \* \*

While he was listening to Rod's plea Mukwe's mind started racing, and when he put the phone down after accepting the request, he said to himself, "I wonder what this catastrophic event could be? It must be bloody serious for him to phone me and ask that I drive seventy kilometres and to meet him at that secret place. Cheez! I hope he hasn't been assaulted by a mob, or something."

Whilst driving he added to his ruminations, "He must have been severely threatened: hell! I'll have to drive faster and get there a.s.a.p." With that he increased his speed to over the limit for that stretch of road, but suddenly remembered that he had to keep a close watch for the narrow, almost secretive track, that led off to the arranged meeting place.

\* \* \*

By the time that he and Monty arrived at the secluded spot, some ten kilometres from Fairhill, Rod was deteriorating in both mind and body, and the bleeding had worsened. Monty kept right close with head against him, consoling him that all would be okay, and this contact helped Rod from collapsing. By sitting firmly on the ground — so that he didn't fall there — he managed to remove the first bandage and applied a second: this time bit more carefully.

Within half an hour he heard a vehicle stop, followed by running steps. Monty barked and rushed out to meet Mukwe, whose steps he well recognized. Mukwe was appalled at what he saw and after sharing some food all round said, "We have got to get you to hospital". It was clearly going to be necessary, so they discussed Rod's situation. Aberfoyle hospital was not an option, but some forty kilometres further along there was a rural hospital in the small mining village of Dunnfold. Mukwe disguised the bicycle and hid it in thick grass, then they all piled into the Pickup and headed for this village.

Whilst travelling Rod said, "Mukwe, you are to keep totally out of this shooting episode — the policeman was acting within his lawful right — even if it were somewhat 'frenzy' driven. You look pretty dubious, but don't be, because my main reason for asking is that you are going to have to look after Monty and my gun, until it all blows over".

"Will you also phone Dad and Mom and let them know that I'm OK, but that you are not at all sure where I am. I'll phone them tomorrow, from the hospital." Mukwe didn't argue — realising and accepting what had been asked of him. And so, the trip continued with only casual chatting.

As they were driving into the outskirts of Dunnfold village Rod asked Mukwe, "Just drop me off on a side street and I'll book myself in through the Emergency Entrance. No argument, just go back to work, until you hear from me. Mention nothing to your Dad at this stage and please will you and your friends keep Monty in a safe and secluded place — tied up when you are not with him!!"

Mukwe undertook to do as asked but gave Rod a big hug and whispered, "Go well Mate". After he had driven away Rod made his way with difficulty, along the little heavily-treed back road to the hospital: it was a fairly small building with a long porch down the approach side which was obviously well dusted and 'scrubbed-off'! He was immediately admitted and the nurses stripped off the bandage, and got to work checking and washing the wound. Sure enough the bullet had exited, so she and the Doctor immediately stitched it up, and he was then shown to a comfortable ward bed.

Chatting afterwards with the nurses — with Rod crossing his fingers behind his back — and lying about how it had occurred he said, "It was an accident down on the farm; I was out hunting when my rifle slipped and went off. Due to my vehicle being a long way in the other direction, I decided that it was best to just walk here." One of them acknowledged his version replying, "Just as well you had a bandage in your bag — it must have been a pretty painful walk up here." They left him to rest, with the undertaking that they would check on him frequently.

Rod suddenly realised that he was exhausted, so he laid his head back on the pillow and within minutes had fallen into a deep sleep. He was awakened at sunset with a very welcome meal, and whilst eating, and chatting with the nurse, asked if he could use the hospital phone, after he had eaten. She agreed and took him to the phone. He first caught-up with Mukwe and brought him up to date on the first-class treatment received. Then he phoned his parents. They were obviously very concerned, both at his admission that Monty had not been tied up, and at the accidental shooting of their son. He was able to put them at ease however, by saying,

"Don't worry Mom and Dad, they have fixed me up really well here at Dunnfold Hospital, including stitching up the wound. I'll sort it out with the authorities, and tell them that Monty just legged it after the shot, and hasn't been seen since."

His Dad appealed, "Okay, but when you come back to take it up with the police, call in and we will support you all the way."

Later in the evening after the nursing staff had replaced the dressings, Rod took the opportunity to grab a good night's sleep. The following morning all went well, and after the doctor had checked on the wound and it had been re-dressed, he was advised that he was free to go and was given a bundle of wound dressing materials.

Before he could organize his departure however, there was a loud discourse at the entrance of the hospital, with arguments and protests coming nearer and nearer. Next thing two policemen barged into the ward, accompanied by angry hospital staff. The senior of the two policemen shouted — "On your feet. We know that you are Rod Cochrane from the hospital register: you are under arrest for what happened yesterday. He raised his hand fully open, and said, Do not say anything, as it may be used in evidence against you." Rod tried to protest, also advising the hospital staff, "I'm sorry about this but can explain their outrage, and assure you that I am not guilty of any crime". Notwithstanding, he was handcuffed; marched out of the hospital and driven back to Aberfoyle.

In that centre a preliminary hearing had already been scheduled to remand him. Seated before the Magistrate (whom he did not know and wondered if he was genuine or just a placement) with a cop on each side of him, he had the charge read out to him. On being asked if he would be represented by a lawyer: Rod said, "No!. I will defend myself — right here and now." The Magistrate declined that, and remanded him into custody for attacking the policeman who had fired the shot. He was then re-handcuffed and pulled around to be marched off to the jail, which doubled as the remand centre. Before leaving the Court room, and in a state of fury at the proceedings, Rod made a mental note of various aspects of the building.

After experiencing the usual introduction into a jail system, and having been told that his 'Open and Shut' case would come up within the next week or two, he settled in for the wait. On the second afternoon of permitted exercise with the other prisoners, in the yard, he was surprised to encounter his old swimming pool acquaintance, Eden. They immediately got to chatting about the Swimming Club and about sport, partying etcetera, of old times in the Town. Once these re-introductions were over, Eden said — "How the hell has a reputable citizen like you Rod, been committed here?". Rod explained the how and the wherefore, and the fact that he had been set-up, on a lie. "Why am I not surprised." Said Eden.

More idle talk and discussion followed– "Look Eden, I

know that you have also been unjustly dealt with, but I am very surprised to see you here." "Why?"

Before replying Rod took a careful look around the compound, to ensure that no one was listening, and also that there were no devices close at hand. He then said — "I'm obviously aware that you have had a couple of very successful prison breakouts, and I thought that you would still be on the run."

Eden replied — "I needed to catch-up on sleep and get some steady food — even if it is a bit 'sus'!. But don't worry, I will be doing it again."

Rod countered, "Hang in there Eden. I'm not confident of what they have in store for me: I could very well be joining you."

"It's tough out there Rod, replied Eden. But yes! I will delay. In the meantime we can be unobtrusive friends." That was the way it continued for the next few days, with their catching up occasionally — in different places throughout the centre.

On about the sixth day they were fortunate enough to meet at the same dinner table. When alone, Rod said — "That window in the Court House, behind the magistrate's right shoulder. The window is wooden in construction and has one of those easy-release type of catches. If it could be left open prior to my trial I could easily escape through it if they start to conclude that I'm guilty. In the time that it would take anyone inside the building to get out the front and around the back, I will have made it across that open area and into the back-garden of that first house."

"Jesus that's dicey. Isn't it?" said Eden.

"No! I don't think so. After that first house, I'll change direction completely because I know another very secluded garden that even has its own little well. If necessary, I could even climb into it and hide."

"How long do you reckon all this will take? asked Eden, because they will have a posse after you, in no time flat."

"About three minutes." Said Rod.

"Okay! Its sounding good. Am I presuming that you would like me to execute my escape during the evening leading up to your Court appearance, and as part of it, to get that window open for you?"

"Exactly! said Rod — and I will meet you under that big culvert, at the end of the wide concrete drain, on the other side of the Scout Hall. If the case is to be held in the morning, as they are indicating at the moment, then I will meet you there anytime from eleven a.m. and before two oclock. If I'm not there by then, get lost."

"Done! said Eden, but we shouldn't meet again until then, because I have alot of preparations to take care of, for <u>my</u> escape."

When he got back to his cell Rod's thoughts were circling around his and Eden's planned escapes, and he remembered that his mother had mentioned that his eldest sister was coming up to Aberfoyle to visit. She would arrange for

Jacky to visit him, as well. This arrangement tied in well with plans, because Jacky knew Mukwe well and he was also going to be a key agent, in what could transpire.

He then applied his mind to working out what he would get Jacky to communicate to Mukwe, in the event that the Magistrate did not pick-up on the falsehood of the charge against him. Essentially there were six key steps to cover with Mukwe:

1. Where and when Mukwe (& Monty) should meet me and Eden.
2. Mukwe should bring two complete army uniforms and belts from their respective wardrobes.
3. That Mukwe should bring the gun and ammo, so that they would be able to hunt and to feed themselves.
4. That Mukwe should bring army water bottles.
5. That Mukwe should bring a modicum of bedding and towels.
6. That Mukwe should bring an Esky of basic foods (including for Monty), and heaps of anti-malaria pills.

\* \* \*

Jacky arrived in town the following day, and was permitted to see him. They had a pleasant time talking about things that each had missed about the others life, since they were last together. She was appalled at what had happened but quite understood the tactic planned, if his case failed. She said. "But what about your leg Rod?" He was able to reassure her that it had been attended to since he had been in jail, and that the exercise had improved it immensely. "Okay, well I'll be with Mom and Dad, and we'll see you when you are brought to Court."

Rod laughed, and then, while looking around quietly said, "Not before I ask you to do some things for me Jacky. If things go wrong and I make a break for it, please contact Mukwe and organize six important things with him. You'll appreciate that they are vital." Rod then mentioned the six items — in order, and giving her the key word of each. He went through them again, and asked her to repeat them in the order of the key words. This she did, and was sure that she would remember them. Soon after that she left, on her way to join their parents.

The next day while out in the exercise yard, Rod heard that Eden had escaped, and noted the agitation that it had created amongst the warders.

The day following that he was called aside by the Commander of the jail, and told that his trial was coming up in two days-time and that he would be collected. The commander added "We'll keep your cell for you — you'll be back."

"But I'm not guilty," said Rod — I'm the one who was hurt, not the Policeman."

At that the Commander shrugged and said, "We'll see, wont we?"

# CHAPTER 9

He was marched into the Court and seated facing the Magistrate. He noted that the Jurors were a really mixed group — both as to race and gender — and that all of them looked tense and fearful, as if they had been stirred up. He also unobtrusively noted that the window behind the magistrate was unclipped and slightly ajar. The case started with the Prosecutor reading out the offense, and the Police version of what had happened. Predictably they alleged that he had first attacked the policeman, who had fired in self-defence.

The Magistrate noted that Rod had no Defence lawyer, and ordered him to stand. He then asked him whether he was guilty or not-guilty. Rod replied "Not Guilty, but I would like to tell the Jurors what actually happened." The magistrate reluctantly allowed him to, but as he was doing so, he noted that the fear was still there, in their faces. Some small talk took place amongst them and they then settled down.

The magistrate then asked them "Is Mr Cochrane guilty of not guilty?" Their spokesman then rose and said "Guilty!"

Before he had completed the word, Rod leapt up onto the desk in front of him; over a partition before he could be restrained by either of the policemen; onto another desk; then he reached up and fully opened the window, and leaped out. The warders also tried to stop him, but were too slow. Chaos ensued within the courtroom followed by much shouting and bellowing of orders. As he was getting up, Rod guessed that he had about twenty seconds to cover the open one hundred metres to the back garden of the nearest house.

As he leapt the fence of the property, he noted that the first of the pursuers had come round the front of the court building. Rod had run in a near easterly direction, towards a main road exiting the town towards "Fairhill": This was a tactic in the plan arranged with Eden. Once out of sight in the back garden of the house, he changed direction towards the South because it was on that intended course that he knew of the friend's heavily hedged garden: the one with the well — if it were needed.

He was very lucky because no one apart from the early pursuers had witnessed the "runaway", even when he sprinted along the pavement of the southerly road. Checking from a hiding spot, he noted that the pursuers continued eastward. When clear, he sprinted across the road unseen into the friend's dense garden, and straight to the vicinity of the well. This was a precaution in case the search became rapidly more widespread. As it turned out, it didn't, and he was able to slowly and secretly work towards the rendezvous point with Eden, using laneways and other back gardens. Once he got into the water of the deep drain channel, he felt much safer, in case the police had already brought dogs into the search.

Half a kilometre down this channel he met up with Eden, under a broad concrete culvert where the latter had been hiding. It was well before noon and Eden exclaimed "Jesus am I glad to see you; I was bloody worried for both of us."

"Same here Eden — damned 'hairy' isn't it? How did your breakout go? You certainly created a stir by the next morning."

Eden could quite believe that and said, "Yeah! Well it went exactly as I had planned. No one actually witnessed it, as I had found a back way out, and over a wall, using a long pole, which I had put in place."

"You're a bloody marvel when it comes to gymnastics Eden", said Rod.

They then discussed their current situation more deeply, anxiously and on 'razor-edged alert' and agreed on a progress plan from their current point. Rod explained to Eden where he had arranged to meet Mukwe, and that it was a long way from where they were.

"How far?" asked Eden.

"Twenty five to thirty kilometres, but don't worry because Mukwe will have everything that we need, including food." said Rod.

"Good! Because we'll be ravenous by the time we get there." Said Eden

Rod agreed, and made the point that they would have to start immediately, and keep going throughout the night. Before leaving their place of concealment, it suddenly occurred to Rod that out of decency, he needed to check with Eden that he really agreed with the plan. "Eden, it is all very well for me to have made plans. Do you agree with them, or can you think of a better way of getting to our destination?"

Eden replied, "No! Rod, I'm quite happy, and remember that I also have to get a long way from Aberfoyle."

Taking every care that they possibly could — by hiding behind any form of visual obstruction — to avoid detection, they made it down to the Aberfoyle river, where there was much more cover, and water to obliterate their tracks. Their route was downstream, and they had to continue to be incredibly careful, because they had to pass a new Suburban Development area; the town's Industrial Estate and the Forestry Department land. The cover afforded was as good as they could have hoped for and they got passed these without a problem, but a new one immediately confronted them — a series of farms with river frontage. Even more secrecy was required, but fortunately better cover was provided by the dense wild bush. Progress was made creeping along the river; sometimes having to cross to the other side when the farmhouse was close to their course, and by evening they had achieved about ten kilometres.

An important thing during that afternoon trek was that Rod noticed some wild small-plums and crabapples, which they were able to pick and eat. As they were winding along the river he also identified some wild spinach that he knew could be eaten uncooked and cold, this kept up their strength and enabled them to continue the trek. Once it was dark, they were able to get out onto the road towards their destination. One of them kept ears glued for sound of traffic coming from either direction, whilst the other concentrated on detecting lights approaching. Every hour they changed these 'vigils'. During light conversation that they were having, Eden suddenly suggested, "Let's jog to keep awake and to increase the distance that we can make." This was agreed and the pace increased.

As sunrise approached and there was a slight brightening in the East, they reckoned that they were within about five kilometres of the meeting point. When the sun did actually rise behind Aberfoyle hill, they were about to return to the river but were overcome with joy to hear hugely welcome barks from none other than Monty, which indicated that Mukwe had anticipated that they would take to the road overnight. After being nearly consumed by the excited dog, and carrying him in his arms, Rod, together with Eden made a very rapid rush to the Pickup — leaping into it, with Monty on the back.

Joyous welcome and proud introductions ensued. Mukwe then did a swift 180degree turn and they headed for the intended hideaway, which both Rod and Mukwe knew from the past. Rod noted that Eden and Mukwe seemed to hit-it-off right from the start, so he asked, "Eden could you enlighten Mukwe on our history going back over the years"? Eden agreed, and spent an entertaining ten minutes or so covering this period.

"We first met whilst at school, but this became a closer friendship when we were swimming and playing water polo. We were both members of Aberfoyle Swim Club and both represented the Club at Inter-Town events. This unfortunately changed when I was jailed about two years ago. But 'Wa-La' who did I unexpectedly meet again? Even more amazing was what transpired from our many conversations: suddenly here was someone else who planned to escape — you beaut!" Mukwe expressed his thanks to Eden for bringing him up to date. It was therefore a very happy trio that arrived at the remote vehicle parking area, close to where they would be camping. While they were sorting out all the gear, Monty made the rounds of the precinct, to get it well onto his map.

The district that they had chosen was at the conference of the Aberfoyle River, with the much larger Culanci River, and as mentioned Rod, Mukwe and Monty knew it well from past fishing and light hunting expeditions. Unbeknown to most fishermen and tourists, was the complete change in the country on the other side of the escarpment, through which this river had forced its way over the millennia. The country down there was tropical forest Government Reserve Land, which was not used for anything at that period, and no people could occupy it. Perfect for the three of them, with Monty, to take the next steps in their lives!.

Although Mukwe would be returning to his job the next day, he insisted on coming with them on this last stage. They made their way down-river to the gorge, but as they got to this highest point of the river Eden exclaimed, "My G.d! the size of the boulders: how do we get down through all that 'landslide? Like climbing down one of the pyramids in Egypt".

"By taking extreme care in the descent, said Rod, although it will amaze you to see that Monty has discovered an almost hidden route down to the bottom." Once they had wound around; hung-over many of the larger rocks and assisted one another to slide down to the side of what would be a waterfall during floods, they arrived at a deep pool, and below that they found a crossing where the river had to flow over a shale bank. Here they met Monty again!

From that point they changed direction to keep under the ridge line — getting further and further away from Aberfoyle. Rod and Mukwe were keeping a lookout for a large cavern that they knew existed in this side of the ridge.

When it came into view, the Group made their way up to it, and were pleased to see that it met their initial requirements. Although the opening wasn't all that large — about the size of a single-car garage- they could make out a much larger cave behind.

First things first though — it needed to be carefully checked to ensure that it was not a Leopard's lair. They didn't think so, because Monty had not shown any untoward interest. Nevertheless, they did search it with gun in hand, but it appeared to be too open for a leopard and they all felt pretty safe.

Time to dump all their gear; get a little fire going for grub and a 'well-earned-coffee', and catch-up on everything that had happened over the last three weeks or so.

# CHAPTER 10

Rod was feeling pretty guilty that he had involved Muk-we in his — now serious — scrape with the law, and offered an apology. "Sorry Mate that I have got you caught up in all of this. You have gone way beyond the call of friendship to help-out me, and Eden."

Mukwe replied "No problem Rod, it has added spice to my life since I raced down to meet you behind Fairhill. But what do you intend to do?"

Rod then addressed Eden. "Eden I hope that this situation isn't way outside the parametres that you've set for yourself, over the last year or so? After all, you havn't been a 'Bushman' before! Have you?"

"No. I havn't, said Eden, but I think I can enjoy this sort of a holiday."

"Muk, before I answer your question, said Rod, have the unfolding events of the last three weeks, compromised you in any way. Are there any indications that the police have you marked?"

"No, replied Mukwe, leastwise not that I am aware of. As you would be aware though your Dad and Mom have been questioned at length, but my Dad says there has been no further visit to your place, since the day after you were shot. Jacky has also had to plead ignorance of why you broke out of the Court, and where you could possibly have gone."

"Okay, well look guys we are in the back blocks of a Reserve: there are no roads into this area, and no Ranger homes or small settlements nearby. What would you estimate the distance to the nearest settlement of any kind, Muk?" On reflection Mukwe estimated that it would be plus/minus sixty kilometres, and that he would bring a detailed map, the next time he came to the camp.

Eden entered into the discussion by asking, "Mukwe you are not in the predicament that we are. Wouldn't you intend to stay with the Agric. Department in Culanci?"

The reply was in the affirmative, He then added, "All the country around this place, is in my Duty Area and I know all the Highways and Byways!. I can get very close to here whenever I visit, without anyone observing, because the veld is very thick, and I leave the road to drive to a hidden parking place."

As the discussion continued Rod said, "Mukwe my mind has been ticking over: we are in the second last school semester, of the year. Would it be beyond the realms of possibility, that you consider going to University in the Capital, next year? It may fit into a plan forming in my mind at the moment, regarding Eden and I". "It will all be paid for!"

"Whoa! Interjected Eden — this sounds a bit in the clouds, for me. I'll need to hear a lot more before I consider going along with it."

Rod put up his hand and said "Understandably Eden, but I remember you saying one day long ago at the pool, that you had managed Matriculation before leaving school. Eden acknowledged that that was correct.

This little issue with Eden had given Mukwe time to think, and he stated, "All right then the possibility of a Bachelor Degree has 'sort of' crossed my mind."

"Good! well let's leave it at that for today, as I need to develop it further. What I can say however to bring things into line, is that sister Carry and Colin have set-up home in the Capital and will be more than co-operative."

"Now we need extra gear and other things! I noticed that you had pen and paper, Muk: let's each make a list for a one month holiday!!"

This they did with one sitting on his 'butt' on the ground; one sitting on a large and convenient stump that they had flattened, and the third lying on his army jacket. Food for them and Monty topped the list. Second-hand clothing for each; sleeping bags with mattress inserts; cooking containers; a large quantity of water for initial drinking and cooking, and many other small necessities including anti-malaria pills, anti-tsetse fly medication and skin creams, filled the rest.

A good item on Eden's list was for a couple of Fishing Rods and Reels. (Easy, as Mukwe and Rod had many of those back in Aberfoyle!). Mukwe added the rifle with ammunition to his, and Rod listed a piece of quality leather plus knives and sharpening stones, for cutting the leather. As they were studying each list, Rod added the need for Mukwe to source an old truck tube and bicycle-tyre tube.

By this time it was mid-afternoon, and they decided to carry out a preliminary survey of the surrounding bush. Almost at once, they were reminded of another potential threat to their situation. The distant sound of an aircraft that sounded like it was flying in their direction. Rod immediately shouted, "Get under that deep cover — pointing directly to where he meant — I will grab Monty and collar him." From the cover they observed it to the South East at some distance: it was flying at somewhere around a thousand metres high, and travelling across the sky, away from their situation. But it could have been so different!

The rest of their afternoon slog was good. The bush was much taller and thicker than they were used to. They saw plenty of small game, much to the delight and short chases, by Monty. Thankfully they did not encounter any of the 'Big Five'. On the subject of the 'large and dangerous' though, they discussed the fact that Rod and Eden would have to go down river — very carefully — and check for Hippo's and Crocodiles. When they got back, they plucked and cooked a guinea fowl that they had managed to 'nail'. No vegetables this time! But in the back of Rod's mind he remembered the wild spinach that was very easy on the pallet. He would have to keep a vigilant lookout...The two bushmen were however teaching Eden where to look for plentiful wild fruit.

Monty had also caught and was eating a small rabbit, at the same time that they were having their meal.

While sitting around the fire and eating, Mukwe and Eden wanted to know more about Rod's plans for the future, and particularly how they affected Eden. Rod chewed steadily while thinking long and hard then said, "Great!. Now, about a possible future plan from next year onwards."

"You guys will remember our Primary School Deputy Head, Mr. Frost? After we proceeded to the various High Schools, that we attended, he became Head Master of the other Primary School, in Aberfoyle. The other two nodded that they remembered him. Rod continued, Mr. Frost was a close friend of our family, including myself and my sisters, with each of them even going into Teaching Music. While I was in jail, I even received a message from him, through the family, indicating that he knew that I would not attack a policeman. Returning to his career, you two might not be aware that he has been elevated to the Inspectorate in the Education Department, and has his Office and Staff in the Capital. Well, when we get there, I intend to go and see him, and respectfully seek entrance to Uni. for you, Eden, and for myself. That is why I would also love you to give consideration to it as well, Mukwe."

Eden interjected at this stage, and said, "I'll go along with you on the plan. However, you seem to have ignored one incredibly important point — the Authorities and Law Enforcement will immediately pick you and I Rod, from our names." Mukwe agreed and was very concerned for his mates.

"I'm fully aware of that, said Rod and it has been burning away in my mind ever since I was remanded. I believe that I can overcome the problem, but you'll have to trust me until we actually get to the Capital. Fortunately we will have safe and total anonymity there, with sister Carry and her fiancé Colin. He was in the same Unit in the Army as Mukwe and I. Eden I promise you, that you and I will get to Uni, next year."

Mukwe and Eden expressed their relief and hope for the fulfillment of Rod's plans, and they all went to their blankets looking forward to whatever excitement could be generated in the thick bush setting, over the next two to three months. As expected, it was a pretty rough tough night, without any form of mattresses!

After a good breakfast of the food brought by Mukwe, he explained, "Look guys, I'll have to get back so as not to create any suspicion. See you day after tomorrow; go easy on the provisions and try and trap some fish or eels!" With that they accompanied him part of the way to his pickup, before cheering him on his way.

Rod and Eden spent a couple of busy days improving and further camouflaging the site. Monty gave off strong vibes that it was time to go bush again, for the excitement of the hunt. They also cut stacks of fine foliage as interim mattresses, which did help — if only partly.

# CHAPTER 11

Intense activity was the best description of Rod's, Eden's and Monty's progress over the next few days — pending Mukwe's return. They built a better fireplace, lining it with carefully crafted rock walls round three-and-a-bit sides. Whilst they were engaged in this, they were talking about This, That and Everything Else.

As they got to the end and stood up to admire it, Eden suddenly said, "I think we should do something else before we head off down, to explore the river."

"Oh! so what do you reckon should come first?" asked Rod.

"To climb to the highest point on that Ridge behind us, he said pointing upwards, so that we can look down on the river, and this Reserve."

"Brilliant! replied Rod, Let's grab a water bottle each and 'head for the hills." As they were ascending the prominence, they got to talking about the best form of camouflage and hiding in case of an emergency sighting. Under the same potential threat they also tied a rope to Monty's collar — giving him only a short lead. Once they got through the bush on the lower reaches, and started on the steep incline, it did become more open. Fortunately there were plenty of large rocks and buttresses that threw dark shadows. Nothing happened to alarm them and after an hour and a half of very difficult climbing, they came out on top. Here, they straight away sought a deep shadow to cover them all, then turned to look at the route that they had used for the ascent, and the opening vista that had become 'their country'.

Both of them were astounded. They were looking out to an horizon about eighty kilometres away, and the view over the country stretched virtually 180 degrees from where they were standing. It was fantastic; dropping away constantly towards the Zambezi River. It was generally heavily timbered and dark green, but with the rivers winding their way across and down towards that line, meeting the sky. There were open Savannah areas, but they were eclipsed by the bush. Rod was surprised that there were no hills or other promontories blocking the view. He exclaimed "What a wonderful decision you made Eden. We get an incredible view of the river, don't we?"

"We sure do." replied Eden in utter awe.

"Another two hundred kilometres over that horizon

is the great Zambezi, and I feel a strong attachment to it." added Rod.

"Yea, but in that landscape we know that there are a heap of game. Take for instance those giraffe, way down there in that second band of savannah grassland." said Eden, pointing them out carefully to Rod. He was as 'chuffed' as could be that Eden had picked them out, and gave him a congratulatory slap on the back. There would have been eight or nine of them, and they watched them for some time, basking in pleasure and looking for other game at the same time. From previous outings and walks with Monty, they knew that there were many small antelope down there, but they were too well camouflaged.

They then carefully climbed out on top and looked in the other direction. Not surprisingly they, and Monty, recognized that part of the country into which they had been born and raised. They could even see the hill behind Aberfoyle, and were sinuously reminded of how vulnerable they were, and the necessity of always maintaining camouflage. During conversation they had a good laugh when Rod said, "Actually I don't think I will be shaving much from now onward, and, I think I will allow a moustache to grow!"

Once they had climbed down — fed Monty and had a good meal, they decided that they would do the first traverse of the river, the following day. This would fit in well with Mukwe's expected arrival, the day after, and hopefully he would be bringing a heap of gear. Eden ventured "We could be taking-up a good part of that day, helping him get all the gear down here. Just as well that we have plenty of good cover, to achieve it."

Rod agreed, then said "Did you by any chance ask him to bring a good pair of scissors?"

"Yeh! I did. Apart from all their other uses — for example cutting our nails — they are vital to help in getting fishing rods properly set-up."

Rod could already visualise his need for them, but didn't expand on it.

The next day went as planned. The river banks were heavily covered by scrub, boulders and dead timber, washed down from previous floods. They did however find some passable openings to the river, which gave promise of good fishing and potentially of swimming — once they were sure that there were no crocs or hippos. Ominously there was no shortage of snakes either, and they even saw a large python making a getaway from them. Rod checked with Eden. "Have you had much to do with snakes?"

"No, and they give me the heebie jeebies."

Rod continued, "Quite understandable, but don't worry about it as they are very sensitive to vibrations, and in most events, you will see them heading away. I'll have to be bloody careful with Monty and the pythons though, as he has had no experience with them. They will attack any medium sized animal. He'd be okay if he managed to get-in some serious bites before the first constricting loop got around him — otherwise they could be fatal, pretty quickly."

Back at the end of the day, they were glad to have a feed and some coffee: plus a chunk of beef and some sadza for Monty, before 'crashing'. The following day, they continued to reorganize and better prepare a place for Mukwe's return that evening, after Soccer! Sure enough he was on time, carrying some stuff in his arms, and with a large haversack, on his back. After greetings all round and dumping his load he said, "You guys are going to have to come back to the Pickup with me, to help get the rest of it." Rod and Eden laughed.

When they got close to the parking area, he cautioned them, saying, "Just hide here, while I go and make sure that there is no one else there." Once clear, they hastened to the vehicle, and climbed in.

Rod then said, " Muk, didn't you say that you could get closer to our encampment, further back — going through thick bush?"

Mukwe agreed saying "Okay we'll go back and approach that way. The vehicle will be much safer there, anyway." The venture involved going back about five kilometres then turning left onto what was essentially a well-worn game track. Mukwe carefully traversed this dense bush for a further five kilometes, but this time going back towards the escarpment, and finally parking under thick cover. They then collected all the rest of the gear, and between them they managed to carry it all around to their 'lair'.

Monty gave Mukwe a big welcome after they had laid it all out, as if knowing that he had brought lots of food for him. Aside from getting out new food for the evening meal, they left the rest for the morrow: instead enjoying comradeship over the cooking and eating of the meal. Once consumed, and coffee in hand, they chatted well into the night, before 'hitting the sack- oh-so-comfortably', on the blow-up mattresses that Mukwe had brought.

Up early to begin the big sort out! It took considerable time, as they cheerfully argued over who should do what. In his eagerness around the fishing rods, Eden went into the fishing gear bag, like a kid into a toy box, saying "I see you've brought plenty of hook combinations and weights Mukwe, but what about lures? Do we have a selection of those?"

"Of course we do. Look a little further in the bag, or in the little zipped containers."

" Ah! Okay, I see," added the latter.

"Aside from the fishing, said Rod — you seem to be delving deep into that box that you've got, Mukwe?"

"I know, replied Mukwe, and I'm looking for that good pair of scissors that Eden will need any moment, and that I will then need, to cut the strips of rubber to make the 'Katties'."

Rod had already noted the truck and bicycle tubes, and

nodded his approval, adding, "This leather will also partly be used on those, to make the 'fellikies'". And so it continued until everything was un-packed and stowed away. All the while, Monty had been nosing and sniffing around into everything, that everyone was doing, until Eden exclaimed, "That dog has now got it into his mind, what each one of us will be doing: which is more than we know about each other's plans. Take for instance that roll of leather between your knees, Rod. You certainly don't need that much to make a couple of fellikies, do you?" Both Rod and Mukwe looked up, and smiled, for they had experienced 'the leather' thing before, on Fairhill farm.

"Three guesses and no prizes Eden, what do you think it could be for?" added Mukwe.

"I wouldn't have a clue — you're going to have to tell me."

"Rod you tell him." suggested Mukwe.

"Okay, said Rod — It's for the Long Bows: we cut thin strips and plat them to make the drawing cord — the action of which, he demonstrated with both hands. Even though we don't yet have the heavy metal arrowheads, there are plenty of nice straight and strong saplings in the bush on each side of the river, that we can use for arrows. Once we have cut them, we have to strip the bark off, and then gradually shape them. Don't worry, you will have plenty of opportunity, to take part."

It was almost midday by the time they had finished the sort, and It was time to give Monty a bone, and for them to organize lunch. Once that was over

they were all anxious to head down to the river, to fish.

Bass were the only likely fish that they would encounter, so each had prepared their individual rods, for this event. So off they trotted to take on the riverine challenge! Surprisingly Mukwe landed a bream at the first site they visited, but after his success the 'bites' faltered, and they moved on. Further down the river they came to a shale crossing and Rod crossed over to other side deeply immersed in memories of how to set up his rod with float/weights/lure and hooks. He came to a point on the bank that he liked the look of.

Mukwe and Eden carried on down the near side, to an area that the latter remembered. Rod got going on the fishing first — using a large hook and small lure, plus a float — just for the fun of it. After five or six casts, he managed to catch a bass. It was female though, and he returned it to the water. He then decided to change to a small hook and to bait it. This meant digging into likely looking riverside mud, until he found an earthworm. Using this one and others, he laboured away for half an hour or so, with many 'casts', managing to catch a couple of bream. Monty was not sure of the catches but Rod said, "You're going to have to get used to fish, old sport!"

On the other side of the river Mukwe and Eden were having similar success, whilst also experimenting with various options on their rods. Eden did succeed in catching a male bass, much to their excitement, while Mukwe caught another fine bream. They all gutted and de-scaled their catches, and headed back to the arranged meeting point. On his way back, Rod was paying close attention to low saplings in the bush all around him. When in sight of the meeting point, he did come across a suitable one point five metre, straight candidate, which he immediately set about cutting down with his knife, which was always kept sharp.

Once together and on their way back to camp, Mukwe who had been ticking-off in his mind the various dynamics, spied an ideal shaped kattie handle — the "V" of which needed to fit a man's grip, and the thickness, about that of a man's middle finger. Eden compared and advised that the handle wasn't as long as 'bought catapult' handles, but was informed by Mukwe that 'African' katties could shoot much further. They had better grip and longer/thicker thongs. Rod added, "Don't worry Eden, we'll give you the full opportunity to manufacture one for yourself: a really industrial process!"

When they got back to camp Rod made coffee, whilst the other two prepared the fish for a late lunch/early dinner. Much talking and laughing ensued about the day. During the food preparation, Rod stripped all the bark off the sapling that he had cut. He then reduced the length to one point three metres, and started shaping the ends of the Long-Bow to be. Finalizing this job would take some days, with strong bending in every direction so as to maintain its flexibility. Once they had eaten, Mukwe and Eden got onto cutting the truck and cycle tubing for the katties, whilst Rod continued working on the first bow.

Monty took his time to get used to fish gut (raw) and flesh (cooked)! The next day, which was the last before Mukwe's return to work, followed much the same routine. They caught a few more fish for Mukwe to take back with him, to enjoy with his soccer mates. They also completed the first 'katty'; with thanks to Rod for carefully cutting a 'fellikie' out of the leather!. Trials with it were 'very hit and miss' by all of them, and required the thongs shortened before sighting some improvement. But as Rod and Mukwe had predicted, a stone the size of a thumbnail could be launched in excess of a hundred metres: dangerous for anything within that range.

By the time that Mukwe found a second one (with bark and foliage still on), Rod had cut two fairly thin strips of leather; woven them together and fitted them to the first bow as its drawstring. He and Eden each had a few trial shots, with light wooden arrows, but apart from the fact that it worked they couldn't make an assessment of its potential without heavier arrows. The next stage would be to lightly roast it above the fire whilst continually taking it off to do the bending process. A great weekend was had by all, with much fun and chatter. A few fish were caught, and Mukwe managed to hit a dove with the 'katty'. A nice extra touch of red meat! He also applied his skills to the bow with the others, and came to the same conclusion. It was definitely time for him to buy a dozen arrows — or just metal heads for same!

For the five days that Mukwe was away, they carried on just as before, except that towards the end of the period they started hunting again instead of just fishing; much to the delight of Monty. While out on these hunts they practiced with the 'katties'. As they gradually improved, they were successful in nailing a pheasant. Monty also managed to catch another rabbit after a tense chase, and was given loud applause for his success.

Apart from these small birds/animals, they witnessed a large herd of Impala watching them secretly through the cover of the bush. Fortunately they were upwind and at quite some distance, so Monty did not smell them. Another notable sighting was a flock of Vultures that had succeeded in gaining ascendance over a kill — probably predated by either a Cheetah, Hyena or a pack of Wild Dogs. They all watched with interest as the creatures fought clumsily to get to the best portion of the carcass, and Eden couldn't help but express his disgust, "Yuk! Look at those revolting things: like they were born straight out of the dirt and dust, and not from eggs."

During discussion and amazement at the goings-on, Rod said, "Eden, those birds are part of a Colony of the same, which roost approximately one hundred kilometres to the South East of here. Once they have had their kill, they will probably fly back over the next twenty four hours or so, and join their 'Kith & Kin'. After that they will repeat outward flights looking for a kill — but it could be in a different direction."

The weeks flowed by with Rod and Eden helping one another in every way, and finding that they could enjoy their wild existence. Monty showed that he definitely concurred. Naturally they each had a hidden concern, deep in the back of their minds. They looked forward to Mukwe's visit each weekend, as the existence of a third party in their midst pushed the angst further to the back of their minds.

All of them enjoyed going further afield each time, and further appreciating the wonder of the river system, and the surrounds. On many of their outings they witnessed some of the unique birds of the country: apart from the abundance of eagles and various hawks and falcons flying overhead, they loved to see the very large, dark brown Secretary Bird plodding through the long grass, looking for small snakes to devour. Incredible that these birds had straight legs, nearly a metre long. They also often caught sight of the beautiful iridescent blue, large Kingfishers, up and down the river, and were always teased from the tree lines by the friendly 'Goway' birds.

Continued practice in the use of the bows with the proper metal headed arrows, and with the 'katties', began to have dramatic success towards keeping fresh meat on their plates, as well as supplementing Monty's diet. Rod had been the first to kill a Duiker, with the bow, and over time the others also succeeded. They quite often hit partridges and quail with the 'katties', and Eden was the first to down a guinea fowl. These accomplishments supplied meat for a week including that required for Monty, and they realised that they could cut down on their hunting. Catching the odd fish, or 'three', also continued!

# CHAPTER 12

On a Friday evening in early October when Mukwe got back to camp for the weekend, he seemed very excited. Rod and Eden teased him into explaining what it was that was pumping him up. "Well, actually quite alot of things," he said, "first of all, I have received acceptance from the University to start my course next year. Then because of that, and the fact that my Department assisted me with my application, I've had long discussions with the Boss for leave of absence while I do the Course. I told him that I needed a break before starting." "So — guess what?"

"From the first of January?" ventured Eden.

Rod on the other hand recognized the excitement as being a portent of what they intended doing, and said, "You are already on leave, aren't you?"

"Yep!" returned Mukwe, " I've already chatted with Mom and Dad, and told them what I will be doing until Uni starts, and the fact that I will be joining you guys on this amazing holiday. Don't be concerned, as it is an absolute secret. And finally, I have come across a couple of canoes in Culanci and we can get hold of them, should we want them." Now the other two were just as excited as him.

"Fantastic!" said Rod, "that does bring up a multitude of areas that we need to work through. So let's have a cuppa coffee; a sit down, and work through them."

Mukwe was the first to put forward a minute, "I didn't mention it, but will be able to keep my vehicle until the year-end, if need be," Both Rod and Eden were extremely pleased with that statistic. Mukwe continued, "and about the canoes? Will they be an advantage?" Rod looked across at Eden, who nodded.

"Absolutely, said Rod, Eden and I have been set on travelling by the rivers to the Zambezi ever since we climbed to the top of the escarpment, and could trace the route. However, that brings-up the complex issue of getting hold of the funds for them and — once we get there, to cover the future. Also, it has been on my mind for a long time, that I will need to contact Colin and Carry about getting all our excess gear back to civilization; plus their meeting us at the dam on the Zambezi and taking us to their home."

When they had all completed their lists, and prepared dinner for themselves and Monty, animated discussion followed and as they were making ready for their sleeping bags, all the immediate issues had been covered in roughly the following sequence:-

1. Mukwe had his work Pickup to cover the immediate future.
2. They were indeed interested in the canoes.
3. All of them grabbed at the opportunity to travel down the series of rivers to the mighty Zambesi.
4. Funding the next eight weeks or so was discussed and Rod made it quite clear that Eden had already paid his way — or none of what they intended would be possible. Rod & Mukwe had the necessary funds, and they would have to work out how to draw down the funds.
5. Rod would somehow have to phone Carry and Colin for transport assistance, at the end of their current stay.

The following morning they all agreed that their dreams had been widely coloured by the previous evening's discussions. At Monty's insistence and demand for attention however, they did pursue their usual fishing and hunting ventures over the next few days, and thoroughly enjoyed the foursome experience — for which he took full credit! They took him to task, and all of them spread out and chased him backwards and forwards across the open space below their camp. At the end of this massive game, he jumped up on each of them, gave them a good licking and thanked them for allowing him to chase them around the grassland!

One day, Mukwe was committed to going back to Aberfoyle for an Agricultural Dept meeting, after which he would catch-up with his parents; draw funds for the canoes and their planned adventure, as well as catching up with Rod's parents. Aside from being able to report on the health and well being of all of them, Rod wanted Mukwe to get his bankcard, through them.

Then on his way back to Culanci, he could make further arrangements in connection with the canoes. He was away a couple of days in which all went according to plan, although finding the 'all important' Card created a difficult search. An extra little gem of interest — particularly to Rod — was that he had met Ed (Rod's cousin) at the meeting, who was in the final stages of an Agricultural Degree, and would be joining the Conservation Department on his return to Aberfoyle.

Mission accomplished, they got down to serious planning. Cash, picking-up and carting the canoes; plus the best strategy for phoning Carry and Colin for the help that they would need from them. Late one evening — with Rod and Eden having blackened their faces and hands, they headed for the Pickup and drove through to Hayes, some ninety kilometres in the opposite direction from Aberfoyle.

Rod remembered having seen an ATM (a cash withdrawal machine mounted in the wall of a Bank) for his bank, in this particular town. While they were driving Eden ventured, "Rod what is this 'whacky' thing that you are going to look for, and there seems to be some confusing myth about it? You can't make me believe that you can go into a town, in the middle of the night, to draw some cash from a teller on the other side of a brick wall!"

Rod and Mukwe had a good laugh at this and Rod said, "Well we're about to do it, so the best thing will be for you to come and watch the 'impossible dream." Thankfully there were no incidents and no problems on Rod's side, in drawing up to his limit, through the machine.

Eden watched the process — scratching his head while muttering under his breath — showing disbelief in the 'magic' of it!.

Whilst back in civilization Rod took the opportunity to phone Carry and Colin from a phone box, inserting the necessary coins, with gloves on. After excited greetings all round he brought them up to date on everything and explained their plans for the next six to eight weeks. First, he asked Colin if he would come down to Culanci. Then bring Mukwe back to the reserve, on the day that he handed in his vehicle, which would be the Friday, eight days ahead. Then he asked them both to come out to Kariba, once he, Mukwe and Eden had arrived at that destination.

The final job was for Mukwe to pick up a beer for each of them for the return journey to join Monty, and for Rod and Eden to have a damned good wash!!

Mukwe headed into Culanci the next day, to collect and pay for the canoes and paddles. Friends from his Soccer Club helped him load them and were intrigued in the fibs he told, as to where and when they would be used. At the arranged time, Rod and Eden made their way up to the hidden parking place to meet him. They were pleasantly surprised at the newness and quality of the two vessels. Mukwe remarked, "They are not kayaks but open Canadian Style canoes, which will be perfect for transporting all our gear." One was a double and the other a single, and surprisingly different in length. With some careful manouvering over the difficult sections, where all three had to carry the double canoe and paddles, they finally made it down through the rocky gap, to their section of the river.

From that point forward executing the plans for the trip were the most important part of each day: exactly what they would need to take by way of gear, provisions and utensils, including plenty of water for the initial stages. All the rest could go back with Colin.

On the day of his arrival in Culanci, Mukwe headed off to hand in his vehicle, and to bid his colleagues and friends farewell and Christmas cheers. He then met up with Colin at the arranged site. It was a loud and boisterous meeting — given the circumstances — and after strong hand shaking and hugs Mukwe welcomed him saying, "Thanks so much for being prepared to come down and help us in the final stages, before we head off."

"No problem Muk, I'm really looking forward to catching-up with the other two blokes and seeing this camp that Rod mentioned. In a way I'm bloody envious of you guys: it would be great to be with you all, but glad to know that Carry and I will be doing our part."

They jumped into Col's station-wagon and Mukwe showed him the route out to the hidden spot! This trip out was not an unusual or weird thing for Colin, as they had all operated in this vicinity, during their army days.

What a super reunion for the Brothers-in-Law, and Monty, who immediately recognized and welcomed Colin. Recollections were flowing through Rod's mind, and he said "Do you realise Col, that it's close to a year since we last saw one another?"

"Yeh!" replied Colin, "and what a major bloody upset for you. What the hell do those Aberfoyle Cops think they are doing?"

"I reckon the poor Cop who tried to shoot Monty, has really been set-up." Said Rod.

Colin was introduced to Eden, by Rod. He then explained the twisted case scenario, as prosecuted by the District Court, and while relating the details of his escape, described how Eden had prepared the window of the court room, such that he could effectively just dive through it. Colin thanked Eden profusely on behalf of the Cochran family and for himself and Carry, as well as for Jacky and Mel.

Now that all four knew one another they had a celebratory lunch, and resulting from the string of questions from Colin, Rod was happy to unburden himself saying, "The first stage will be the intended canoe trip, following the three rivers to the Kalupati River. That one you know, don't you Colin?" That worthy nodded vigorously, indicating that he had fished it often. "The next stage will be a short stay at the Dam Tourism area, culminating in the arrival of yourself and Carry and the hope that you will be able to have a mini holiday with us. Then finally returning to the Capital with you and Carry."

Colin also followed Eden's line of months before, asking, "How do you and Eden expect to get into Uni, with your spooked names and identities?"

Rod mentioned Mr. Frost (whom Colin had also known briefly) as being the first part of the 'hurdle race', and held up both hands with fingers crossed, saying, "I'm pretty sure that I can organize the second, vital, part of the race." They were all pretty flabbergasted — but all had faith in him.

They gave Colin a wonderful couple of days of fishing, and hunting with Monty. He was fascinated with the effectiveness of the bows and katties, and after trying them all a few times said, "Make sure that you bring these out with you: I'm looking forward to practising with them while you guys are at Uni. Then I'll challenge the lot of you, during your vacations." Over this period their greatest concentration was on fishing in a myriad of spots, up and down the river.

Colin taught all of them a great deal more than any of them had known before, as it had always been one of his family's favourite pastimes. He had brought a 12V refrigerator in his car, and once it was connected, it was loaded with a variety of fish for his home journey. The threesome also had plenty for the start of their trip. Once they had got their excess gear and equipment up to Colin's car, they bid him on his way. Rod parted saying, "Thanks a ton Sport, and we look forward to seeing you and Carry in plus/minus seven-weeks."

Up early the next day, they carried all their gear down to the canoes which were parked on a sandy beach with their bows already in the water. Having loaded them they returned to camp for a final grilled fish 'brekkie'. They then poured water and heaps of sand over the coals, and took the last utensils etcetera down with them to the launching site. The canoes were packed evenly, leaving appropriate spaces for the rowers, and for Monty — who would always be with the single rower.

# CHAPTER 13

The rainy season had only just started, so there was not alot of water in the river. This meant that they would have quite a few portages, of shortish distances. Guess which one of the four, didn't mind that prospect at all ...? Whilst Colin had still been with them, they had discussed the journey ahead and between them they estimated that they would have up to three hundred kilometres to canoe and port. Rod's impressions were that the early stages would be the most difficult, due to the river still being pretty low. He advised them that there would be two more similar confluences, to the one above their camp, but that the one after that would be much bigger: that one would take them into the Kalupati River, a substantial tributary of the Zambezi. He enjoined his mates to try and achieve ten kilometres per day to start with, which would require early starts and sunset finishes. Potentially pretty tiring — but they were all 'fit as fiddles'.

All were eager to embark, although Monty definitely thought the mode of transport — *a bit strange!* However, once Rod had got him onto the canoe and ordered him to 'Sit', he realised that he was committed.

As expected, the journey downriver was complicated, because every portage was different. Some of them caused the canoers to divert away from the river through short sections of thick bush; others involved traversing granite slopes over which the river spread and cascaded in a very shallow flow. Still others had muddy sections — but thank goodness for progress — others were mere shale embankments that only delayed them for ten minutes, or so. At about midday they stopped and ate a proper lunch before continuing. Importantly they were all thoroughly enjoying the adventure, and achieved their estimated ten kilometres.

A further three days of similar rowing and encumbrances of riverine terrain, brought them to the next river confluence. While debating their journey so far, they discussed the fact that they had already seen a fair amount of game, including a small herd of Kudu. (a large and powerful African antelope, the male of which has a mighty set of twisted horns). Clearly they expected to see many more types, and were mindful of more dangerous ones

A storm coincided with their reaching this confluence, and it reminded them that rain of this magnitude could bring about some change to their progress. It was a good 'ole tropical downpour', which they could hear crashing through the bush towards them. The blackness of the storm cloud was also something to witness — as if it intended to just cover everything forever! Notwithstanding, they didn't stop paddling until they had got well into this new and bigger river. Once they did stop, the canoes were emptied out and beached upside down. What they had experienced was a keen reminder of the very heavy cloudbursts that often occurred up on the Highveld.

First things first, were to dry-off then cook-up a feed for all. After the wash up, it was back to the river for a 'wetting of the lines'. The new river seemed to be deeper so they adapted their rods to suit, but it took ages, plus many changes to type of hook, weights and baiting. Mukwe decided to use a lure and Rod changed to a 'runner' type reel — casting up-stream and allowing it to gradually work downstream. As it turned out, Eden was the first to catch a fish big enough for their eating stock. After the second catch, by Mukwe, Rod grabbed the rifle; loaded it and headed out with Monty. He didn't shoot anything but Monty did catch a grouse and ate it on the spot. Rod kept talking to himself, "The magnificence of the forestation which is so varied — both as to size and type. I reckon that we have now entered an area in which Teak flourishes." Monty enjoyed himself just as much — wildly sniffing around and chasing anything that moved. They arrived back to a wonderful smell of fish being cooked for the evening meal, and a happy couple of guys who had supplemented their stock with a few more fish caught.

During discussion over the meal, they estimated that they had covered between forty and fifty kilometres over their first five days, and both Mukwe and Rod expected their speed in the canoes to improve, now that they were on a larger river. The portages should become less and easier, due to the wider reaches, and stronger flow.

Eden then came in with a question out of the blue. "Rod you have just been out bush alone with Monty, for a couple of hours: how do you make sure that you don't get lost?" Mukwe and Rod exchanged glances, which clearly inferred that they were bloody good at just that.

Rod replied, "I'll leave it to Mukwe to give you the Surveyor type detail, but one of the main personal rules that an individual should consistently adopt, is to frequently look back at the route that he has been coming along, and try to identify certain very clear, or bold features. Another rule is to always be aware of a large promontory, rock formation, or towering tree, so that you can judge where you are, in relation to it. For instance, if we climbed up that large boulder over there, said Rod, pointing to the feature, and looked over that way — pointing more or less in the direction of the rivers they had been traversing — we would still see that high ridge under which we had our main camp site. Another thing that one can do is to strip some bark off a tree, or build a small peak of stones on the route that one is following, and keep a lookout for it, on the way back." He then looked across at Mukwe, and signaled for him to carry on.

Mukwe continued, "Rod mentioned the word surveyor: well, let me alter that slightly Eden to put your mind on Maps. They show North, East, South and West, very distinctly, with North always at the top of the page. Now bring yourself back to earth, and always be aware of the direction in which the sun came up — that is East. Opposite that is where the sun will set — in the West. North and South are at ninety degrees to those two. Take a look at the position of the sun now, and you will realise that it is not directly overhead, but slightly to the North thereof. This is proof that we are in the Southern Hemisphere, and that the sun appears to track anti-clockwise for us."

Eden interrupted by pointing at the sun and asking, "But how do you know that that is North?"

"Because as I mentioned– you must always be aware of where the sun rose in the morning, and which you should remember was over there — said Mukwe, pointing about ninety degrees to the right. Now back to the map and imagine that you have a compass in your hand: the needle will always point to Magnetic North. Being South of the Equator, we always have to look North during the day to see the sun, so we are pretty lucky compared to those in the Northern Hemisphere: they have to look South for the sun. Mind you, we have to admit that their Northern Star is much more accurate for North, than is our Southern Cross, for South. One last trick that Rod and I have worked out that we reckon is better than judging shadows, and proves the theory of what we have both laid-out, is to use the twelve (12) and the hour hand of your watch. If you don't have a compass with you, you point the Twelve (12) of your watch, at the sun, and half way between that and the hour-hand is North. There you are! Now you will never get lost."

Eden replied, "Maybe! But thanks for all that — I'll try to remember it. Presumably if one were in the Northern Hemisphere, you would have to face South with you watch?"

"Exactly, and their sun appears to track clockwise."

Paddling the canoes the next day was so much easier, and sheer joy — as the portages were fewer and shorter, although they did have another granite slope to navigate. On the second day after that, they all had to take a sudden left turn to the bank after a shout of "hippos" from one of them. He had espied a school of hippos in the middle of the river, up ahead. Had they not had Monty as a passenger they may have tried to circumnavigate them, but Rod, quite rightly judged him as an unpredictable factor. Having to get around them on land, provided a rather long and difficult portage, and so it proved for the next few days, when they had repeated sightings. While executing one difficult portage, they found an excellent camping spot and decided to use it for their 'over-nighter'.

Eden said, "I saw a perfect fishing spot a bit further back, so I'm going to take my rod and bag of gear and head back there." Rod and Mukwe set-up camp, built a fire and got going with a big feed.

When they were just about ready, there was a bit of shouting and a great deal of clamour from down Eden's way, followed by crashing through the bush towards them. Monty didn't show any particular interest so they wern't too concerned, until Eden lobbed into their midst with blood streaming down his arm, and shouting, "That bloody bird!"

Once they had calmed him and wrapped a clean cloth around the wound, he explained the odyssey. "While I was quietly fishing a small flight of large birds settled on the beach, not far away. I was intrigued, as I did not know what they were, so pulled in my line and went down to investigate — giving a 'bit-of-a-hoot' as I got near. Somehow they got a 'helluva' fright, and the biggest of them lifted off and came straight at me. I lifted my arm because it was flying straight for my head, and the next thing I felt was the sharp cut on this arm: that was when I let out the bellow!" Rod and Mukwe were pretty worried for him, until he let out a laugh and exclaimed "Well at least it didn't kill me!" They encouraged him to sit down and have a bite explaining that it was a Spur Winged Goose, and that, as he had discovered they are not to be trifled with. After the meal and amidst some joking and laughing, they went back with him to collect his rod and fishing gear — plus the one Bream which he had caught.

On about the ninth day they also saw a small herd of

Elephants, and were able to watch them from the middle of the river. Thank goodness there wern't Hippos, just there. Meantime, storm activity was increasing menacingly, including a number of thunderstorms. Whilst they were in the water, these didn't seem to threaten, but while fishing or hunting — well they could only pray that they wouldn't be struck by lightning.

Good solid progress was made down this third river, and they all, including Monty, enjoyed every aspect of it; from the fun of their comradeship, to the wealth of animals seen, including many schools of hippos, crocodiles and many different types of antelope. Fortunately none of the crocodiles that they had witnessed, were large, so they weren't too concerned while out on the water. They loved the fishing, which was improving in both size and the number caught. This meant that they could return more back to the water, including Barbel, which were deep feeding — mud sucking fish, and not palatable.

Theirs, and Monty's hunting had also become more organised. If one of the other guys accompanied Rod on these walks, he would make sure that they carried the rifle, whilst he improved his skill with the two bows. Looking back, he succeeded in hitting either a small buck, or a wild turkey or a guinea fowl, on each outing.

It was on one of these hunting mini expeditions, when Mukwe, Eden and Monty had walked out armed in the same way, that they saw a Leopard in a tree not far away.

Fortunately, Monty did not see it straight away and they were able to call him to their sides, and apply his lead. They did not venture closer, and eventually the leopard decided that to attack as large a group, could mean coming off second best. So it jumped down, gave them a disgruntled look and trotted away into thicker bush. On their return Rod was most disappointed that he had not been with them — but was able to show a 'Yellowgill' fish, as a first, and a 'beaut' meal for that night.

Whilst sitting and enjoying this meal conversation raged in all directions: about their progress and timing; about the escarpment that was now in full view, except when guiding their canoes through densely forested sections of the river. Eden suddenly popped-up with a memory from school days, and said "You know there is an ancient African tribe, somewhere in this region of Africa. They originally lived in the Zambezi valley, with fishing being their main source of food. Then they had to be moved because of the building of this dam, which would flood their ancient tribal areas. Understandably they were apparently pretty 'bl....y' upset about it, and threatened that their River God would wreak havoc on the dam building." On further discussion they all realised that these people were much further South West from their current position.

Mukwe acknowledged exactly what Eden had raised, and mentioned the name Batonka, as the tribal name. He also added, "The name of the river god is Nyaminyani, and in their eyes it has supernatural powers: so, watch out you dam builders."

The next day it seemed that Nyaminyani had exploded onto their peaceful adventure so far. Only it wasn't the River God, it was a band of heavily armed insurgents — remnants of a past political war — still creating havoc and mayhem out in the backblocks of the country.

During this attack the canoers were fortunately travelling up the West side of the river, which at this point, was nearly a kilometre wide and flowing strongly. Rod and Mukwe immediately became aware of the attack because they heard a rocket mounted grenade fly overhead. Action stations, because the next shot could very well be lower. Rod stopped rowing, ordered Monty to lie down and then caught sight of some six to eight attackers — partly dressed in camouflage but with odd bits of coloured shirts visible, and with black caps. They were somewhat protected by straggly dark green bush, that extended down to the water on their side. He picked up his rifle and a magazine and was in the process of loading a round when he heard Mukwe scream in fury at these attackers — in his African vernacular, "Stop shooting you stupid bunch of bastards: we are all together as a canoeing group and are no threat to you, or any anyone else." African men are able to project their voices over very long distances, so the group of insurgents would have heard his violent reaction. However, there were loud shouted retorts to his message, with a couple more scattered shots being fired in their direction. Their firearms were however AK47's, which were not good long-range weapons.

The shambled delay gave Rod time to complete loading his long-range rifle, and to aim and fire very close into this band. He then called across to Mukwe and Eden, "Turn end-on to them, and go full bore for the bank. Then you cover me and engage them." Eden then entered the fray — scratching his head and enquiring in some alarm, "Who the bl--y hell are that mob"? Mukwe replied, "Just a stupid band of Blockheads." Rod saw the attackers leap up and fire wildly towards them — giving Mukwe time to make the bank and then repeat Rod's action, which scattered them into retreat. Both fired a couple more shots into the bush and then Mukwe and Eden got their canoe going again and — joined by Rod and Monty — all made best possible speed out of the zone. They didn't stop for about five kilometres, which happened to be the next portage.

In the process of carrying the canoes to the next clear section of river Rod said, "I don't trust those bandits. They could cross over one of these portages, and have another go at us."

Mukwe disagreed, and reassured his mates that the insurgents would still be on the run, and that the canoeing group would be O.K. as far as *that* band was concerned. He did however say, "We will have to be far more vigilant from now onwards, as the bastards could be anywhere". With that warning they rowed on late into the evening before beaching on the far side of the river. At the first opportunity in which Eden was out of earshot, Rod and Mukwe agreed to take turns on two and a half hour guards, through the night — from then onwards until they reached the Zambezi.

After another three weeks of amazing rowing — in which each double stroke carried them about twice as far as when they first started — they were hyped up with excitement, and they were paddling around a long curve of the river when suddenly –Wa La! — there was the Kalupati River ahead of them. This was the tributary of the Zambezi: their final river to row. The conference of the two was so large, that it was like paddling out onto a lake. They decided to continue, and made about four kilometres before the first portage obstruction. Once they had carried the canoes through this, they decided to stop and set-up a camp for the night.

Mukwe suggested by way of a reminder, "Rod, Eden we are now in 'Big Cat' territory, and will have to take well thought-out precautions whenever we're on land, and particularly at night. Adding to that he pointed to some Mimosa thorn trees that surrounded their camp, and said, "In fact I'm going to go and cut some branches right now." The others offered to help him and when they returned dragging a number of mimosa branches to the fire, he was able to show them the long and dangerous thorns, on such a branch. Using these branches they surrounded their camp, and from then onwards if there were mimosa trees near each camp, they engaged this practice.

ROBERT COX

Their continued progress down the river, confirmed Mukwe's warnings: they did see a great deal more wild life, in addition to the frequent sightings of hippos and crocodiles. Elephants, buffaloes, zebras and more different species of antelopes were the most frequent sightings. On one occasion while rowing, they did see a Lioness with her two cubs, and were able to watch from the center of the river. From then on, they took even greater precautions — especially when executing portages — which were just as well, because one evening whilst making camp they heard a mighty crash in the bush not far behind them. Fortunately, the offender had been scared and was running off. Once their situation settled and they were able to discuss what caused the mighty din, the consensus was that it had been a Rhino: most other large animals would have been in herds. Monty tried hard to impress upon them, that he — and the canoes! — had much to do with their safe passage!

That was it as far as the game were concerned, because for the next few days the environment changed completely. They had entered a deep band of dense, dark green forest. In some sections — where they were probably passing through what would have been a transverse ridge — the Teak and other indigenous trees seemed to be so tall and overhanging that it was like progressing through a canyon. The three friends agreed that it was an enthralling experience, and that they were but a microcosm in its midst.

They had experienced many rain events and it was

becoming very clear that the high country behind them must have been enduring even heavier rainfall, because the river was now beginning to flood. This meant faster travel and fewer if any, portages further down, but it was also a warning for extra care and vigilance. After another week or so of this exhilarating canoeing, fishing, hunting adventure, they became aware of the Zambezi Escarpment. It was a very hot day and they were enjoying their midday break in a largely open area, when Eden suddenly remarked, "Surely there aren't two sets of escarpments — one further away than the other?"

Rod lifted himself from his 'butt' and took a closer look, which soon turned to amazement, and said, "You're right Eden, except that they are not two sets of horizons: that is a classical 'mirage'. The heat; the effect of moisture rising from the feature, and the angle of the sun, create and lift that mirror image, so that it is identical to the one below. The only other time that I have witnessed the same, was when I was driving on just such a day, as today, and suddenly the end of the straight road that I was travelling on had an extra end to it." They all viewed this dual-horizon with renewed interest, and discussed the probability that the Kalupati River would wind its way through the massif that they were looking at, before running out into the Zambezi River.

Late one morning, as they were approaching the escarpment, they saw that the river had indeed worn a gorge through the escarpment. Sensibleness, rather than foolhardiness prevailed, and they beached the canoes before venturing further.

Actually, they had two reasons for this: the main one being to make a careful assessment of the flow through the gorge, but the other was to take account of a narrow concrete bridge, under which they had paddled. They climbed up out of the river course and found, unsurprisingly, that a narrow, single track dirt road ran in each direction away from the bridge. On discussing it, they all agreed that it was probably a Professional Hunter's and Ranger's road.

Having assessed that, they returned to the river but climbed up a steep rugged rock face to a higher viewing point where they were met by a sullen roar from further down the precipitous gorge; like a dragon sounding its warning!. This was no surprise to Rod, as he knew that they were still way above the Zambezi and the dam down in the valley. They were all unanimous that it would be too risky to continue, because apart from rapids, there could quite possibly be one or two waterfalls. Thus, they had reached the end of their river canoeing, and it looked like the only option open to them was a day or two carrying their canoes and gear, along the road towards the dam wall. By their reckoning it was twenty five to thirty kilometres from this river crossing, to the tourist village at the dam wall. Over a little fire for 'the all — important coffee', they repacked their haversacks, roped the oars to the canoes, and spread the guns and bows between them. Rod looked at Monty, and jokingly said, "it's a pity we havn't got a little four-wheeler trolley with reins. You could have pulled most of this along, for us, couldn't you Monty?"

For which Rod got the 'Eagle eye'!

# CHAPTER 14

After a few difficult hours of carrying, a pickup approached from behind them, and obligingly stopped and offered to help. The driver was an employee of the Water Authority who had been up-river checking on the rate of inflows. His greeting was "Hi! Where the hell have you blokes come from?"

Rod quickly replied "We've paddled across from the other side and brought the canoes and ourselves around to that bridge, back there, hoping to paddle down that river and into the dam. But it sounds a bit too dangerous for ordinary guys, like us."

"Too bloody right — you wouldn't have made it: you would have all been crunched, including the canoes....... and the dog. Anyway, scrub that. My name is Charles and would you all like a lift around to the town?" They readily accepted, and introduced themselves. He climbed out of the cab to help them. Once the canoes were loaded and tied down, as well as they could with what they had available, he suggested that two should climb in the back, with the dog, to make sure that the canoes didn't move. Eden and Mukwe leapt into the back with Monty, so quickly that Rod had no time to even offer a suggestion! Rod then got into the passenger seat and the driver got going. Rod filled the travel time by asking the driver a myriad of appropriate local questions.

It only took him half an hour to reach the Dam village. Dropping them, and canoes at a Boat Anchorage, he helped them to unload, then said "There are a couple of good Motel type places further up, one of which also accommodates animals, I think. Also, there are two good Pubs, and I might see you all at one or the other. Cheers! And enjoy yourselves." They thanked him profusely for the lift and for the information, and with a wave he drove off.

After searching for a boat booking-in-office and not finding one, they zipped the covers over the canoes, and anchored them on the beach close to all the other boats. Reloading the rest of the gear between them, they started walking up the hill towards the accommodation precinct.

On the way up they were deep in conversation, and one of the subjects was that they were going to have to assume other first names. This caused much mirth, and even Mukwe decided to have a different name. After a couple of non-starters they came up with Pik, which he insisted upon as the best option for him. Rod decided upon Thomas (Tom) and Eden liked Peter. They practised these names with each other, as well as surnames — dragged out of the blue! Once they found the Motel that had an outside kennel area, Pik and Peter booked the three of them into one room — asking for an extra bed, whilst Tom took Monty to the kennels; unloaded the dog's blankets and gave him some food and filled the water container. He left the dog and whilst locking the gate gave a cheerful "See ya tomorrow!"

When he got to the room Tom found the other two lying on their beds in a state of exhaustion and he quickly followed suit. Desultory chatting followed, which to Rod's (Tom's) mind indicated that they were both physically and psychologically tested again! By this time it was evening and they suddenly realised that they would need to shower and get out some clean clothes. While Pik was showering, Tom and Peter entered into joking conversation, "Peter why don't you shape your moustache; square-off your beard so that you look like Captain Hook, the Pirate King"!

Peter added, "Maybe I would if we had the correct clothes! and added, "If you're going to darken and extend you're eyebrows, you should do the same with your beard and moustache, so you look like a bandero!" Tom remembered that he had rolled up some very fine, very black ash, for that job. Again the good scissors came into use! Once they had finished their trims, all agreed that they indeed looked like Tom, Peter and Pik! rather than their previous identities.

Showering finished and camouflage completed, they made their way to the dining room, where they barely received a glance. A gorgeous meal — being so different from everything over the last four months, was enjoyed by all of them.

They paid close attention to conversations close at hand, to try and ascertain what was going on in the world, and it seemed that little had changed. It was worrying to hear that there was much unprovoked violence and thieving still being carried-out.

After the meal — which included 'sweets' — and they had finished their coffee, they went through to the Pub which, surprisingly, was pretty clean and classy with a long highly polished hardwood counter. They ordered beers and absorbed the atmosphere in the pub which was very different from that in the dining room. In no time at all they were talking to other folk — mostly men, but they did engage with some ladies, girls and 'grandmums', all of whom they found pleasantly entertaining.

Rod took the opportunity to go out and phone Colin and Carry, to advise that they were now at the Dam. Apparently it was a Wednesday, and they agreed to come across on the Saturday. They were especially pleased that the three of them were safe and well, after what Carry described as 'their ordeal'. Rod assured her that it was anything but, and that they had thoroughly enjoyed most aspects of it — except for one which he would tell them about, when they arrived. A bit more chatting occurred and then they each hung up, with Tom returning to the pub and purposefully addressing Pik and Peter by name.

Over the course of the evening they met some interesting guys, and there was genuine curiosity that they were canoers. Tom noticed one prominent man who had been watching him, and who seemed to have picked him out as the 'leader' of the three of them. His mates called him Dan, and Tom anticipated meeting him again — unless he and they, headed back to where they had come from, before the following evening.

Next morning they purposely went down to the boats, after picking up Monty, and made as if 'busy' with the canoes — even to the point of Eden taking the single canoe out through the heads of the little bay. Later on, the other two took the double out for a paddle. Various fishermen and or boaters came down, and they were able to talk to some and discover that this little village was primarily a Fishing Resort. Occasionally hunters used it as a starting off point.

Unsurprisingly to Tom, Dan and a mate did come down, and they evinced an interest in the canoes, as well as just generally chatting. A subject that came up quite strongly with them, and with the other boat people, was Tiger Fishing. One bloke who was about to head out in his boat queried, "How are you guys going to use canoes to tiger fish?". The three were able to put his mind at rest. Peter retorted, "Canoes are not for Tigers!" However, their interest was being really hyped by all this talk, and they remembered that Colin had talked about it, with a glint in his eye. There was no doubt that Tigers had a reputation as being ultra-fighting fish. Maybe they could hire a boat, and go out with he and Carry — provided the boat had suitable cover against the fierce sun.

That evening they went to the pub before going to dinner, and enjoyed a beer each, with some of the guys that they had met. Dan was amongst them, and in addition to talking about the day's events, mentioned that there was a card game, after dinner, in the Activities Room. Tom said "I don't play cards, but I'll come through and watch: Pik and Peter may want to play". The three of them went through after dinner, and sure enough the card players were betting on their prowess. Eden joined in with a max of $10 and enjoyed playing until it was used up. It continued for about another half hour, at the end of which an unknown person won the largest pool, but Dan was second in winnings.

The card party split up, and looking across at Tom, Dan said, "I bet you — for your canoes — that I can wipe-you-out at Poker."

"No doubt you would," said Tom, "but I don't gamble at cards. However, I will take you on at Fifteen Matches."

"Oh! What is that?" enquired Dan. Tom explained the game to him, "Well there are fifteen matches on the table, and the two players, alternately, can take one match, or two, or three, and the ultimate winner of each game is the player that leaves one match on the table. Each sortee consists of five successive games, with alternate players starting". Dan checked back with Tom on aspects of the game, then said "Yeah okay, that sounds pretty right. So the winner of three games out of the five, is the overall winner." Is that right?"

"Yep!" said Tom

"Okay let's go," added Dan, "provided that you are prepared to bet your canoes."

"On two conditions — one that I start the first game, and two, that your bet is acceptable"

"I bet $500".

"Accepted" said Tom.

They located fifteen matches, and set them up on the table. Tom started the first game, and away they went into the sortee. He won the first and second games, and felt secure that Dan didn't really 'cotton-on' to the science of the game. He therefore deliberately erred in the third game, Allowing Dan to win it. The fourth game was therefore critical, especially as Dan was starting it. Tom managed to win it, proving that Dan didn't understand the game. Dan gave up, saying "You've won three out of the five, so I can't win. Wow! what a game: here you deserve the $500." He then counted out the notes and handed them over.

Tom thanked him and said "Come down to the canoes tomorrow — I'm sure that we can work something out." Dan headed back to the bar, while Tom, Pik and Peter said "Good night" and made for their room.

Eden closed the door behind them, and said "We should double-lock this tonight!" However, no problem occurred, nor was it genuinely expected.

The following morning they were down at the canoes with their fishing rods, after an early breakfast, They had fitted these out with free running reels and colourful lures, as bait. Various fishermen had given sound advice to them, but they were all dubious as to success. "If any of you catch a tiger from those boats, It'll be a first." Dan came down with a friend before they had rowed out, and Tom got him on one side, while his friend got involved with Pik and Peter.... and the rods!

Tom said "You were very courageous last night Dan, and I would like to make you a revised offer, if you are still interested in the canoes?"

Dan replied that he was, adding cautiously, "But I'll be pretty wary of your new valuation."

"Naturally! The $500 that you bet and paid to me, covers their value. What I am hoping is that you might be able to help out Peter, and I, in your business over the next few years. We are going to Uni next year, and part time jobs during the holidays would be great, if you can see your way to organizing them? I'll be completing my Accounting degree, and Peter will be doing Secondary School Teaching."

Dan was rapt, and said "That's a generous compromise on your part, and I'm quite sure that we would be able to fit you both in, for part-time vacation work. They shook hands on the deal and then he jokingly said, "Now I suppose that you want to take them out to 'fight the tigers?!"

"Exactly". said Tom, and they agreed to meet again that evening, so that Dan and his mates could load them up, for their return, to the capital.

Although they had fixed their rods to troll, canoes really weren't the right craft. The disadvantage of being at right angles to the expected catch, and not being able to stand, to fight fish that are capable of launching vertically out of the water to try and throw the hook, was more than any of them could handle. But they were excited at the prospect, and again hoped that Colin and Carry would be in it. Solution? Change back to their old reel, hooks and weights design, and paddle in towards inlets. It wasn't long before they were catching bream again — three for their evening meal and a couple for Monty's. They arrived back at the anchorage mid afternoon, unloaded and cleaned off the canoes, then went to find Dan and his mates to give them a hand loading them. Once the canoes were very securely fixed to the trailer, the fellows left for their return journey to the Capital.

# CHAPTER 15

There were no great plans for that evening, other than taking their fish to the kitchens to be prepared for their evening meal. Somehow, they tasted a bit more professional! They again enjoyed the company and general conversation in the bar, but retired early to plan for Colin and Carry arriving the next day.

All of them with Monty, spent the morning discovering the small town and various excellent views of the Lake. Although much further from the town, they also walked down to the massive dam wall and were all unequivocally amazed at the sheer size of the structure: it was strongly curved into the lake and had a dual-carriageway road across the wall. Once they arrived immediately above the wall, they were astounded at the height of the wall and the depth of the gorge, and the frightening thought that this whole vista was threatened by the Batonka's River God, Nyaminyani.

While discussing the issue Tom had a sudden flash of memory — passed on to him by cousin Rick, who had been an Engineer on the Dam — and he related it saying, "That threat was not base, because the first time that the flood gates had to be opened, after catastrophic rains, the force of the water falling down over two hundred feet into that large pool at the base — to which he pointed, caused massive damage to the rocks at the base of the wall, and into each embankment. The builders had to urgently bring-in under water Concrete Specialists, to repair the damage. Apparently it took them about six weeks of constant plugging to cure the problem. The floods also engulfed and carried away a small footbridge that had been erected across the gorge and had been crucial up to that point." Mukwe and Eden found it difficult to believe that such advanced science could be implemented, in this remote place.

Once back in the town they awaited the arrival of their future host and hostess.

Many hugs, kisses and welcome handshakes were exchanged on their arrival, particularly between brother and sister, and between the newcomers and Monty, who well remembered them. Carry said, "Rod I nearly died at the thought of you being in jail, especially as we, and Jacky and Mel, would be so far from you. As you know, Mom and Dad were equally devastated."

"And so were Muk's parents. Still it didn't come to that and I owe a fantastic debt of gratitude to both these true-blue

Mates of mine."

Eden in somewhat confused state, suddenly said, "Hey! Carry weren't you a year ahead of me at school; I had never really established the connection between Rod and you. What a great realisation: and what a lucky bloke you are, Colin: she was top-o-the-pops at school, or should I say 'top of the classicals?!" Carry likewise, suddenly put the association together, and went as far as giving him a hug and kiss on the cheek. With that they all went into lunch to continue the joyful get-together.

Initially conversation revolved around the two groups, and just how well they had been doing. The three 'bush' guys were eager to learn how Colin and Carry were getting on at Home Building, and in their careers. They were ecstatic that all was on course. Colin and Carry on the other hand, fired questions at Rod, Mukwe and Eden about their journey with the canoes; and on their health — both physical and mental. All three assured them that they were 'fit as fiddles' but Eden suddenly interjected saying, "But did these two jackasses tell you about the mini-war?"

"No, what was that?" asked Carry.

"We had to blast a bunch of insurgents off the edge of the river, and back into the forest." said Mukwe

Carry and Colin were staggered and looked at Rod for further information, which he gave in detail and which absolutely horrified Carry. Colin on the other hand, said "Jesus I wish I had been there, and also armed with a rifle!"

"Okay, okay! said Carry, so you are all bl...y fighters! but what I want to know is how the 'dickens' you guys are going to get things right?". Rod asked that he put that 'on hold' until their drive back to the Capital, at which time he promised to lay it open and to get Carry's wisdom on his plans.

After the intensity of all that, Rod demanded with a big smile, "Now we are going to go Tiger fishing in a big boat, aren't we?" He then lied saying "The boat is already booked for tomorrow!" The weather was beautiful, so Colin and Carry were very excited, and Rod had to admit that he had told a 'fib'. They got on the phone right there and then and booked the boat which the boys had already looked at. They spent a happy afternoon walking around and chatting endlessly, with Monty probably the happiest of all — it was a long time since he had had so many family and friends, all around him. Before heading to the Dining room Rod had to inform Colin and Carry, that in there, and at the pub, they were known as Tom, Pik and Peter, and asked them to please memorize those names. Dinner at their 'digs' was also memorable, and they all went to bed looking forward to the next day with great anticipation.

The boat that they had hired looked massive after the canoes, but certainly lent itself to comfort and efficiency. The 'bushies' were a little anxious, but for Colin it seemed to be 'of second nature' and off they powered into the centre of the lake. When they reached a position that he, Colin, thought had good prospects they stopped. He dropped

the boat into neutral saying. "Now!" "this Tiger Fishing
is absolutely something else! We start moving forward at
about ten kms an hour and your lines with the lures on, will
be dragged. The fish are very fast attackers and will hammer
the bait (lures) and go under. If hooked they are famous for
leaping out of the water vertically — sometimes as high as a
couple of metres: be ready for that and give your reel some
massive turns." "Okay!" "go for it."

With smiles all round Carry gave him a thump on the
shoulder and said, "You'd better jolly well catch one now."
All rods were set-up and they cast out into the inviting water
with floating lures, at which point Colin got the boat moving
gently forward. There were many anticipatory strikes but
for a while they came to 'nowt', until there was a gasp from
Eden and they all caught the flash of a vertically flying fish,
(beg your pardon) tiger fish! That one he lost, but it gave
them all a lift. Some twenty minutes, of hard concentrated
fishing later, Colin nailed one, and the excitement aboard
was like watching a thriller movie. He instructed Carry on
how to use the net, when he finally lifted it out of the water.
After that, he turned the boat around one eighty degrees,
and the whole process started again. Throughout the day,
all of them managed to catch a tiger, with Colin managing
three. All the fish but one were let back into the lake, as they
were not considered good eating fare. To complete the day,
Colin took them in closer to the bank to view the game. It
was a vast shallow embankment and an array of animals

were in the water, up to just over their hooves — mostly elephants — but with a few large hippos, buffalos, and a sprinkling of smaller game. Monty was the most excited, and Rod had to have a hand on him for the duration. Close to the game viewing point Colin located a site at which he had previously had success with bream, and they fished the rest of their sojourn there, catching enough for the night, and the week ahead, at their home.

The evening ahead was very pleasant, both in the clamour of the bar, and the lovely meal that followed: Carry even asked their waiter to compliment the Cook on his scrumptious preparation of the fish. Between them all they chatted quite late into the night, before retiring to get a good night's sleep, ahead of the long drive back to the Capital.

Colin and Carry were proud owners of a Station Wagon, which enabled them to house Monty behind the rear seats, and Rod got into one of those so he could put an arm around him, to settle him, if it became necessary. Departure was soon after breakfast, and they made very good time on the bituminized road. With a good deal of amusement and teasing, as well as relief, they were able to drop their hoax names, and revert to who they actually were. Phew!. To start off with, they were travelling through similar country to that through which they canoed, but once they hit the higher country it changed to savannah with lower msasa trees, almost to their relief. However, they still studied it closely and with interest, and were surprised that the small town of Monahan apparently had a deep cave with an underground water complex.

While they were motoring along, Rod engaged Carry in conversation and appealed for her considered opinion — apologizing for not going into detail while at the dam — on how and why he believed his deep plan to obtain new names, for he and Eden, could come to fruition. Everybody's ears shot up, and Carry exclaimed "it sounds pretty way-out Rod, but let's hear it."

"Right then!" Said Rod, "going back to a time before you left Aberfoyle, do you remember a girl by the name of Kim, with whom I was very friendly?"

"She wasn't a serious girlfriend, was she?" countered Carry, "but I think I remember her".

"No!" said Rod, "but I knew her well enough, to also have a good relationship with her parents. They thought I was ... should we say — good contender material! Anyway, out of all that she owes me, like 'Big Time'. Importantly she is a long-time employee of the Immigration Department, who as you know, are tied to the Department of Human Services, in this country. Well I intend to go and see her and put a proposition to her: to create two absolutely new citizens: not only Christian and Surnames, but full documentation as well. That is stage one. The second stage will be to approach Mr. Frost, and see if he can 'winkle' these two new candidates, into Uni."

"Now before any of you take me to task or ridicule me,

let me add a bit of background — even if you consider that same will still give insufficient impetus, to go ahead with my plan. Kim and her family would not be where they are now, if it were not for me. I am not seeking fame, or extra thanks from them, but feel that an approach may work."

"Holding my thumbs, as before! In the case of Mr. Frost — and I've already mentioned this to Mukwe and Eden — he was in Aberfoyle on duty while I was in jail, and asked Mom and Dad to convey his sympathy, and to tell me that he knew that I wouldn't strike a policeman. So there you have it: I will not go in demanding of either of them, but rather with a gentle, thought out proposition."

Mukwe chaffed Rod by saying "My G.d, she must have loved you — to expect such a favour!". They all laughed at that, and Rod had to protest denial.

Carry then cautioned "Okay then Rod, maybe she does owe you to that extent, but you are going to have to be extremely careful in the manner of your approach. Any presumption on your part will be fateful."

"Believe me, I know that full well," added Rod, "it will be very cautious and exploratory."

Out of the blue then, Colin dropped a hopeful possibility. "Hang on you lot, the first person that Rod and Eden should see is Kathy. Rick's sister. She works for Births, Deaths and Marriages; if she could do 'under the carpet' Birth Certificates for each of them Rod would stand a much better chance, with this girl Kim."

The subject was left at that, as they were entering the outskirts of the Capital, and the discussion started to revolve around the best way of accommodating the three of them, and Monty. As they drove southwards out of the built-up section of the city they were confronted by a 'wide flatly bulldozed area of brown earth' — the Development of the new suburb, with only a handful of houses erected or under construction. Throwing his arm forward and pointing Rod said, "I hope one of that small clump of houses over there with the neat little gardens and planted trees, is yours?" Carry lent towards him with a proud smile and replied, "Yes! The one with the biggest trees and the prettiest garden." Everyone had a good laugh.

Carry and Colin already had two dogs, but they were well trained and friendly towards guests and other dogs. So they all witnessed a very special canine event, when the hosts took Monty across to their dogs, and effectively introduced him, to them. To Rod , Mukwe and Eden, it seemed that the trust that their two dogs placed in the fact that their owner's knew Monty, was enough for them to befriend him. For that is exactly what happened, with much sniffing, licking and tail wagging. First hurdle crossed. Carry then said "You guys are going to be a bit squashed-up until we can work things out a bit better."

"No problem, said Rod, we would like to help wherever we can, and are quite prepared to pay rent to you and Colin."

"That won't be necessary, countered Colin it's just an

incredible pleasure to have you all with us, instead of at the bottom of the Zambezi, or even worse in the stomachs of crocodiles or hippos. That six weeks plus, waiting for your call, was more than an anxious time for both of us — particularly Carry, as she hadn't witnessed your preparations. Nor did I realise that you would have to use those rifles to defend yourselves. Many a time, I had to reassure Carry that you blokes were well prepared and safe — which it now turns out, was a bit of a lie."

So, with that warm and friendly welcome they all set-to; unpacked the vehicle and got it all under cover. The threesome were then shown a large Bedroom, which seemed like heaven to them. Once they had got all their gear to it, they helped with the evening meal and with feeding the animals — now three dogs and two cats ...!

Before heading off to work the next day, Colin reminded Rod & Co. "Don't schedule anything for next weekend, as you guys are going to start teaching me how to use those bows of yours."

Mukwe quickly added "And the katties, as well!"

That first week back in civilization was one of settling-in and getting used to the fact that they weren't constantly busy. There were lovely parklands in the vicinity, so they took all the dogs for long walks, without the need to place leads on any of them. At other times, when Mukwe and Eden were occupied reading or tinkering in the workshop, Rod started to put together details of their forward plan. He made an initial call to Mr. Frost, just to acquaint him with the fact that he had arrived in the Capital, and enquiring whether a future meeting may be possible. He was very relieved, that that worthy looked forward to such a get-together. He also contacted Rick, to say Hi! Carry took over the call, and asked them all to come-round on the Sunday, and to please bring Kathy with them.

As he and Eden would need new names, a fictional idea started to form in Rod's mind based around the fact that they had been travelling through Africa from England. They had migrated from there because each of them had reached a point, where they no longer had any family back there. On their way down through the African continent a catastrophic event occurred, and after many weeks they reached the Zambezi and crossed It.

Apart from telling Carry that he was working on it, he decided that any in-depth discussion could wait until the weekend.

After breakfast on the Saturday, Colin had them out onto a very open section of one of the beautiful parklands, for the highly anticipated instruction with the bows. All three were very conscientious with their advice, and practical instruction, and slowly he started to get the hang of it. When they demonstrated, he was astounded at their accuracy, and he realised that he was going have to persevere, to try and achieve same. They then continued with the dogs, for a long walk around the park and finally back home. They all enjoyed this first Saturday in the Capital, at Colin and Carry's home –watching a good film on the TV.

Next day, Rick and his wife Lil, together with Kathy arrived and entered the family reunion. Rick and Mukwe knew one another from school days — having hostelled some fifteen kilometres apart — but he did not know Eden. Following introductions between the three of them, they spread themselves around the tables, to enjoy Carry's morning tea. Some of the conversation clearly, described the bows and katties, so when tea was finished both Rick and Kathy insisted on seeing these infamous weapons, in action.

Back out to the area of the park in which they had been the previous day, and they took a couple of large cardboard boxes with them. Again the instruction was very clear and precise, and when the "bushies" demonstrated with the Bows, the "City-Slickers" applauded, and were very vocal at the fact that most of the shots hit the cardboard boxes at sixty/plus metres. Rick and then Colin again, insisted on having a go, and to start with, were way off the mark. However, they really applied themselves to it, and eventually Colin managed to hit the box, and Rick scored close to it. Kathy also expressed a strong desire to give one of the bows a try, so Rod took her about twenty metres closer. Although she wasn't successful in hitting a box, she just revelled in the opportunity to try it out.

The rest of the group came up then, and when the katties were unpacked, Rick exclaimed loudly "Hey Rod, these are our design, from school, and I'm sure Mukwe would have remembered them." The two culprits laughed in total agreement.

Eden added "Okay, come on Rick, if you designed these, let's see how good you are."

Rick threw up his hands and said "That was about ten years ago, but give me one and I will give it a go." The fact that he was as good as any of the threesome, was ample proof of his original workmanship, with Rod and Mukwe.

He then added, "Did Rod tell you his experience after just finishing one of these; it was back at High School and on an exit to Railway dam?" Mukwe and Eden shook their heads so Rick continued, "He was pretty chuffed with that particular katty, and after some practice found a perfect round stone about the size of my thumb nail. We looked around because he was engaging us in 'blah', only to see him aiming vertically into the sky, and with a massive pull flung the stone towards the heavens. For a while he just stood there looking up but then he let out a yelp; dropped his head and covered it with his hands. The stone had come hurling straight down and landed about a metre from him. As you can imagine, we all just collapsed with laughter."

All present had a good laugh.

At this juncture, Colin suggested to Kathy that they head back to the house with Rod, and as they were walking along said, "You'll be aware Kathy, that Rod and Eden have a unique problem now that they have arrived back in civilization — hence their beards and moustaches. I must also add on behalf of Rod, that he would not be here, if it were not for Eden: but he can fill you in on that, later."

Kathy acknowledged the facts, and said, "I'm sorry Rod, it hadn't really penetrated just how caught-up you and Eden must feel. Please acquaint me with all the facts and how you reckon I can possibly help you?"

Colin interjected, "The main thing Kathy, is that they will not be able to use original identification papers, but Rod believes that he has a way of getting new Passports — as exotic as it might sound!. But let him fill you in on the whole problem."

Rod thanked them both, and as they were just about to enter the house for lunch, asked Kathy "Will this afternoon suit you?" She replied that it would, and they went in to catch-up with Carry, and lunch.

Rod and Kathy retired to the study after lunch, and he told her the entire sequence of events, including the shooting; the arresting and jailing, and the Court case. He also explained why he was not prepared to go to jail, for a crime that did not exist: hence his escape (and the part played by 'escapee' Eden). Because he knew that she would appreciate the adventure of their camp (Lair) and of their canoe trip, he gave her chapter and verse, of that as well. He told her about the lie they had told the Ranger, to the effect that they had come across from the other side, when that worthy picked them up. At that point, he said "It has been going through my mind Kathy, that we enlarge on that 'coming across from the other side'."

"How do you mean?" She asked. Rod then outlined the myth that he had worked out in his mind, of he and Eden being of English origin, but with no further living family; travelling down through Africa, in their car: of having been hijacked; their car and all their belongings having been burnt, and of their escape in the clothes they were standing-in, whilst the fire was being lit. That they had fled, virtually without stopping, until they came upon the Zambezi. They had crossed it and continued their way until they came upon the road, where Colin and Carry had picked them up.

By this time Kathy was laughing, but stopped to say "Man I just love that — but I don't know whether it will do us any good. However, leave it with me Rod: I'll need to think it through. What I am interested in though, is how you believe that you can get hold of Passports: a process that will be just as difficult, as what you are asking me to do."

Rod then told her about Kim, and the fact that she worked for Immigration; adding, "She and her family owe me a pretty big debt of gratitude. Obviously I cannot guarantee that she will be able to help, so my approach will be very cautious, but also desperate. I'll also invite her out a few times, before tackling this ticklish question."

"Okay then?, I'll keep you informed on that side, and of course on the names that Eden and I choose. In the meantime, it will be quite okay for you to discuss this with Rick as he and I have been close cousins, forever, as you know." So, they closed the issue there, but Rod had definitely got the impression that Kathy had taken it very seriously.

On the Monday evening Rod did contact Kim, and she was surprised and delighted to hear from him. He enquired straight away, "Are you aware of the strange circumstances, in which I now find myself?"

She confirmed saying, "Yes, my parents contacted me immediately after the breakout, and I was extremely alarmed by everything that lead up to it."

"Well, I can tell you Kim that there was no crime committed: the policeman accidentally shot me whilst aiming at Monty." Kim started to cry, and wanted to see him as soon as it could be arranged. She had a previous arrangement for the next night, but arranged that he pick her up on the Wednesday evening.

This he did, having borrowed Carry's car, and as soon as Kim opened the door of her flat she surged out with tears running down her cheeks, "Oh Rod!, it's so wonderful to see you again, Please come inside." She threw her arms around him and cried again as they hugged tightly and eventually kissed, while Rod stroked her hair until she stopped crying.

To step into her lounge was like going back a year or two: she had quite a few items of furniture, cushions and pictures that he remembered from her Parents home in Aberfoyle. Their re-acquaintance likewise, was if they had never been apart and they were able to happily chat away whilst she enquired into all aspects of what had happened. Although totally absorbed in his account, she couldn't help asking, "Rod, can I see the wound, from the shot?" Fortunately, being summer he was in shorts, and therefore easily able to slide them up to show her the front and back of his thigh. She gulped, and her hands automatically flew up to cover her mouth. She then asked, 'How were you able to get to treatment, and stop the heavy bleeding?"

He covered the immediate aftermath of the shooting saying, "Initially I found a large dressing in the bathroom cupboard and bound it on myself. Monty and I had to get away from Fairhill very quickly, so I phoned Mukwe and we arranged a meeting place — that we both knew — and Monty and I raced there, by bicycle. Thank goodness Mukwe arrived not long afterwards, for I was in 'a bit of a state' by then. He rebound the wound and then delivered me to Dunnfold Mining Hospital."

At this juncture Rod said, "Look Kim I know a nice Restaurant not far from here." So off they went to enjoy dinner together. The rest of his, Mukwe's and Eden's journey was covered, and then Rod asked, "What were the circumstances of your coming to the Capital?"

"Oh! I was transferred by my Department and given a slight promotion. When I got here, I had to rent a flat and make new friends; both at work and in the community; and I'm slowly getting used to it." They talked on into the night;

sometimes recalling their days back in Aberfoyle, and of his, and her family.

Eventually she enquired, "With the desperate situation that you are in, what do you and Eden intended to do, to get back on an even keel?"

He was able to divert the enquiry by saying "I'm not quite sure yet, because I've also got to think of Mukwe and Eden; but there are 'no two ways', we are going to need some help. This beard and moustache and the military type clothing that I'm wearing, are really camouflage, and Eden has had to do exactly the same thing. What we are going to have to achieve is new identities: I've chatted to Kathy, my cousin, who works in Births Deaths and Marriages, and we are trying to take it from there. Kim was about to respond, but Rod stood up and offered his hand saying, "Come on Kim, I must take you home; it's getting late. Please can I take you out again, it's been so wonderful?" She agreed, and was delivered home, where they parted with a kiss, and with the next date set for Friday.

Every day was enjoyable in the company of Carry and Colin, but the three guys also talked non-stop between themselves. On this Thursday, Rod raised the question of what names he and Eden should adopt for the future saying, "We've got to think very carefully about this, because they will be on Birth Certificates, Citizen Certificates and finally Passports." Many names were bandied around, with Mukwe suggesting many outrageous names, and all of them ending up in a rough and tumble.

"I like 'Peter', from our time at the dam," said Eden.

Rod agreed that he liked that name and said, "I think that Antony is a possible first name for me." Then they had to get on to second names and Surnames, which were much more difficult. They were engaged for a full hour — this time with genuine help from Mukwe. Rod finally came up with Robin, and Colhoun, as the last name, while Eden decided upon Adrian and Deighton. After all of that, Carry called them for lunch, which was thoroughly enjoyed, and then they took the dogs for the 'all important' walk. Whilst doing so Rod reflected, "How happily the other two dogs have accepted Monty, into their lives. Fabulous!"

When they got back, it was time to phone Kathy with the names that they had chosen, and for Rod to see whether she had given any more thought to their problem. As always he enquired if she was in conference and sure enough she was busy, but not to the extent that she couldn't say, "But I'm very interested in taking the names, and will arrange a meeting with Carry for this coming Sunday, and we can enter into further discussion." He also informed her that he had made first contact with Kim and was satisfied with progress so far. She was rapt at that and said, "That's great — I really must meet Kim."

Rod added, "I will be meeting Kim again on Friday and will arrange it — provided that things are on-course."

Not only was their next meeting on course, but it was Kim who took the initiative. "You mentioned on Wednesday that your cousin Kathy works for Births, Deaths and Marriages. I'd like to meet her: please don't get me wrong. I'm sure she is a lovely person, and we will get on well together, but I have 'business' to discuss with her."

Rod was somewhat taken aback, but felt that he should get right onto the problem, and said "Does this mean that there is a possibility that you might be able to help Eden and I?"

She replied cautiously, "I'm hoping so, and that is why I want to meet Kathy. Don't say anything to anyone — not Mukwe, not Eden, or your sister — until Kathy and I have met. Only then will we know the possibilities. Now, I have made dinner for us here and I am looking forward to our 'old style' date, of talking joking and playing. We can also catch-up on one another's parents." And so it was another very happy get-together. She informed him, much to his relief, that she had a boyfriend who was away at the moment, and who would be kept right out of the current dilemma until — hopefully- it was settled.

Rod responded to that by saying, "I'm glad for you Kim, and would like to meet him then. The three of us bushies are intending to go to Uni. provided that Mr. Frost — whom you will remember from Aberfoyle — can get us in. It would be another wonderful achievement if he can manage it as a senior Educationalist. After that we have all separately decided that we would still like to travel. Eventually Australia is beckoning Mukwe and I." Kim raised an eyebrow and said "Snap, for Trevor and I."

Before leaving, Rod asked Kim to join them all at Colin and Carry's on the Sunday, and arranged to pick her up. This he did, and they all met and enjoyed morning tea together. Kathy and Kim had briefly talked, and after tea asked to be allowed to leave the group: Colin took them through to the study. They were gone for an hour or so, and by the time they had finished this first meeting they each had screeds of hand written notes. On rejoining the group, Kim looked across at Rod and said "Well Antony! We are on the way."

Kathy caught Eden's enquiring look and she added, "Nearly Peter!, but we still need to get together a few more times. However, all of you, total silence concerning all of this, otherwise the two of us — indicating Kim — could really be 'in the cactus." This was appreciated by all, but there were audible sighs of relief.

After a beaut lunch, and amiable chats over coffee, Rod took Kim home, and thanked her profusely, adding "When you and Kathy have achieved this, and we have our new identities, I would love you and Trevor to become close friends, with all of us." She thanked him for that request, and for the day. They parted with a brief hug.

Nothing more was heard from the two girls for the next ten days, until Rod and Eden were asked to meet them in town at a secret location, to sign documents. These were the Citizenship papers, and once that was done the girls congratulated them on being Antony and Peter, and that they would be presented with those, and the other important documents, at a date to be advised. Kathy informed them, with a glance at Kim, and a twinkle in her eye, "I have already arranged the presentation 'ceremony' at Carry's, on Sunday next." Neither of the girls could spare more time off work, so after handshakes and hugs all round, they went their various ways.

Life at the house between then and Sunday, was a case of using, and getting used to the new first names, with Mukwe being the one, doing the most addressing. Sunday, with the additional attendance of Rick and his wife, was stupendous, and with everyone clutching a champagne Kim and Kathy shared the delight of presenting Antony and Peter with their Citizenships, Birth Certificates and Passports. Naturally there were informal speeches, with Antony and Peter thanking Kim and Kathy. Peter also said, "Although I have always had great confidence and faith in Antony, I never thought that this momentous event could happen." Mukwe also thanked everyone, as the best friend of each of them.

Colin closed the ceremony by calling, "Three cheers' for all concerned." A very happy afternoon was spent, but before Kim left, Antony (Rod) advised everyone that the next time they all got together, Kim would be accompanied by her boyfriend who was due back soon.

# CHAPTER 16

N ow that they had their new identities, the final piece in the puzzle was to re-approach Mr. Frost. After a few days Antony did this, and was able to give him a preview of what he would like to see him about. They arranged a preliminary interview at the Inspectorate of Education Offices. Antony went along and was astounded at the impressive 'white walled/red tyled building'. He was shown to Mr. Frost's Executive Office and It was good to catch-up again, with Antony opening by saying, "Thanks Sir, for the message received whilst I was in jail."

Mr. Frost reverted to 'family friendly' attitude, and immediately asked, "What the dickens happened to you in Aberfoyle and how did you stage everything that has happened since — to get you here to the Capital?" Antony (Rod) covered everything briefly — including his meeting Eden (Peter) in jail — their dual escapes; the rivers trip and finally meeting-up with Carry and Colin. Mr. Frost did remember Eden, and the twisted circumstances leading to his jailing: however, he was unaware that Rod had been shot and was aghast, as well as for the attack on them whilst canoeing.

Once they got to 'the arriving in the Capital' point, he continued, "How are the new identities for Rod and Eden progressing?" and was delighted that all that was in place. "Okay!" So now you want to know if there is any chance of my organizing entrance for you two, into University courses?"

"Exactly!" said Antony.

"Well, if it hadn't been for your concocted story that I got from Carry, there probably wouldn't have been. I just loved that, the same as she did and because of that I am making initial arrangements for entrance papers: for you to complete Accounting/Business Management and for Eden to undertake Secondary Teaching. I'll give you a call as to when the two of you can come in to complete those, in your new names." Antony thanked him, and they parted on the same relationship, that each of them had previously valued in the past.

Towards the end of the week, Mr. Frost's Office contacted Antony and requested that he and Peter go to the University Entrance Offices that afternoon, to complete the entrance forms for each of their courses, and to receive the paperwork relative to Semester 1 of their courses. Mr. Frost was there to greet them, and in shaking hands with Peter, remarked, "I remember teaching you in Primary School." As soon as Peter saw Mr. Frost, he remembered him as well. All paperwork was completed, and Antony could detect the utmost respect, with which Mr. Frost was received. Good omen! They left with high thanks to him, and an armful of the work they would be doing in the first term!

All the official entrance papers were received a couple of weeks later, by which time they very definitely were, Antony and Peter!

At about that time also, Kim contacted Antony and told him that Trevor was back, and that she would love them to meet: no background! Antony was chuffed because he had begun to plan a final celebratory Dinner in the City, at his expense. Everyone concerned was invited. He told her of this, and asked that she and Trevor come along to meet with the whole family.

In discussion with Colin and Carry, it was decided that they would also try to get their Mom and Dad, as well as Jacky and Mel, to attend. As it turned out Ed was also coming up to the Capital that weekend, to stay with Rick and Lil.

Carry asked Peter if he would like her parents, to bring up his Mum. He was most appreciative, but asked if he could have a little time to think about it. Later he expressed concern to Antony, that his Mother would not understand what had transpired: as far as she knew, he was still on the run — somewhere in the other Province.

The party went off better than Antony could have expected. It was great to see his Mom and Dad again, a sentiment entirely endorsed by Monty. They had slipped out of Aberfoyle with other people, in an unknown car. Jacky and Mel also made it, and their company was also wonderful. Jacky had stacks of time to talk to Antony, because Mel discovered that Trevor was a like 'Train and Modeling' buff!. Kim was very amused at this, and it helped in their being absolutely accepted into this new and growing 'family', in the Capital.

Mukwe took the opportunity to phone his parents, and have a long catch-up chat. They also informed him, that Antony's parents were so excited at this opportunity to be with him, and family again. Antony reveled in the fact that everyone including Peter, talked to Kim and Trevor and they later came up and made the same observation. It was 'on for young and old'. Whilst in the Capital, Antony's Mom and Dad made a point of calling on the Frost family, whom they had known for ages; his Mum had actually worked as a secretary, in the school of which he had been a Teacher. This rekindling of friendship would also help in the long run.

The three of them fitted into university life right away, and because the lead-up had been so profound, they found that they applied themselves immediately, both in class and outside in research. Mukwe surprised both of the others, by signing up for a second degree, in Information Technology (IT). The way he explained it, "Look it would be such a 'cinch' just completing a final year in Agriculture, and anyway I also want to hang out with you guys, for the three years ahead."

Antony renewed his connection with Dan, from the few days they knew one another at the Dam. He apologised for 'bullshitting' about his name, but gave the excuse that the gambling had been a concern, because his family forbade it. Dan 'came good' on his undertaking to give them casual work, when there was an opening. Over the two years that followed, they frequently worked their vacations with his company, and they could probably thank Mukwe for this, because Dan's company carried out work for farmers, and Muk fitted into that slot beautifully. Rick's company also gave them casual work, and between these two sources, they were able to keep up their rent to Carry. She kept saying 'not necessary', but they insisted, loudly announcing that she had the best meals in the country! It actually worked very well, as they were frequently able to keep the animals exercised and fed.

When not studying; writing exams or playing sport, Colin and Anton in particular, started to plan and organize the building of an outside 'bunkhouse'. Anton and Mukwe drew the plans (from past experience on Fairhill), whilst Colin handled the City Council and their myriad requirements. Anton and Mukwe would not let Colin carry the expense, and they went 'fifty/fifty' with him, on the project. By the beginning of the final semester of year one, they were able to make a slow start on it, and had the concrete floor down by the end of the semester. This meant full-bore building of the walls during the holidays, and getting the roof in place before the rainy season started. Monty and the other two dogs had plenty of input, especially driving the point that mid-afternoon was time for walks.

Almost simultaneously with the roof being water-proofed, their exam results for the year came through, and amid much jubilation, they had all passed with flying colours. Peter exclaimed, "Well I never. This is a paradise that I never dreamed of — yes I do want to be a teacher!" What a great opportunity for all to get together, and 'have a ball!

Aside from the building of the Bunkhouse, all of them would head out to either the large dam that was not far away, or to many known spots on rivers in the vicinity of the capital. Here they continued their love for fishing. All the dogs would be part of the group and much fun was had by all. Now however, any fish of the right size that were caught, were for human consumption — not for dogs! Anton always felt that Monty and the other dogs couldn't have cared less.

In the middle of their second year in the capital, and post first semester results, they all dived into finishing the bunkhouse. Colin also took leave and between the four of them they were able to finish it sufficiently to a point that the threesome could move in. Colin had a 'dig' at them saying, "Well I've done my bit — now it's up to you guys to fight over finishing colours, for both inside and out."

Peter quickly suggested, "Gold". But was tackled by the other two, with Anton enquiring, "Wow who are you intending to impress?" Not long after that, the filling and painting were completed. This took alot of pressure off Carry and allowed her space to 'swing- a cat'. They still paid their rental/catering and Carry still loved to do the meals, so it was a happy-plus situation, with the animals still benefitting.

During Anton's second year he met a young guy named Brendon, doing Economics, who hailed from the Lowveld. His Dad had a ranch down there running pedigree cattle, but who was also engaged in an unusual game trapping exercise, for Zoos around the world. Being knowledgeable about game, he had discovered a very rare antelope breed on this large ranch, and was carefully trapping young females of the breed, to be shipped around the world. They became good friends at Uni. and would often chat over lunch or a coke. At this stage Antony asked Brendon to call him Anton, which he preferred, and he invited him to Colin and Carry's place, one weekend. Their friendship however was mainly at the University.

The second half of the year was 'heads down and bottoms-up' with their academic studies, and their interim results proved this. It was during this period that Mukwe let on to everyone, "Myself and a colleague are researching a small transportable communications item, at Uni." On being questioned, he wasn't yet able describe it, and deliberately put-off further probing but suggested, "We should be able to 'nail' it by next year for our Final and PhD theses."

The year progressed in this vein, and in 'no time flat' their end-of-year exams were upon them and they applied themselves, with an almost total exclusion of conversation — other than at the dinner table. Massive sighs of relief from all once the exams were completed, and then they were looking forward to Christmas. Carry demanded that Anton give her a hand — or rather a shoulder — which she grabbed and pulled him into the study saying, "Colin and I would love to have the same large 'family,' around here for Xmas, but this time you must be the principal 'Inviter'!"

"Ah Great!" replied Anton, "I'd love to, and can't think of anything more fulfilling at this moment in time." So, he immediately got down to preparing Xmas Card/ Invitations to the whole group, which were posted out within the week.

One couple whom he did follow-up with a phone call, was Kim and Trevor, and he was very happy to hear that they had become engaged. On an excited note he enquired, "When will the 'wedding date be?" They told him that it would be sometime in the following year, but that heaps of arrangements etc., still had to be made. They would however, be available for Carry's party.

. In the case of Mukwe, he quietly asked Carry if she would mind, for this occasion, if he travelled back there, to enjoy Christmas with his parents. Naturally Carry was very happy for him, and a special present was sent to them, from the capital 'family'. Peter's Mother confirmed that she would be able to make it — having created a diversion.

As before, the Xmas party was a wonderful success in terms of fun, dancing and meeting with everyone again. Anton and Carry felt sure that everyone had chatted to everyone else, and that the parental figures had also mixed in beautifully. Kim and Kathy had reignited their close bond, and Trevor and Mel, had got together again, to talk about their mutual hobbies. Peter's Mom was now also accepted as part of this group and between the two of them, they were able to easily fit in. Anton made a toast to Mukwe and his Parents , and in no small measure to Colin and Carry. He spent a fair amount of his time with his Mom, Dad and Jacky, and bringing them up to date on all that had occurred during the year — exam results, bunkhouse, exam results!

The bunkhouse was the first thing that his Dad wanted to see, the next day — that sort of project being right-up his alley. Colin and Carry, Anton and his Mum and Dad did inspect the bunkhouse, the next day, and the non-builders were impressed. Mind you, in typical Dad frame, he offered some pointers to the 'builders'. Everyone laughed, but accepted same in the true spirit that it had been advanced.

Before they returned to Aberfoyle, from this Xmas visit, Anton asked his Dad to absorb his (Antony's) car into his Motor business, to which request his Dad agreed, adding, "When you do buy another car, obviously I will help finance it."

Having discussed vehicles that morning, Anton mentioned

to Peter, after lunch, "You know, there is something that you and I have not yet taken care of?"

"Oh! said Peter, what could that be?"

Anton replied "As the final cog in this whole personal identification thing, we need to apply for driver's licences. In most instances, they are the 'quick' identification." It was agreed, and over the next ten days, they each, independently applied for, did their Drivers Tests and received their licences.

The final year of Uni also proved very demanding, but by applying themselves deeply and conscientiously, they were very successful in their mid-year results. In the long vacation that followed, it transpired that each of them did quite different things:- Peter was assigned to a Secondary School, to undertake Teacher Training, in situ: Mukwe and his colleague were deeply engrossed in their research, and Anton broke the trend, and went with Brendon to his Dad's ranch in the Lowveld. They were able to travel down and back in a Station Wagon, and Brendon was perfectly happy that Monty accompanied them — imagining just how he would enjoy the chase.

They travelled South West through rich savannah bushland encompassing a wide range of trees and shrubs, which gave off a quite different aura to the forests through which he and his Mates (and Monty) had rowed. After 'some' one hundred and fifty kilometres the route turned due South and much of the shorter and denser bush was left behind. However, the incidence of rivers increased to the point where Anton reflected, "Hey Brendon! The rivers are much more numerous down here and also seem to flow more strongly."

"Yes! they are, answered Brendon, and I'll tell you the story of a friend who was travelling just where we are now — but in the middle of the rainy season. He had just crossed over the Tokwe, that last river that we came over — and it was flooding at about bridge level." To quote him, — "when I got to the far side I was so relieved, that the storm and all else just left my mind. Then I got to the next one (the Lundi River) and everything rushed back with a vengeance, because it was in violent flood — well over the bridge, and I had to turn back. However, when I got to the first river it was also well over the bridge by then. I was stranded! And could only hug the steering wheel of my car in desperation."

It took them best part of a day to reach the secluded ranch, where they were welcomed by his father Mr. Kent, and a brother. Both of them also welcomed Monty, as they had been told that he was no ordinary dog. He was properly accommodated and fed, and then they followed with a most welcome farm-like meal. Over a late-night cup-of-tea Mr. Kent amusedly enquired, "Antony, has Brendon let you know how early we get going each day?".

With a smile, Anton said, "That makes no difference to me."

So, next day they were up for an early breakfast, at which

Brendon's brother Gordon effectively took 'the stage' and told them exactly what would be expected of them: "Brendon, you and Anton will take one of the Quad-Bikes (which also has a seat in the back for Monty!), and muster the left — or nearside — of the herd of antelopes: Dad and I will do the same on the far side. The herd will then be driven down to the camouflaged corral, that has been erected. There will also be a few on-foot drovers on each side, plus those at the back, who will scare the herd into virtual stampede." Apparently, the distance from start to finish could be as much as six kilometres, through the heavy bush.

Anton enquired, "Are there were any rocky outcrops, dongas or difficult streams to negotiate"?

"No! said Brendon, the area is fairly flat and definitely our main problem will be controlling the herd."

All three vehicles travelled quietly out to the site, and got ready for the muster. A single shot was fired, way out behind them and they knew that the drive was on. It was now a case of keeping very alert to make sure that the antelope didn't break either way. The Drovers were very good at anticipating this, and passing the info onto the vehicles. After approximately three minutes they picked up the first rushing sound of the approaching herd, which seemed to be tracking slightly away from them. They started up, and moved across slightly, knowing that the opposite would occur petty soon, as the vehicles and herdsmen on the other side veered them into line again. Sure enough this happened, and they had to be prepared to go back a bit first, and then turn and pace parallel, with the fleeing herd. Monty helped greatly in this, by barking loudly. This wild and anxious process continued for twenty minutes to half-an-hour, with the vehicles on both sides sluing and racing to keep the antelope moving in the right direction, followed behind by the chanting drovers. They finally got them through the corral opening, and sped in after them, such that the drovers could close the pull-round barbwire gate, and hitch it up tightly, to contain the herd.

Once that was achieved, and father and brother had ventured forward to make sure that the herd had not broken the far side of the corral, they all got down and had a well-earned brew, carried in the brother's vehicle.

The BossMan had got a good look at the herd, and the father estimated that there were at least half-a-dozen young females, that could be exported to zoos. The next procedure was to separate these from the rest of the herd, and get them into a smaller and tighter enclosure, from which they could easily be loaded onto trucks. Having had about a year's experience in this 'game', they now knew that they had to allow the herd to calm down, for a day or so, before the separating process.

The remainder of that day was spent at the house, with father and brother doing odd jobs, whilst Brendon and Anton chatted on the verandah drinking coffee! In the afternoon Monty was taken for a good long walk, and Anton took his bow along in case of guinea fowl. They didn't actually see any, but Brendon was fascinated at its (Anton's) accuracy, and had a few shots himself — being further amazed at the distance that it could reach. Anton told him that Rick and he had developed the design at high school.

That evening at dinner and afterwards they talked non-stop amongst themselves with Antony and Brendon's Dad, eventually becoming separated. The latter was most interested in the fact that Antony was doing Accounting and Business studies, and that Brendon and he, enjoyed certain common subjects. He then informed Antony, "I have been a Corporate Executive." This was a big surprise — though nothing compared to what was coming — and Anton made the observation that he was very young, to have retired.

Clearly Brendon must have conveyed high respect for Antony, because his father then related an incredible sequence of events that led to the family being on this secluded ranch. A non-related prelude to the events was the fact that he had lost his wife — the boy's Mother, some ten years before, and therefore the urgent move was in no way slowed–up.

Hesitating at that point, Mr. Kent said, "Antony, what I am about to tell you is an absolute secret, and must not be mentioned outside of these walls. At the time of the events, myself and the Boys received death threats." Anton immediately gave that assurance., The man then continued with the 'story'. "I worked in the site offices of a Diamond

Mine in the Orapa area of Botswana. It was the first of the diamond mines in that country, but certainly showed the potential. A much bigger mine was being developed by the company, which would eventually see this prime 'Site Office' move to the new mine. However, before that move I was confided in by one of my native Botswana staff about illicit diamonds being smuggled away from the mine. He wanted protection — as I also did later."

"I made an immediate appointment to talk to top Mine Management, the next day. I was able to convince them, and they contacted Head Office in Johannesburg who, in a very short time had Interpol and the Botswana Police on site. Once they arrived I persuaded my staff member to utilize accommodation where I was living, and that small move alerted the hierarchy of the smugglers, to penetrate the protective ring, and deliver threat letters to both of us. In each letter we and our families were threatened with death. My boys were away at Boarding School, so to me this was catastrophic. The Board of the mine also recognised the seriousness of this threat, and probably because they were already planning the site-office move, advised that they would prepare something right away."

"This they did, and astoundingly they purchased this ranch, paying a substantial deposit against it. I was told about it and asked whether I, and my staff member, would disappear onto it, and thereby be totally protected from anything happening outside. Obviously separation payments, and that sort of thing came-up, and I for one was a bit disappointed at the amount of mine. But not for long, because when the documentation arrived for my signature on the property, I discovered that I was a fifty percent owner and that there were provisions in it for my staff member. That was nearly five years ago, and there have been no threats since."

Antony responded, "Thank you for your trust: I'm absolutely amazed at the story, and can assure you that it will go no further."

The following day they all went back to the corral, where they found the antelope in a pretty calm state. In discussion the previous day, it transpired that they and the herdsmen had tried various options to get the eligible females into the smaller corral, but none had been effective, with some minor injuries occurring. Finally they decided upon anaesthetic shots, which were provided by their Veterinary Officer. The neatness of this method was that as soon as the nominated females lay down in a drugged state, all the rest could be let out, back into 'their country'. So, again that was done, with Brendon and Anton witnessing it. Neatness was the right word, and the anaesthetized females were rolled onto stretchers, and carefully carried into the smaller corral, from which they would ultimately be transported.

At the end of that week, Brendon, Anton and Monty returned to the Capital, after what -Anton was able to reflect on — as an extraordinary visit. Having been dropped off he was welcomed home, and during the evening meal he told them all about the antelope capturing, and what it was like down in the lowveld; four hundred and fifty kilometres from the Capital. He then quizzed Mukwe and Peter on their progress, adding "So do you still want to be a teacher, Peter?"

Peter wiped his brow and said "There are a couple of fifteen-year-olds in the class, and boy! I hope that I wasn't like them: one really has to employ some psychology to keep them under control. Apart from them however, I thoroughly enjoyed the experience, and have to do another 'prac'. next vacation."

Everyone then listened to Mukwe as he recited progress at Uni. on his 'sort of chip,' to communicate between two people. It sounded revolutionary to the listeners, and that it was coming-on apace.

When Anton got to his room and was looking through mail, there was an invitation to Kim's and Trevor's wedding, for all five of them. He completed the invitation, but instead of posting it he phoned the lucky couple, and arranged to deliver it instead. The following evening he rocked-up at their place at the appointed time, and was received with much excitement and pleasure. His main reason for needing to see them before the wedding, was to make sure that they weren't stinting themselves. They gave him much detail to absorb about their preparations, and these were as happy and complete, as anyone could wish, but he still insisted that if they needed any help or funding he would love to do so.

When the day arrived, Bride and Groom were a beautiful

couple. The ceremony went off like a song: everyone was there, Antony/Carry's entire' Capital Family', with large contingents from each of Kim's and Trevor's families. For Anton in particular, it was super to meet these folk for the first time, and Kim's parents for the first time in nearly four years. What a send-off for the couple on their honeymoon.

Final half-year at Uni was, predictably, a period of extremely hard work and dedication. They received every bit of assistance from family and friends, which certainly helped, but it was just a case of total application to their final subjects. In the end, they all did well, and achieved their degrees. Peter applied for a teaching position, and was told that he had every chance of securing it at a good school. Mukwe returned to the Department of Agriculture, but instead of being sent out to some minor station, he was employed in the Capital, in their Research Division. Antony joined one of the Big-Four Accounting Companies, and because he now had two qualifications, he went in as Manager of an active team. All were happy in their employment, but funnily enough, still preferred their Bunkhouse, with Colin and Carry, rather than seeking new accommodation.

Life for each of the threesome carried on fairly quietly into the New Year: Antony and Mukwe in fully employed jobs, and Peter doing part-time, either at Dan's business, or with Rick's. As the new University year approached Mukwe asked, "Anton would you be prepared to consider a small — same day — bit of surgery?" Anton asked what it would be, and whether it would be the same as that on his, Mukwe's arm. He continued, saying, "Yes, and a small chip will be inserted just below the skin, leaving a flap." He showed Anton his insertion and explained that the chip had some communication potential, but that its current use produced a green glow for 'All Okay', and a red glow for 'Be Alert-Not, So Good' — activated by a small vibration. Whilst this sounded fairly funny to Anton, he agreed to go ahead with the surgery — having the utmost faith in Mukwe.

Once the wound had healed and was perfectly normal, they arranged a test between themselves, across the widest parkland. Mukwe had a small mirror, and faced the sun: Anton went across the other side with Monty and as soon as he saw the first mirror flash, his arm started to vibrate mildly and Monty barked. He then lifted the flap and there was a green glow. He gave an agreed signal back to Mukwe, who then switched that signal off. Another mirror flash: another vibration, another bark, but this time the glow was red. Again Anton signaled, and the vibration ceased. They then joined up with Mukwe and went back to the bunkhouse for a cup of coffee — and biscuit for Monty.

And so City Life continued — as it does! They all either played sport or continued with Gym workouts, and had many 'get-togethers' in Sports Clubs, or Pubs in the city. The 'city family' had many gatherings –some without parents, and some with — but all enjoyed to the full. The animals also had many outings to lakes and fishing spots.

Anton purchased a good second-hand car with the help of his father's promise, which gave he and Peter more mobility.

Peter was now a full-time Teacher and getting alot of satisfaction from it. The jobs of the other two were predictable, but enjoyable due to the large group of compatriots, with whom they associated each day. Anton and Mukwe often conferred about progress with the 'Chip' research, at the Uni. and all that the latter could confess was to say "We are increasing the distances that the two chips can be apart."

Towards the end of the year Brendon breezed into the Capital one day, and contacted Anton. "I will be in the City for a few days, and will be as busy 'as hell'. Would you and friends like to return with me to the ranch?" Anton agreed to pursue it and found out that he *could* take a first bit of annual leave, and was naturally excited about it. On talking to Mukwe that evening, Mukwe smiled and expressed great interest: he also looked into the possibility and managed to secure leave. It was therefore a matter of getting themselves, and Monty, ready for the trip ahead.

# CHAPTER 17

On the day of Brendon's completion of City duties, Anton phoned to enquire of the meeting point, and to re-affirm that Monty would be welcome. He also asked if he and Mukwe could bring their rifles, as they would love to do a bit of 'small stuff' hunting. Brendon agreed with aplomb and indicated that he would join them, if not busy at the time. At the end of the day-trip down to the ranch, with Anton, Mukwe and Monty following Brendon, the first thing that caught Anton's eye was a new, very high Security Fence around the homestead. On enquiring, Brendon said, "There have been a few occurrences of attacks on lonely farms and ranches, by insurgents from over the border. Don't worry though, all of the ranchers around the Lowveld are connected by Citizen Band radios, as well as high frequency sirens that alert each of the other ranchers, down into their homesteads."

They were all welcomed, and after unpacking their gear, feeding the dog and cleaning themselves up, were treated to a scrumptious meal prepared by brother Gordon and their Cook. They all talked well into the night, over a wide range of issues. Mukwe had been well received, and Mr. Kent was most impressed with his academic and scientific achievements.

They were into the second stage of a muster, and the new arrivals were asked to be ready for an early start. After an early breakfast, they all packed themselves into the Station Wagon and headed down to the small corral. It was exactly as Anton remembered it, and he was able to brief Mukwe very clearly on the anesthetic darts that would be used in the number of young female antelopes that had been captured. It seemed to happen all very quietly, and once the darted females lay down and 'went to sleep', all the other antelope were let out through the main opening. At that stage the group left to return to the homestead, and Mukwe was told about the loading of the small female antelopes onto trucks, and under veterinary care, taken to the export point.

They kept themselves busy throughout the week, until the next muster, by helping out in the workshops and sheds, as well as going hunting, which of course Monty thought was wonderful. Mukwe did manage to shoot a small antelope with his rifle, because the house was running out of venison, and Monty caught some kind of large bush rat, which they took home, for his evening meal.

When the next muster was organized, Mukwe was with Brendon, while Anton was with Gordon on the other side of the muster route. As before it went well, but with an anticipated hiccup here and there, which the drovers were able control, once they got the main herd stampeding in the exact right direction. Mukwe was 'blown away' in his excitement — as Anton had been, for his first Muster. On one particular occasion he lept-up grabbing the top of the windscreen, and shouted, "They're racing this way fast, Brendon." To which directive the latter immediately applied corrective action through the Quod-bike.

Stage two was completed the following day, with the same successful results. Ironically, Mister Kent mentioned that night that a long break was now scheduled from that day, to allow the herd to regain numbers to their ideal strength.

All the young men went for a hunt later that week, armed with both rifles and bows. Gordon took them due westwards to an area that they had not previously hunted, and although they only 'nailed' one buck, one guinea fowl and Monty a well-chased-after- rabbit, they came back well satisfied, and were in agreement that the companionship had been great.

On entering the house all were surprised, but particularly the two sons, that Mister Kent had all their various firearms out on the lounge floor where he had been cleaning them, and checking the magazines of the automatic weapons. Brendon exclaimed "Gee Dad! I didn't expect to see these out." To which his Dad said, "Well I had nothing to do, so decided that as they hadn't been cleaned for quite a while, I would do the job. But we can pack them away again — now that you are all back." The two boys did this, leaning them against the cabinet in the passage.

While they were doing it, Mukwe remarked to Anton, "We should also clean our guns and refill the magazines."

The following day was busy, with the son's catching-up on various odd jobs, assisted by their 'city' visitors, plus Monty. Anton and Mukwe also brought their rifles across to the house to work on them over 'lunch'. Mr. Kent spent most of his time in the Office, working on the books, and only making occasional ventures outside to see what the rest of them were doing.

There were the usual jovial get-togethers inside, particularly after the evening meal, until there was a sudden blast out to the right at the front of the house, followed by the distinct 'crack' of weapon fire. Immediately thereafter there was total onslaught of shooting towards the house, from the East on the other side of the fence. Thanks to brick walls none of this initial fire penetrated badly — except through windows and doors. All inside were galvanized into action; running through to the passage and collecting their weapons, and loading them.

At the first tailing off of the assault, Mr. Kent leapt up, with one of the automatics, shouting "Gordon, follow me but go right: Brendon, you cover the back." Both of them also grabbed automatics and obeyed his instructions. He shot out through the front door, immediately engaging the attackers by spreading fire across the front. Gordon copied his example, spreading his fire between one o'clock and three o'clock of the clock.

Anton and Mukwe got going down the passage, and out to the left. As Anton ran out into the night he was fairly sure that he heard a scream from the other side of the fence, way out to the front. Just then he saw the flash of gunfire over to the left, which Monty also saw and raced across barking furiously, but it had also resulted in a definite gasp from Mr. Kent. The next thing there was another flash from the same point, aimed at, and hitting Monty, who let out a strangled bark and crashed to the earth. Anton had however noted the exact position of the flashes, and fired two quick shots at the position, followed by one slightly lower. There was a scream from there, but Anton was already on his way down to where Monty was lying; at the same time loudly employing Mukwe, 'Please go across to Mr. Kent; he is lying in the drive."

When he got there Mukwe grabbed the FN Automatic, and the spare magazine jutting out of Mr. Kent's pocket; knelt against the trunk of a tree close by, and with Gordon firing full tilt on the right of him, sprayed the attackers from left to right and back. There were more screams and then silence. Brendon and Anton had also been busy, and this devastating counter attack caused the enemy to flee, leaving casualties.

All of them then ran across to the father, who had clearly suffered a terrible wound low down the front. Brendon covered him, while Gordon ran inside to get on the Citizen Band and engage the siren. As soon as Anton was satisfied that Brendon had his Dad comfortable and talking, he raced back to Monty. His wonderful dog, and Mate, had been hit in the shoulder, and there was no exit wound, which really worried Anton. Just as he was able to ascertain that Monty was not dead, Mukwe came across from where he had been shooting, and helped in getting him to the house. The four of them then concentrated on getting Mr. Kent onto a mattress, at which juncture the Citizen Band 'awoke' again, and Gordon ran inside to talk. Between the three of them, they got Mr. Kent into the Lounge on the floor, still on the mattress. He was awake, but in considerable pain. Anton ran across to Gordon who was speaking on the radio, and asked him to request that a Veterinary Officer, also come out. When Gordon returned to the lounge he relayed, "There will not only be a group of other ranchers coming out by vehicle, but the Army are also coming out by helicopter, with Paramedics. My Dad will be flown back to Mobridge Hospital, in the helicopter."

The other Lowveld ranchers arrived about an hour later, and had the 'nouse' to set-up guards at each corner of the house. They were taken coffee and relieved every two hours. This happened on, and off, until the helicopter arrived.

Anton had excused himself and gone to cuddle Monty, and to make him as comfortable, as possible. The Kents all expressed their dismay at the fact that Monty had also been hit, and hoped that the Vet could get there quickly. Soon after the Paramedics had attended to Mr Kent, and loaded him onto the helicopter, for his urgent trip to hospital, the Vet did arrive. He straight away got down on the floor next to Monty, to inspect the damage. He was so gentle, and talked to Monty as he worked, and then gave him a strong pain killer. While he was waiting for it to take effect, he asked, "How old is Monty?"

Anton and Mukwe both had tears in their eyes, but the former knew this answer, because he had been working it out, and said "He is in his sixteenth year."

The Vet replied "I can see that he was very fit, but that makes him an old dog. It will be touch and go, as to whether we can get him to pull through."

Anton accepted the advice, adding "Yes, I realise that, but can only hope."

When Monty had quietly lain down flat, the Vet said "Antony, I am going to take him back with me in my vehicle to Sapphire, so that I can operate on him: I trust you can come through and be with him." Clearly Anton's answer was in the affirmative.

Once the Army unit had arrived in the helicopter that night, with the paramedics, they immediately assembled and very carefully inspected the whole area of the attack. Sure enough Anton had managed to kill the attacker out to the left of the homestead, but they also came across two wounded enemy. They patched them up as well as they could, and left them securely bound, until they returned. They then pursued the attackers out into the night, taking the dead attacker with them, to bury him well away from the homestead. As it turned out however, because the attackers had left their wounded they had fled at the run, and the unit could not catch them — as they were currently set-up. They immediately radioed their base and explained the whole thing, asking to be picked up, and for two permanent guards to be brought down, as well. Their final statement to HQ was that they had two wounded enemy, who would have to come back with them. While this call was proceeding, a soldier with the most nursing training, was checking on the state of the two wounded, and re-bandaging their wounds, and issuing pain killers. There were no chances they would be released.

There was a bit of an exodus the next day, with Anton and Mukwe making for the town in which the Vet had his practice, and Gordon heading off to be with Mr. Kent. They were satisfied that Brendon would be safe, because apart from the other ranchers, two Police guards had also been brought down, for added protection. All of them however, felt reasonably safe, due to the army having been so quickly on the scene, and the fact that the Citizen Band Radio system and siren had worked so well.

It was mid-afternoon when they walked into the special High Care section of the Vet's rooms in Sapphire, and saw Monty bathed in bandages and gowns. He was still under the effect of the anesthetic, so was not aware of their presence. It was a distraught moment for both of them, but they held the tears at bay. The Vet told them that he had operated and removed the bullet and stitched the wound, but would not know of the success until Monty woke up. Fortunately he had not lost alot of blood, but internally along the trajectory that the bullet had taken, including one lung, the congealed blood and damage was severe. The Vet was busy with patient animals, so asked them if they could come back again, later.

They went across to a restaurant for a meal in a sombre state, and took the opportunity to phone Carry and Colin. Peter was also there, because he had heard the first broadcast of the attack on a ranch, and felt that he recognized the name. Anton gave them a quick synopsis of what had occurred; of Mr. Kent's and of Monty's serious wounds. Carry started to cry when she heard the news about Monty, and handed the phone across to Peter, who was devastated. He said he would get the details from Carry, but asked if they needed his help down there, and that he was quite prepared to fly down. By this time Mukwe had taken over the phone and declined Peter's offer, with heartfelt thanks from both of them, advising that they were on their way home in the next day or two. During their meal, they only talked about the animal who had been their mate, for so long, and whom they both loved so much.

When Anton and Mukwe returned to the Vet's Centre,

he came in from the back looking serious and sad. He indicated to the surgery behind, and as they walked in he said, "Monty has woken, but his vital signs are weakening: his heart rate and breathing are also failing." Although the two had more or less expected that statement, they were nevertheless very downcast at the news. Monty was lying flat on a comfortable, padded 'dog-bed', but they could see that he was having trouble with his breathing.

They went down to him straight away, with one on each side, and gently stroked him. Anton put his hand gently under Monty's head, and bent close to his ear saying "Hi! Monty, we're here with you." Mukwe was also at his head by this time, and added "You've done well sport: and we've come to get you". Anton lifted Monty's head slightly, and put his against Monty's snout. There were a couple of very laboured wags of his tail, and he looked straight into Anton's eyes. His eyes smiled, as did his mouth and a message was passed "Good to see you both, and I'm so happy." Both of them replied that they were also happy to be with him. Another slow wag of the tail, and another contact of eyes between him and Anton through which he conveyed, "But I must say cheers, as I am on my way." Anton quickly pulled Mukwe round the front, to also look into his eyes: there was a last wag, and last glances at Anton and Mukwe, and he slipped away into dog heaven.

The Vet quickly checked his pulse and a little mirror to his nose, and said "He has passed away." Anton and Mukwe acknowledged that, and the Vet concluded saying "I'll leave you two with him." With his head against Monty's head, Anton started to cry. Mukwe put an arm around Anton, and also started to cry. When they had each passed their respects in this way, they gazed down on him lovingly, and Anton said "You were part of our lives Mate: God bless you and have a happy journey."

When they went out front wiping their eyes, it looked almost as if the Vet and his assistant had also been crying. Once everything was concluded, Anton asked the Vet if Monty could be heavily frozen whilst in the mortuary, as they would like to take him back to the Capital, to be buried in their garden. The Vet agreed and gave them 48 hours to return and pick him up. Mukwe said, "Not until we have all had a coffee together — I'll go and collect."

When he came back with the cappuccinos they had a final chat over everything that had occurred. All of them were chuffed that the Army had widened their presence in the entire district, and had sent strong support down to the Ranch.

From there the two headed for Mobridge — some eighty kilometres away — to which Mr. Kent had been 'casevaced'. They had phoned ahead and Gordon met them in the carpark of the hospital, with hopeful news of his dad, and they all proceeded down to the High Care section. On the way Gordon informed them, "Dad has had serious surgery and will not be able to see us yet." There was an area set aside for tea/coffee, and while they were waiting for their order, Gordon chatted to the senior nurse, and was assured that the prognosis hadn't changed.

While chatting over their coffee, and an enquiry from Mukwe, he confirmed, "Brendon and all the others down at the ranch are safe and okay, thanks to the quick response by some of our neighbours — alerted by the sirens and Citizen Band contact, and for the immediate action by the Army. May I say however on behalf of the family, how devastated we are to hear of Monty's death."

Rod acknowledged saying, "Thanks Gordon, and I can assure you that his last weeks were some of the most exhilarating of his life."

From there they booked into an hotel and took a well-earned rest, until the next day when they again got in touch with Gordon. He was able to advise that post lunch, would be okay for a brief visit. They kept this appointment, and it turned out well. Both paid their respects, and thanked Mr. Kent for hosting their stay. He was only just able to show his appreciation, and invited them to come down again, if they were able. After a short visit, they parted and Gordon accompanied them to the door of the ward. They promised to keep in touch with both he and Brendon.

Early the next day they went back to pick-up Monty, and then made the long trip back to the Capital. Carry, Colin and Peter were wrought by what had happened, and were so glad that Anton and Mukwe had brought Monty back to be buried near to his canine friends. Next morning they all got involved in the grave digging and the burial, and Colin said that he would make a plaque.

# CHAPTER 18

I t had been a long and sad trip up to the Capital, ascending
to the Highveld, all the way. There were many sections
on which they had to exercise extreme caution due to the
steepness, and the many tight bends in the road. During the
course of the journey Anton outlined to Mukwe the first
rumblings of a plan, "I have always had a keen desire to visit
the Orapa and Okavango districts of Botswana. Its right out
of the blue, but as we still have two weeks remaining of our
leave, what do you think?"

They discussed visiting the new diamond mine where Mr.
Kent's ex employer had its new Mine Offices. Anton felt that
it would be good for the Management of that company, to
know what had happened to Mr. Kent. Mukwe agreed and
said, "Yes! He deserves that respect, and I hope that the
Company acknowledge what we tell them. Meantime an
extended holiday trip won't go amiss."

Because it was the other side of the world (nearly anyway!!), they decided to fly to Gaborone, and take the bus from there to the mine. They chatted to Peter about the plan, but he was in the middle of a school term so couldn't contemplate joining them. Flight and Bus tickets were purchased, followed by some careful packing by each of them. Hopefully they would also be able to join a game tour to the Okavango, so would need rough clothing for that experience. Pullovers were not high on the list, but Anton did say, "Mukwe, just in case; do take your suit and tie, as they may want us to attend a meeting at the Mine."

After a farewell kneel at Monty's grave, and cheers to the other two dogs, Carry took them out to the airport to see them off, with the final advice of, "This time try to keep out of trouble." Anton kissed her, and they all had goodbye hugs. The flight had a stopover in Pretoria first, before re-directing to Gaborone.

Mukwe was agreeably impressed with Pretoria and the Witwatersrand that they flew over, and received a friendly belt on the shoulder, by Anton, who said, "So you should be — it's a first-world producer."

At Gaborone Airport there was a bus waiting to head 'out-desert' to the Diamond Mines. They already had their tickets, so grabbed their baggage and boarded. A very interesting journey followed — flat as a board — and with only part of the way being on a sealed road. Initially there were a few African villages which seemed to be doing good trade for their populace, but apart from a few 'get-offs and pick-ups', the bus did not make a scheduled stop. Mukwe was busy reading up on this district of Botswana while Anton was taking it all in. There was a dirty wind blowing with large clouds of light brown dust billowing across from one side to the other, which cavorted a myriad of tumbleweed across the road — something which Anton had never before experienced. Not only were he and Mukwe sweating but most of the passengers were showing signs of the extreme heat outside: there wasn't a cloud in the sky — which was only just blue, and he estimated the temperature out there to be in excess of 40 degrees 'C'. Most notable was the lack of any rivers in this part, and the constancy of the dry savannah for the rest of the way. They did however see a fair amount of game, principally Zebra and Wildebeest, but the rest were foreign to them, and generated much discussion amongst the occupants.

On arrival they were shown to an hotel and booked in, then enjoyed an evening walk before dinner, followed by seeking their beds for a well-earned rest.

Next morning using two phones and many attempts between them, Mukwe finally managed to reach the General Manager/CEO's office, and handed the phone to Anton. He was speaking to the CEO's Secretary and introduced himself and Mukwe as Executives from a Central African country to the North, and that they had a letter addressed to the CEO, which they would like to deliver right away, as it was of immense importance. She agreed to receive it.

Dressed in their Number Ones (Best suits with ties) the taxi dropped them off, and they were impressed at the fine four-story block of offices. They were taken-up to the CEO's Office where they handed the letter to the Secretary, again expressing its importance. She said that she would take it in to him right away, and asked them to wait.

The GM (Mr. Sansom) came out with the Secretary, opening the letter in annoyance and enquiring what they were seeking. They got the impression that he would have sent them on their way, until, clearly, he saw the name Kent on the letter. He guided them through to the lounge — waiting area — explaining that he could only give them ten minutes due to an important meeting about to take place in the Boardroom.

Anton leaped at the opportunity and asked if they could be admitted to the meeting — for quarter of an hour or so, to pass on information about a previous Executive, Mr. Kent. Mr. Sansom's eyebrows lifted, and he said, "Obviously we do know of Mr. Kent. Is it important information?" Anton replied to the effect that not only was it very important, but that it was 'top secret' and had occurred on the ranch.

The GM accepted that, stood up, and asked them to follow him. He took them straight into the Boardroom where many members had already congregated, and said, "To all of you, once we are all here, I would like to introduce these two gentlemen." Almost simultaneously with this introduction, the last two members came into the room and Mr. Sansom introduced Antony and Mukwe, with their surnames, as well, saying "We need to listen to them and their account, because it concerns Mr Kent, whom you should all remember, was an Executive Member in our Office at the Old Mine."

Anton stood, and thanked the Board Members for being prepared to listen to them. He then briefly related what had happened to Mr. Kent, and the fact that he was currently recovering in Hospital, from his severe shooting wound.

In answer to a question put by one of the Members as to how they knew about this, Mukwe replied stating, "Because we were there and took part in the action, with Mr Kent and his sons." There was silence for at least ten seconds, until Mr. Sansom said, "Members of the Board we are not in our meeting yet, so we should just talk through this, and cover it from our perspective".

Before getting into deeper discussion, Anton requested that the Kent's be afforded total privacy from the Press, in connection with the attack upon them. All the perspectives were then covered for a further ten minutes, with notes being taken by the Secretary. At the conclusion everyone stood, and Anton and Mukwe were officially thanked: each received a couple of taps on the back, as they followed Mr. Sansom out.

He thanked them again and told them that if they needed

anything while they were in the mine town, to please let him know. They enquired if there were official tours of the Mine, and when he replied that there were, they promised that they would make arrangements to join one. But, in the meantime they were going on the Okavango Tour!.

It was a half-day trek northwards to join the tour at Orapa, through country that was almost identical to that of two days before.

They were welcomed into a happy band of International tourists of both sexes, among whom were two Australian girls, Patricia (Pat) and Lynn, whom Anton and Mukwe both liked the look of — which 'eyeing' appeared to have been mutual! They had all come across from Francistown, to which city they had flown from Johannesburg. They also exchanged names with two young guys — Darren and David, as well as their driver Stewart (Stew), to whom Mukwe immediately exclaimed, "Boy! Are we impressed with the Four-Wheel Drive vehicles in which you will be carrying the party."

The Tour left for Maun soon after, as they had a long journey ahead of them. The first night's stop-over was to the West of the Ntwetwe Pans, and as they had been travelling for a good part of the day through very flat featureless, hot dry desert country, they were pleased to pitch camp, and clean-up. Afterwards they enjoyed a splendid meal and had their first social get-together. Not only did they enjoy this camping experience, but they realised that this Touring

Company also provided Four Star (4*) accommodation and meals — in fact everything.

During the evening the Senior Guide informed them, "The Delta province have received some good early rains, and this fact will significantly improve most aspects of the tour. Likewise the rains have also broken far to the North, in Angola and the Congo, and we the guides are hoping that the first flood flow will come down the Okavango. However even if it doesn't quite reach the delta, all the elephants, buffalos and other game — notably antelope large and small — are already on the move towards the Delta, to take advantage of the extraordinary growing season of the grasses, reeds, and all other plants native to the depression in the land."

The following day they carried on to Maun, and it was noticeable how the country started to change. Primarily it was the trees that created this sensation: they gradually got bigger and thickened into bushland, but it was the dense green and freshness that impressed. On arrival in Maun they were surprised that the town actually had some gardens and seemed to be very well kept. Lynn expressed their mutual admiration saying, "Gee! Look at all these beautiful flowers along the median strip, and mowed lawns, as well."

David had also noticed and been amazed, and added, "You're right I certainly didn't expect such a show."

'What a dazzling range of colours too, said Pat, and I also

noticed Oliander which I thought were Australian: as they are grown extensively in the 'Outback.'.

Anton remembered some 'expert' horticultural gems passed on by this Mother, "Get with it, you lot! Africa can also be very beautiful. You are 'spot-on' Pat with the Oliander: they will flourish anywhere in the world, in conditions such as these, and in your Outback."

By this time the Guides had left to top-up the vehicles, so the tour party happily took a break and found a restaurant where they could appreciate this real rural town of Maun. As well as re-fuelling the 'Rovers', the guides also had to replenish the stores. That afternoon they were transported right to the Delta. The closer they got, the greener the whole scene became — almost akin to admiring a thousand square kilometres of Lucerne.

The permanent camping had been set-up on a slight rise to avoid it being inundated, and as they approached it, they increasingly noticed the water was beginning to invade what had been the vast arid desert. Its widening spread seemed almost impossible; as did the millions of swamp and lake type birds including many varieties of ducks, geese; herons, and plovers taking advantage of this bonanza of delta creatures coming up through the newly formed mud.

This phenomenon was also a recognized attraction of the Okavango Tours. People who had a deep interest in fish and other strange molluscs and crustaceans of the water, could have a bonanza studying this very unusual gathering of such creatures. Apart from the fact that the millions of predatory birds were frantically gouging down to seek their individual preference, the floods coming down from the North also brought a variety of medium to large 'hunter fish' that preyed on the various sizes of minor fish etcetera, in the chain. It was a predatory stairway. Much conversation ensued between those on the Four-wheel drive vehicle.

Reaching the campsite each couple were allotted tents with the appropriate toilet facilities alongside. During this process Pat and Lynn insisted that the four guys in their vehicle be placed close to them, and this was done. Meals were served in a common area such that the full touring party could be seated together at the tables. Superlative. Based on the excitement of events during each day, the wide conversation in this common area increased loudly and wildly and caused much mirth during meals.

From this axis the tourists travelled out in every direction. For the first few days the guides took their groups in the Four Wheel Drive vehicles to areas where they could show Hippos and Crocodiles: the latter taking up the challenge and doing their best to eliminate anything that moved in their zone. The portrait of hippos and their dreadful reputation had everyone spellbound: Stew explained, "Hippos are very unpredictable and dangerous anywhere near water and more people are killed in the African bush and rivers by hippos, than by any other African animal."

Lynn was horrified and exclaimed, "I hope that we don't have to enter the water anywhere near here."

Back at camp after the second day out and congregated for the evening meal, the great news was that the group in one of the tour vehicles had witnessed a massive Fish Eagle swooping down and catching one of the bigger invading fish. One of the occupants offered in disappointment, "It all happened so quickly that no one was able to take a photograph."

As the flood increased they had to convert to powered boats, and on the first day the group were able to cross North Eastwards for about ten kilometres to approach the savannah bushland in that direction. At the site that the guide had selected they got to within half-a-kilometre and were able to view herds of Elephants already on the move. "Just look at that spectacle, said Mukwe, I've seen many herds of elephants but nothing to compare with that." Anton agreed and the entire group concurred vociferously. They watched them for a long while, noting that there were also a couple of baby elephants. Some of them came down to the water to drink, and seemed incredibly close. However, it was obvious that their main destination was still some way off. Although the group kept a close lookout, no other major movement was visible on that day.

That night back at camp after the meal — and the exit of many of the tour group — with cups of coffee in hand, Lynn who had obviously been contemplating something, suddenly said, "You know, when our family were travelling in our car along bush roads, Mum taught us a little game to keep us awake and to take an interest in the passing environment. To quote — it was I spy with my little eye, something beginning with — then a letter of the alphabet. Those in the car had either seen same, or had to make educated guesses."

Everyone suddenly remembered the oft played 'poetic challenge', and Anton suggested, "We must use it when we get back to the game watching, and the winner can request a small prize?". There were loud and humorous retorts to this idea.

"Yeah, but if Pat or I are not the winners, we will not be the prize!!" Everyone had a good laugh at that and notwithstanding, it was decided that once the game movement increased, they would 'play the game'.

On the second and third days they travelled to the other side, and witnessed massive herds of Buffalos; many varieties of antelope including the epic Sable and Kudu, plus Zebras and Giraffes making their way towards 'food heaven'. They did play their game during these visits and had lots of fun — especially at the expense of Stew, who hadn't previously heard of the game. Over the final days the guides sought out prides of lions plus a few leopards and cheetahs that were preying on the weak within these vast herds. The Tour members couldn't believe their eyes at what they saw, and Darren expressed it saying, "I don't think that there could be anywhere else in the world, where one can see such a bonanza of animals conglomerating towards one epic delta".

Everyone agreed with him heartily and they even witnessed a couple of 'kills', and although astounded at the dramatic action, were somewhat appalled and horrified with same. Pat expressed this mutual sentiment saying, "The lions, leopards and cheetahs are so beautiful when they are calm and just enjoying the day, but agh! they appall me when they go into killing mode."

The last camping stop of the ten day tour was back at the southern Resort, where there were covered sleeping areas and showers. It was relief to the whole tour party to be able to have a major clean-up, and to go out for an evening meal and drinks. It was the last opportunity for all of them to have a fairly wild party together. Pat and Lynn were standouts in the crowd; certainly for Mukwe and Anton. They each had on beautiful 'just below the knee' dresses and had used make-up tellingly, for the first time. As both had achieved lovely tans during the tour their lipstick was almost illuminating. Pat had let down and brushed her dark hair, to the point where it beautifully outlined her face. Lynn on the other hand had curled and brushed her gorgeous lighter coloured hair, to compliment her make-up, and to Anton it worked appealingly. Both the guys had dressed well, and immediately moved in to be close to the girls.

There was naturally a great deal of chatter, comparison of experiences etcetera, but everyone found the crocodiles repugnant. This brought back memories to Anton and Mukwe of their canoe trip, which they casually recounted — adding that two members were missing! Predictably, one of the girls asked "Oh! Who were they?"

Mukwe replied saying "Our other mate Peter, who is a High School Teacher, and- looking at his watch — will just be finishing school, about now". They all had a good laugh at that.

Lynn then interrupted asking, "And the fourth?" Anton then relayed the story of Monty, and of his being fatally wounded in an insurgent attack. Clearly everyone was saddened by that account.

The party continued apace, with members gradually heading for bed, until Anton, Mukwe and Lynn and Pat were the only four left. The wild and intimate party continued for them, long into the night, with them all retiring to Pat and Lynn's sleeping area. In the early hours of the morning when they left to return to their own, the girls gave them their addresses and telephone numbers in Australia.

Later in the morning, hugs and kisses with the two girls and 'cheerios' were exchanged all round, with the international guests heading back to Francistown Airport, and the Twosome catching the bus back to the Diamond Mines. On the trip back, Anton remarked that the tour that they had just completed was the start to his 'travel' aspirations, and enquired of Mukwe, "What say we chat-up Mr. Sansom about giving us jobs, back at the Mine? It's geographically pretty central within Southern Africa, and we could either travel North to our Country; East to the Transvaal and Natal; South to the Cape, or West to Namibia."

Mukwe's eyes lit up and he said "Very interesting! I'm getting used to being a free agent again."

After further discussion, each of them felt that their Employer's would grant them extended leave, and anyway, If Not — So What! Both felt confident of finding the job of their dreams and the girls of their dreams! They also agreed that they would keep in touch with Peter, and not go anywhere overseas, without giving him the opportunity of joining them.

# CHAPTER 19

On arrival back in the Mining town, they booked into the same Hotel and had a good night's rest. Next day they booked for the Diamond Mine tour, which was scheduled for a couple of days later. This gave them time to go on an exploratory walk around the town, and to locate the various Service Shops that they might use in the future. Included in their discussions, they agreed to invite Mr. Samson to join them for lunch at their hotel.

They managed to get in touch with him and he was surprised at their invitation, saying that he would speak to his wife, and get back to them. The CEO and his wife did accept the invitation, and arrived at the hotel for the 'specially prepared' lunch. Mrs. Sansom mirrored the high respect that they had for her husband. She was dressed beautifully; was equally charming and became absorbed into the conversations. "We are so pleased that you have booked for the Mine Tour tomorrow, and feel sure that that you will be impressed." Said Mr. Sansom .

Anton added, smilingly, "I'll be interested to see how it compares with the Kimberley Mine, in Northern Cape Province."

Mr. Sansom's amused reply was, "We don't have as vast an Open-Cut yet, and ours isn't as old!. Mind-you what will happen in the distant future, is anyone's guess." They also covered Anton and Mukwe's stay on the Kent ranch, and what fine people the Father and his two sons were. The conversation progressed to the fact that the Kent's were catching and exporting rare antelope, as well as running pedigree cattle.

Mrs. Sansom then asked, "What type of antelope are these?" Anton replied that they were Bontebok. Late in the course of the lunch, they talked about the careers of these two wily travelers, tackling the desert areas of Africa! At the end of which, Mukwe casually enquired "If you have similar openings here at the Mine, we would love to be considered for them." That was a big surprise to Mr. Sansom, and they could see that he tucked the 'gem' away. The lunch finally concluded and they parted on a very happy note.

Mine tours can be a bit boringly routine, but not this one: efficiency of all processes, and broad engineering support were paramount. A few of the tourists were prepared to go down the shaft in the lift, to level one (1), where the guide indicated the comprehensive Explanatory Board and went through all aspects of the mining processes. Some questions were asked, and answered, and it was interesting to hear that the mine was confidently aiming to be one of the richest in the world. Back to the ground level and they were directed to the Jewellery display shop. It was a fairly modest building from outside, and Mukwe even remarked, "I didn't expect to see an armed guard out here." Once inside it was decidedly different, with all timber polished to perfection and such an incredible array of diamond jewellery that the whole place seemed to glow.

Whilst making their way between the counters Anton noticed Mr. Sansom, signalling for them to come across to him. They did so, and he said, "You both indicated yesterday that you would be interested in taking up jobs here?" Both Anton and Mukwe replied that they were. The GM accepted their willingness, and said "We have an opening in the Finance Section, to be part of the team researching improved Computerised Accounting, and a similar one in IT, down at the Mine-Head Office." Both of them accepted, and were prepared to start the next day. The GM said that he would organize the persons that they should report to, in order to complete the employment paperwork, salaries, etcetera.

That afternoon they phoned their employers back in their Capital, to advise that they were overseas and were seeking extended leave for an extra six months. Although the news was not happily received, each of them got the feeling that they would be re-employed, on return. Later in the evening they contacted Peter, to advise that they would keep in constant touch with him. Carry was pleased for them, and agreed to pack extra work clothing for them, with Peter's assistance, and to send same down to them. She also added on behalf of Colin, that she would send down a photograph of the plaque that Colin had made, for Monty's grave. Anton promised to get back and thank Colin, after they had seen the photo

Some weeks later the cardboard box did arrive with work clothes, letters from family and some home baked biscuits! Above all, was the picture of Monty's grave and the shield shaped plaque, on which Colin had carved "We applaud you as a champion!. From, all your loving friends — both human and canine." Both Anton and Mukwe wrote back to Colin and Carry, expressing their total admiration and love.

Over a period of about eight months both Anton and Mukwe enjoyed the work, as they each felt that their individual contribution to their team's efforts, were very worthwhile. They bought a good used-pickup vehicle between them, and on long weekends took the opportunity to travel into the Western Transvaal; the Northern Cape province and they also took a one-week holiday down to Durban and the Natal coast, to catch-up on swimming and surfing. One thing that struck them during this travel was that Agriculture, in one form or another predominated, as it did in their home country.

Actually, they made a second trip into the Northern

Cape (just over the border), because Anton was able to convincingly persuade Mukwe of his reasons for wanting to visit Mafeking.

"We must visit Mafeking Muk, for two important reasons:- One! that the head of Scouting in the world, Lord Baden-Powell, was the General in charge of British forces in the town in the late 1890's when it was besieged by the Boers, during the Boer War. And — Two! that Kathy's and Ed's paternal family, have always lived in the town. So, you can see it is vital that we visit there!! Actually we could drive across to a rail station and climb aboard a train heading South, which would get us there in a few hours."

"'Come off it' Anton! was Mukwe's rebuke, you've just got itchy feet! Still, I'm with you because it certainly sounds an interesting little dorp."

At the end of their first year of work at the Jwangeng Mine they decided that they would visit home, and travelled into the country on an extreme Eastern route, Making for the Dunnfold Mining Town. On the way in they noticed a very attractive Caravan/Camping area surrounded by, and designed with, tall Acacia trees. Left turn! And straight-in, where they booked three side-by-side sites.

Each of them phoned their respective parents and persuaded them to come out to the mining town; reminding them that it was the same town at which Anton had had his wound repaired and requesting that they each bring out the large tents that Anton and Mukwe always used.

Their folk did this, and a few wonderful days were spent together, from which location all of the other members of family and friends were contacted by phone. Peter however, took the opportunity to come down and join them, with his new girl-friend Elle. Wide ranging introductions all round and a lot of catching-up was done, and a great deal of interest in their current venture. Anton and Mukwe also took immeasurable delight in all that was happening back home — particularly the fact that Peter had achieved well, and was a highly respected Teacher at his School.

After taking leave from their parents, family and friends, they drove away from Dunnfold during the night and took a dangerous route (for them), out of the country down towards Botswana. On reaching Francistown they bore West, embarking on a very long and lonely trip of about one thousand kilometres across to South West Africa.

Initially, with Mukwe driving, their chosen route took them through familiar country as their respective High Schools — of years before — were only about a hundred kilometres away. The terrain was flat but heavily timbered with medium sized rounded-Mopani and towering Teak trees predominating, as well as savannah scrub. They also recognized Marula and other wild fruit trees. Suddenly realising that he was hungry at the time, Anton said, "Let's stop and go pick some fruit, Muk. I could die for some marulas and their medium 'plum' size; but 'greeny-brown' colour and gorgeous juicy green flesh."

They made their way into this bush and identified really ripe fruit: "Look at that tree, said Mukwe pointing, those ones are absolutely ripe." "You're dead right." replied Anton. Both immediately indulged themselves with exclamations of scrumptiousness! They had a hessian bag with them and filled it with the marulas and crab-apples but could not get enough in, so Anton whipped off his boots saying, "It's only desert sand back to the car — so we can fill my boots as well!". On the way back to the car they also saw the well-known wild spinach, and picked some of that as well.

Progressing westwards via Maitengwe the dusty road again took them to Maun, where they located a pleasant Camping/Van area and stayed for the night. After a well-earned breakfast they turned South West to virtually cross the Kalahari Desert.

Initially there was some scrubby bush which gradually faded away. As the day heated-up they had to accept what their choice now provided: thousands of square miles of flat, cream-coloured sand, and gentle dunes rolling away — one after the other in every direction. The intense heat hammered down and they experienced the strong scent and sensation of this dry desolate sanctuary, belonging to the Meer Kats and African Bushmen.

At a petrol stop they were informed that there was an area — some hundred kilometres ahead — where they might see game digging for water. This reminded them to check on their water storage — especially the radiator of the pickup!

The desert dunes became more intense, and as the sun dipped over towards the west they provided fascinating black triangular shadows. The few water courses they crossed were dry as bones. Some game were sighted but nothing to get excited about.

Eventually they came across the viewing-point described, and were fascinated to witness a medium sized Elephant digging down to the moisture with it's feet and trunk. The reminder of the herd was leaving and heading up the 'hollow' back into the desert. The amazing thing about the elephant 'drinking' scene was that they could not even see the water at the bottom of the sandy cone.

During the second days travel with Anton driving, Mukwe suddenly and excitedly exclaimed, "Slow right-down Ant, there is something up ahead, in the bush on your side: It's pretty thick down there and I can't make-out what it is. Pointing forward he exclaimed, there! That movement down there".

Anton replied, "Yes I noticed a movement down there: hang-on I'll ease forward to get a better view."

"Got it! said Mukwe, It is very small, but I think it is a human and there seem to be more than one. The first one is coming up to the road now. Boy! That is courageous — especially as we are in a Pickup."

Anton stopped the vehicle and they both got out and stood at the front, and watched the very small Bushman carefully approach them until he got to within speaking distance.

Mukwe put his right hand straight upwards and greeted him in 'his' African language, "Hello! We are Mukwe and Anton; pleased to see you." He had very little hope that this black, little four-and-a half 'footer, had understood him.

However, there was a reply in a language that neither of them understood, followed by a big smile on the little guy's face. Mukwe put his arm forward with hand extended and the Busman did the same to connect with Mukwe's hand. Smiles from both and Anton did the same. The Head of the group then called down to the point that he had entered the road' and within moments five more little 'hunters' came up and joined them. They could be classified as that, because they were carrying carcasses of small animals.

There was much two-way talk and laughing but with little understanding other than the pleasant environment that they were all experiencing. Mukwe pointed to the carcass of a hare and asked a question about it. In reply to his enquiry the hunter approached him and passed the dead hare to him. Much head and hand movement expressing grateful thanks, as well as many laughs. Anton then opened the back door of the pickup and pulled out two large bunches of spinach and handed them over to the Senior guy. Again, very happy acknowledgement of the food swap by way of talk and laughing.

Parting was harmonious with many strange hand-shakes and incredulous looks on the faces of Hunting Party' as the Pickup started and moved away. Whilst covering the last one hundred kilometres towards the South West African border Anton said, in a state of sadness, "Gee it's a pity that we didn't catch sight of any Meer Kats." Mukwe nodded in full agreement.

The food issue became very alive when buying in the towns of Ghanzi and Butapos, in Botswana, and later when they crossed into South West Africa and were able to supplement with Pumpkin, Corn and Oranges, from Gobabis and finally Windhoek.

Anton's Uncle had been able to tell him something about this small City, but Mukwe was just astounded. For a start most of the buildings in the main street were double-story or more, and the Germanic architectural features came across strongly. This city left its mark on the two, because even the city squares and parklands were so different from any other centre that they had previously visited. The people that they met and talked with were also decidedly Germanic, but very kind and interested.

At a German restaurant that night, they got talking to a local group at the next table: with introductions all round, they were asked to join the group. During the course of the wide-ranging conversation a particularly interesting fact came-up, when one of them enlarged on a subject, saying "The Benguela Ocean Current runs northwards all the way along our coastline, and it is a very rich as a fishing resource."

Mukwe was quick to add, "Yes I had heard of that, and the fact that your Province are massive exporters of edible fish as well as fish-oil for agriculture."

"Yes we are! But that was totally exploited, and we are proud of the fact that Namibia has been one of the first countries of the world to impose a strict International Embargo on fishing: South Africa followed suit, and the embargo on the Benguela Current is vigorously enforced."

"How is this done?" asked Anton.

"It is done from the port of Swakopmund where there are Customs buildings and enforcing staff, as well as regulatory Navy staff and many sea-going craft."

Eventually after a wonderful night of good food and company and the ending of their 'meeting', Anton and Mukwe left with the strong impression of what they had heard, and made the decision to head down to the Port, the next day.

Notwithstanding the full conversation of the previous night, they didn't realise that the final part of the journey down to Swakopmund was again through genuine desert. Mountainous dunes and not a tree in sight and this continued for some fifty kilometres! On arrival they not only booked accommodation, but also a Tour of the full facility for the next day. Before cleaning-up and dining, they plunged at the opportunity of a dip in the Atlantic Ocean!.

The arranged tour the next day did not disappoint in any way. It covered the Official Buildings, with details of what processes occurred in each and a land tour of the Docks which impressed as being substantial, and very military. All of this was brought into real and propelling discovery as they journeyed out through the heads in a thousand tonne Customs Enforcing ship. On the way out into the Atlantic the tour guide also spoke strongly about the International Fishing Embargo imposed on the Benguela Current, and the very strict enforcement thereof. It was an unforgettable experience, as they had never been out to sea or to a dominant current before. At the conclusion of the tour and whilst driving around Swakopmund our guys also noticed that there were many official signs that clearly signalled the penalties for transgressing.

A 'Couple' who were also on the tour, joined them afterwards for 'coffee' in the lounge of the Hotel, and they were all high in praise for the event. During later conversation it transpired that he worked for one of the South African Diamond Mines, and that she was in the Medical profession.

Anton very quickly followed by saying, "We both work in Information Technology, over the border!"

Later in the evening after a bit of a wander around the town, they met up again in the bar and over dinner. Everyone was introduced, and shook hands — giving their first names. His name was Johaan and it was clear that he was from Farming stock'. Her name was Liz and it transpired that she was a Doctor. The conversation covered many subjects and occurrences, one of which was a short account of Anton and Mukwe's canoe adventure with Eden and Monty, given by the latter. Johaan spoke further on the coastal roads going down towards the Cape Province border, "There is the main Highway, and then a parallel road right on the coast. Surprisingly this one is closed to general travellers, and referred to as a Restricted Diamond zone."

He enlarged on this by saying, "Much earlier in diamond mining history in South Africa, official prospectors had discovered that alluvial diamonds were washed down the Orange river and out to sea. Then they discovered that the sea washed them back onto the beaches. This information leaked into the general public and before long many an adventurous character — or two, or three — attempted to make the dangerous journey across the Namib Desert to the beaches. Some succeeded and probably got away with what they had done, but many died in the process. Which ever!, the Diamond Mines quickly got onto it and had the whole coast line from the border to Swakopmund, declared as a prohibited zone, as I mentioned. Initially this still didn't stop the 'smuggling', and the Miners had to erect the many policing posts, and install the Xray equipment capable of exposing 'swallowed' or 'inserted stones."

Soon after this, they all said goodnight and headed for their respective night accommodation.

After this revelation Anton and Mukwe decided not to attempt to travel down the coast road, but went back up to Windhoek, and took a more southerly and parallel route back to the Botswana mine. They found it extremely interesting but very remote country, and were surprised to see a sign pointing to Augrabies Falls (on the Orange River).

Anton who was guiding Mukwe (who was driving) suddenly 'blew it out', "What a bloody awful road this is! How can the South African Government expect tourists to try and get in here. They need to up-grade this track and possibly build a landing strip." Continuing their travel through semi-desert and sparsely treed plains they eventually reached the Falls.

Wow! Nothing they expected could be more different; they were viewing a kilometre long and powerful waterfall. The extent of granite boulders of every shape and size from high-up and way to the East, all the way down to a straight, deep granite ravine to the West. The Orange River was flowing strongly with decidedly sandy coloured water, and they praised their endurance for sticking to their plan.

Months of dedicated and hard work followed their return and they felt that their joint decision to give 'Diamond Mines' a go, was like giving an expensive bell, a gentle tingle. But suddenly that Bell resounded to a loud toll! Anton was tapping away on his computer in the office, when the chip in his arm vibrated. He lifted the flap, and the skin was pulsing Red. He acknowledged by pulsing back in red, then quickly saved his work.

He ran across to his Team Leader and said "Something is wrong down at the Mine Head." That worthy acknowledged, saying, "How do you know?"

"Never mind said Anton, just let GM know." With that, he departed in a rush.

As he approached the mine head Mukwe was waiting

for him outside the buildings, but he drove around behind an opposite building, not wanting the two of them to be seen together in that precinct. Mukwe hurried after him and jumped into the car with him. They had barely started to talk, when Mukwe noticed Mr. Sansom approaching — slightly faster than normal. He interjected, and said "What is the GM coming down for?" Anton explained that he had called him, to follow. On his arrival, they both climbed into his car and he went further, and out of sight of any workers.

He immediately demanded what this was all about, and Mukwe explained what had happened. "I was coming back from the actual mine area, and needed to go to the toilet — to sit down — so used the workers toilet down there, locking the door behind me. I heard two men come in and go to the urinal: they were totally unaware that I was there, and were talking fairly loudly. It seemed that they knew that a guy by the name of Kronk, had stolen diamonds over a period — before the stones had gone to the Selection Process — and that he was leaving at the end of the week. They were discussing how they could get the diamonds off him, before he left — even to the point of killing him, if he resisted. I was pretty bloody scared, so didn't come out until well after they had left."

"Then I contacted Anton privately."

The GM immediately asked "How long ago was this?"

Mukwe looked at his watch and said "Twenty minutes ago." The GM then asked whether the men referred to, were Africans or Europeans. Mukwe replied, "Difficult to tell exactly — the man doing the talking was speaking in Afrikaans, and the other could be either African or Coloured."

'Would you recognize the voice, if the police put you in a position to do so?" Mukwe said that he thought that he would be able to.

"Okay! Said Mr. Sansom, I don't think that anyone has witnessed us here. I'm going to call the Police right away, so you guys go back to the Main Office, and I'll see you there." They returned to the office that Anton used, and not long after Mr. Sansom arrived and they went out into the main office area. He reported that the Police were on their way.

He then asked," how the hell Anton, did you get that message from Mukwe?"

"He beeped me". Replied Anton, while looking across to Mukwe, and giving a slight nod.

Mukwe continued, "For my Bachelor Degree in IT, a group in our year — including myself, designed and developed a communication chip, for use between friends. Initially, and purely for fun it only worked on a green glow for 'Go' and a red glow for 'Stop'. In our final year, we got it to pulse, as well, and eventually I'm hoping that we will be able use Morse-code."

The CEO asked in a disbelieving tone, "What's this thing that glows or pulses?" So they showed him where the chips were inserted below the skin, and told him that they would give him a demonstration, at the appropriate time.

When the police arrived, the CEO went out to have an initial meeting with them, and to advise them that he had also contacted the Johannesburg Office, to send two 'Diamond Detectives' out to the mine. Anton and Mukwe were then asked to attend, and a preliminary session was held with the local police, in which Mukwe again recounted what he had heard. The Police informed the meeting that they were taking it very seriously, and would be working closely with the Detectives arriving the following day. They had two and a half to three days to recover the diamonds, and apprehend those responsible. With that, the CEO and the Police withdrew to continue planning for the following day. He came back soon afterwards, to advise that the local police would start on some unobtrusive, preliminary investigations, right away.

Soon after the Detectives arrived by helicopter, Anton and Mukwe were called into the meeting with them, the CEO, the Mine Manager and the local Police. The police were able to confirm that a person of interest had been identified. The Mine Manager endorsed this, saying that they knew who was receiving final pay and was leaving the Company and the town on the Friday. The police and the detectives would also be seeking out the other two men, and might require Mukwe to try and identify their voices.

The CEO followed on by saying, "The Company have long been suspicious of diamond heists from our mines, and we know that other Diamond Miners are experiencing the same problem." The meeting adjourned, and Anton and Mukwe went back to their usual jobs. Two days later, Mukwe was interviewed by the investigating officers, who had brought with them a recording of mine workers whom they had 'taped' whilst they were working. They had particularly aimed at dual friends working together, or supporting one-another. Over the course of the two days, they believed that they had had some success.

Mukwe listened to the recording, and suddenly recognised the two voices that he had heard in the toilets: he immediately put up his finger at that point and said, "I think that's them." They continued playing through to the end, but Mukwe asked them to replay, and stopped them at the point where he had previously put up his finger — "Yep! I reckon those voices are recognizable." The detectives thanked him, and asserted that his identification supported theirs, and that the two suspects would be arrested. They also mentioned that Kronj had been arrested, and that he had handed over the diamonds.

Deep investigations continued for a further two days, at which time the Officers left with their charges — securely hand-cuffed. Mr. Sansom called in both Mukwe and Anton, and thanked them for their participation in securing the arrests, as well as their respective alertness. He also asked them to be on standby, in case of further developments.

Work and leisure continued; they both got satisfaction

from the jobs they were doing because their knowledge of the up-to-date digital technology was being extended, in no uncertain terms. However, they still got a 'kick' out of their usual exploration thing.

Anton noticed that the CEO was away for quite considerable periods, but didn't really attempt to fathom it. Some three weeks to a month after the attempted diamond heist, he was back at the Mine Offices. A couple of days after his return he called Anton into his office, closed the door and said, "You've probably noticed my absence, and I might add that it is unusual."

Anton answered 'Yes I had, but obviously I didn't attempt to find out why."

"Well to put it in a nutshell, most of the Diamond Mining companies have been meeting in an attempt to get to the bottom of this missing diamonds dilemma. We have had Interpol, our own Specialist Detectives and executives from the International Diamond Bourse, attending the meetings to try and strategize a solution."

"However, there is one thing that the Companies from Southern Africa — whom I might disclose supply over sixty percent of the world market — would like to do, and that is to set an International Trap. We have got Interpol pretty interested, and only have to complete the exact details of how to achieve it. Not only will they assist, but will police and monitor the plan which we jointly come up with. Knowing you and Mukwe reasonably well now, I must add that execution of the ultimate strategy, will be extremely dangerous. All the parties that I have mentioned though, will provide enough plain-clothed support officers."

Anton, who had been listening with avid interest, interjected at this point, and said "Am I right in saying that you — 'The Good Guys', would like me and Mukwe to be involved in this strategic planning?"

Mr Sansom replied, "I'm glad you asked, because it makes my undertaking to the Group easier. Would you and Mukwe consider it? If you are prepared to, you would both be working with the Detectives in the Mining Investigation Unit, based in Johannesburg: but you would still be members of my staff and paid by us. Don't worry your salaries will be reset, and all airfares and other travel expenses will be refunded."

"I'll certainly talk with Mukwe in absolute privacy, Anton replied, but it does give us the opportunity to extend our travels, which is our aim for the next couple of years. For security reasons, we had better let you have our answer by tomorrow, shouldn't we?"

"Call him to come-up here now, Mr Sansom added, and then make an appointment with my Secretary, to see me as soon as I'm available: that'll provide that 'appropriate opportunity' for me to see how your 'chip' works!!"

"Okay, responded Anton, but can we go just outside the front door now, and I'll give that Morse-code, a go." With that they proceeded outside and with the Boss watching,

Anton applied pressure to the cover over the chip; lifted it to check that it was pulsing green, and then "Yes?" — in green Morse, from Mukwe. Anton then followed that with intermittent Morse-code for "Come up now for CEO." Answer — "OK!" — in green!

"He should be here within five minutes", Anton said

"If that's genuine, and he does pitch-up, it's absolutely bl...y brilliant. We'll have to build those-sort-of-things into your 'operational' pay. Within about six minutes Mukwe arrived — in a Mine vehicle — which Anton thought was priceless ... Okay, said the CEO, shaking his head, let's go through to my office." When they were seated, he again went through the reasons for his 'times away' from the Mine, and then looked across to Anton to continue.

Anton did so, looking at Mukwe and saying, "The Joint Diamond Mining Group in Johannesburg, want to know whether you, and I, will consider being involved in formulating this strategy, by working with the Mine Detectives. I personally, am interested. What are your thoughts Muk?"

"I would like to hear much more detail, but Yes, I'm interested", Mukwe replied.

Mr. Sansom then took over, and reiterated that they had arrested the three workers connected with the intended heist. "We have the full interrogation results from them, and those form a very modest base from which to build the plan." Some of the other Miners have lesser bits of info, as well. Clearly the Detectives and Interpol, have commenced investigations, both here in Southern Africa and Overseas. These will be continued, and fed into an overall strategy to be formulated in Johannesburg. As their work develops, they have indicated that they will need the likes of you two men, to assist them."

Anton added "I omitted to mention Mukwe, that we will be re-employed by this Mining Investigation Unit, and will therefore have the full protection of this policing force."

"Now I'm becoming more excited, than interested, said Mukwe, and provided that I know that my back is being covered at all times, I'm all for it. When do we commence this work?"

"Pretty well right away, said Mr. Sansom, in fact I would like to fly you blokes out a s a p, because in my opinion you face danger by staying. How soon can you wrap-up your belongings, to be ready for an exit by helicopter? The Company will settle outstanding rentals etcetera." The reply was that they only had suitcases to pack, and would be ready by the following morning.

Anton got a quick word in at this point. "Two things — One (1) presumably the interrogation outlined, considers that there could be a dangerous element here, in this mining town; and Two (2) The Detectives should have a very private, but deep, questioning session with one of the most prominent Jewish Jewellers, in Johannesburg. They are renowned for being among the largest sellers to the

International Diamond Bourse, and in my opinion they would have a wealth of knowledge, of both the local scene, and of the European one."

The GM made a note of this observation, and said "Good! Now get back to the hotel and start packing up: I'll assign a local policeman to be present with you. I'll also book the helicopter now, for an early departure for tomorrow morning. Be seeing you both, then."

# CHAPTER 20

The helicopter arrived early the following morning, and the' twosome' were seen off by the CEO. His final words were, "Thanks for joining with us; keep safe and I'll see you in Johannesburg fairly soon."

It was a fairly long flight, but over country that they now recognized. Initially the land in both Botswana and Western Transvaal was ranchland — lightly forested and with wide stretches of savannah which were ideal for grazing. That suddenly ran-out as they passed into large areas of agricultural cropping land. Gradually that merged into a North-South ridge of high-rugged hills with dense pine/cedar type forest below the peaks. As they flew over these Anton pointed forward and exclaimed, "Geeez! Mukwe those farmlands below seem to go on forever; well at least to where the sun rises!"

The retort from Mukwe was, "Yea! And I can see that the

growers really know what they are doing."

In Johannesburg they were met at the landing point on top of an high-rise building, by Dennis, the detective who had been out to the mine. He welcomed each of them with a firm handshake, "Hope you had a good flight and don't mind this small landing strip?" He also thanked them for becoming involved in the groundwork of the plan.

Mukwe accepting the handshake excitedly said, "Yes, it was good for both of us but t's the first time we've dropped out of the sky onto a vertical landing, half-way-to-heaven!!"

They were then taken inside to the Investigation Unit offices, and introduced to the other detectives, including the 'Boss' William, and the two Interpol staff. Coffee was ordered and brought through, but William had already started quizzing Anton and Mukwe, about their discussion with Mr. Sansom, "What has been arranged, and to what extent are you prepared to participate?" He, and all of the others were very pleased when the two stated that they were prepared to go all the way, provided their backs were covered at all times.

Detective Dennis then took them through to the Employment Office, where they went through the usual 'signing-on' procedures, plus sleeping accommodation; insurance et al. When they returned to the Investigation Office, they were asked whether they were ready to go over the strategy, so far. Anton agreed that they were, saying, "Mr Sansom has so far advised us that you have interrogated the three guys that were brought back from the mine. But we are not aware of how much more you have done."

William expressed satisfaction, and said "That's good, and we can tell you that we have started the much wider investigation, both here and overseas. The big mines in the Cape Province, Transvaal and South West Africa, have also recorded cases of attempted smuggling: some bigger and some smaller than this one in Botswana, that you guys blew-open. The extent of these and whispers that we hear around the trade — both here and in Europe, would indicate that the problem is a serious one. Now you Anton suggested to Mr. Sansom that an approach should be made to a reputable Jewish jeweller, in Johannesburg?"

"That's correct." said Anton

"We <u>would</u> have got to that point with our investigation, but havn't yet, so why don't you and Mukwe start with that? We can go through each of their advertising pages with you, and select the one that you, and our team think would have the most explicit knowledge of diamond trading, both here and overseas."

Both Anton and Mukwe agreed, but Anton added, "We will be received with higher respect, if we are accompanied by an Interpol Officer." There was general consensus with that, and the team set about getting all the paper work that would need to be studied. This progressed throughout the afternoon, and had to be continued the next day. A second group was studying other Jewellers. Finally a best prospect was selected, and there was detailed discussion on the date; the time and the method of approach. At this stage the Belgian Interpol Agent who would be interviewing the Jeweller, joined the group.

While this part of the plan was being developed, another group within the Unit was attempting to find local and international illegitimate diamond buyers, and associated gang-type enforcers. Understandably, they were only having moderate success with this more difficult category, but warned that the team going-in would need to be covered.

Early in the working day of the intended visit, Anton phoned the Jewish Jeweller and made an appointment for he and Mukwe to come in about selling legitimate diamonds.

Actually, the three of them went down to the address — with their journey being closely monitored by the 'armed' Second Group — and arrived without incident. On entry and introductions Rod opened with, "My name is Anton; and this is my mate Mukwe. We are representing the Joint Diamond Mining Group, and working with the Detection Unit. Right at the outset we would like you to know that you, 'the Jeweller', are in no way suspected of anything. You have been identified as being the most knowledgeable person on the local and International (Belgium) scene, as well as being one of the largest sellers to the International Diamond Bourse." Anton then introduced the Belgium Interpol Agent, who verified what Anton had just laid out.

The Jeweller acknowledged their introductions, and said,

"My name is Ellis and thanks very much for coming in, for like yourselves, I am aware that the international scene is not what it should be. Both on the home scene here — where I get a surprising number of individuals (and traders) offering beautiful uncut-diamonds to me, for very reasonable prices; as well as the unmistakable 'Gray' pageant that oozes into one when visiting the diamond scenes overseas. For me, I get the same feeling whether it be in Europe, England or America."

The 'questioning' then began, and copious notes were taken of the answers, and all other information that Ellis was able to convey. They also passed on snippets to him, which would increase his world-wide knowledge. At the end of the session and demonstrating the utmost respect, they all shook hands and thanked him for the breadth of his information, and that they would get back to him with their eventual final report.

A busy time followed, with the sub-committee of the Miners (including Mr Sansom), the Interpol Agents, and the appointed group within the Detectives Unit, fully analyzing all information that had been gathered, within Southern Africa and Internationally — particularly, Antwerp. They finalized the Ten Million Pound Sterling (value) rough uncut diamonds strategy, to uncover those criminals whom the research had identified, and set the details of their 'trap'. The diamonds would be deposited in a Bank vault in Antwerp. This whole plan was double-checked, and improved to the point where they would be able to present it to Interpol in Paris.

A final undertaking of the Miners Sub-Committee through their Payroll appointee, was to award each member of the penetrating team Ten Thousand U.S. Dollars, with reduced awards to the Helpers.

Travel to Europe, was to more-or-less coincide with a Meeting of International Diamond Miners, in Antwerp. As would be expected, Mr. Sansom and more Senior members of his Company's Board of Directors, would be attending that Meeting. About a week before that, Anton, Mukwe, William the Senior Detective of the Diamond Miner's Unit, and the Interpol Agent who had worked with them, flew out of Johannesburg bound for Paris. It was an uneventful trip; covered principally overnight. On arrival they were driven to the impressive renaissance-type Interpol Head Office.

In the days immediately thereafter, the plan was presented to a full Committee of Interpol, for 'digestion' and final verification. It was accepted, but with far more detail on the exact policing and protection of members of the penetrating team. They needed to be aware that there was the potential for close monitoring, from the moment they arrived in Antwerp and booked into their hotel.

At each stage, double rooms with adjoining doors would be booked — as one room only, and the detectives and agents would be in the adjoining room, heavily armed. On travelling from the hotel to the suspected Diamond Buying warehouse, and return, they would be afforded helicopter surveillance, as well as a following Detective/Interpol team.

The drive to Antwerp was remarkably short, passing through much of the country besieged during the First World War. The team booked into an hotel, securing a second floor double-room, with the planned inter-joining door. Anton and Mukwe moved into the prime room, with the Detective Unit, secretly, through the door.

Next morning Anton phoned the Diamond Buying Agent company, and made an initial appointment for he and Mukwe, to discuss selling the uncut diamonds. 2.00pm the following day, was the time scheduled for the appointment. They primed the detectives with this information, and that they would leave, without the diamonds, about half an hour before the time set.

At 1.30pm the next day, Anton and Mukwe set out on foot for the well-known Buying Agent Company, and arrived there pretty well on time. They were aware that their surveillance team was following — from behind the hotel — and in broken formation. On arrival and looking from side-to-side and upwards Mukwe made the observation, "Not quite the citadel I expected; only two stories high."

They made their way inside through a broad well-lit hallway, and from there into a very smart Reception Area, where Anton approached the desk and stated, "We are here to sell diamonds and would like to be put on-to the correct person."

The Lady phoned internally and asked them to wait for one of the buyers: who, when he came in, took them into an adjoining office. Initially there was some very general conversation, then he asked, "Where do the diamonds come from, and what is their estimated value?"

Mukwe advised, "They are from South Africa, and possibly worth ten million Dollars." That detail seemed to please him and the deal went into its early stages. The next thing he asked was to be able to see the diamonds. To both of them, this seemed too rapid and pretentious, and Mukwe spoke-up, "They are still in a Bank vault, and we have come on this first visit to find out the process for selling them." In reply to this the Buyer explained that the Expert Assessors inside, would view them first and value them.

Anton quickly interjected, "We will only permit that, provided that we accompany them!" The Buyer then phoned through — speaking 'Belgian', ostensibly to get permission for this; listened for a short duration, then agreed that it would be okay. Anton then put the proposition to the Buyer, "We would like the payment to go straight to the Bank, and to receive proof of the transaction, in our hands."

The Buyer agreed and said, "That is our Company's method of payment." Anton and Mukwe thanked him very much, and made an appointment for 9.00am the following morning, to proceed with the transaction. They then left, and headed for the Bank.

The trip to the bank was a ruse, because they had no

intention yet, of withdrawing the diamonds. One of their team — in a very plain suit — had been stationed behind the counter in the Bank, and already had an appropriately sized Bank Box, for them to take out when they left for their hotel. They chatted with him for about fifteen minutes, then phoned for a taxi. Their trip was closely monitored, at road level, and from the air, and they were advised later in the afternoon, that there was a strong chance that they had been followed.

This prompted a meeting of all members of the investigative team, in Anton and Mukwe's room. William and one of the French Interpol Agents controlled the discussion and decided that two plain clothed members — one in a suit — would be stationed in the foyer, immediately the meeting was concluded. The remainder of the team would be through 'the door', and ready to barge in the moment they heard the code words. The fourth member of that group, would then immediately exit into the corridor outside, in case one intruder was left outside to guard the scene. Anton and Mukwe were instructed to dive over the back of the settees with the diamonds, as soon as the armed intruders appeared. In that event Plan two, would have to be implemented.

Nothing occurred before dinner, with the two Interpol Detectives remaining in the rooms. After post dinner coffee and a small liquor each, which was the signal to the team to station themselves, Anton and Mukwe returned to their room — with their hearts in their mouths, and were making desultory conversation, when there was a sharp wrap at the door. Mukwe got up to look through the reverse peephole, and unsurprisingly saw a figure in Hotel attire. He signalled to Anton, and opened the door — but to three large, masked intruders. He was snatched away from the door and shoved across towards Anton, and the leading figure demanded "Where are the diamonds? We need them now."

Anton replied in a somewhat quavering, but loud voice "What diamonds?" This was 'the code', and the intervening door flew open, and the Detectives rushed in with their guns drawn, shouting "hands-up, and do not move". Anton and Mukwe took two or three steps and were diving over the backs of the settees, when there was action from the entrance door, with the intruder's No. 4 barging in, with his weapon drawn, shouting "You two smugglers, get ..." That was as far as his demand got, before he was struck on the head, from behind, by the Fourth Detective. They immediately hand-cuffed each of the intruders, and officially arrested them. The Antwerp Police were then phoned, and already had a vehicle standing by, to take them to jail.

After the Police had departed with their prisoners, and everyone was back in the room, there was a good deal of back-slapping and congratulations, followed by Mr Sansom and the Mining Team from RSA and Botswana, being advised of the success, so far. They requested permission to come over — as if they needed to? — and join in the

'Celebration' in the 'Room'. The Senior Detective agreed, and felt that it would be extremely good for them to be contributing for the final stage, next morning.

The 'stage was set' for Anton and Mukwe to front up at the Diamond Buyer's Agency, at 9.00am, with the Bank Box. The rest of the team (including the Managers, representing the various Diamond Mines) would have already, and most furtively, taken up positions, around the building. The two walked-in and without giving their names requested to see the Buyer, to whom they had spoken, the previous day. The receptionist phoned through for him, and said "He's on his way."

The moment he opened the door there was panic, and he backed out slamming it behind himself. Mukwe quickly ran to the front door and gave the signal, for this occurrence. All members of the interrogative team, stationed around the building were alerted, as were the Police. Mr Sansom and the other Mine Unit Managers, then came-in and demanded to see the General Manager/ CEO of the Company. Again the receptionist phoned, but this time was told that they had all just left their Offices. Some minutes later, they were brought through the front door, in the hands of Police. The RSA and Botswana Mine's Managers accused them of seriously promoting diamond smuggling, and that they would see them next time, in Court. A total of some twenty members of the company, were taken from the scene, as remandees.

On the final day of the prestigious International Diamond

Miners Meeting held in a large Convention Centre within the City Hall precinct, all members of the Diamond Miner's Investigative Team, including Anton and Mukwe, were asked to dress-up and make themselves available. All were brought-up to the stage and sincerely thanked: the Interpol and Mine Detectives were advised that recommendations would be made to their employers. Anton and Mukwe were each presented with an envelope, and an attractive diamond necklace, with the inference that their future partners would really be able to appreciate and value them. All were invited to join a celebratory function, about to commence.

In the experience of Anton and Mukwe, it was an incredible gathering, and they met with and were thanked by many of these Top Executives from all over the world. Apart from Mr Sansom, and a couple of the other South African Diamond Mining bosses, they were intrigued that an Australian CEO, was also prepared to spend some time with them. In general conversation Anton mentioned, "We are going on to London from here, and for a long time have been considering a working-viza trip to Australia. What do you think of our chances?"

He was amused and pleased at their enquiry, and gave them some tips about approaching the Australian Embassy in London.

In the middle of the afternoon, they sought out Mr Sansom and Anton opened the conversation saying, "We feel that it is time for us to head-off, as we need to get to the bank before they close. Thank you for your support and for this experience." Mukwe also thanked him and they both received sincere handshakes.

Before exiting the building, they checked the envelopes that each had been presented with: they did contain Bank Cheques, for the amount previously advised, plus closing salary amounts. No short-term problems with funds!!

Once they had deposited the valuables into Safe Deposit, with their reputable International Bank, they were free to head down to the station, and purchase train tickets to London for the following day.

# CHAPTER 21

A nton and Mukwe had no long-term plans for London, so headed down to the well- known area, inhabited by visiting 'Colonials", and booked a room for a week in the Hostel accommodation. Initially they just wanted to visit the historical sights; see some good shows, and probably catch-up on watching some good sport — especially soccer — given Mukwe's love for the game.

At their first meal down in this residential and restaurant precinct, many introductions were made with 'guys and girls' sitting at their table. Unsurprisingly it turned out that their aims were the same, so Anton's and Mukwe's outings were often in the company of girls. This arrangement definitely made the visits and shows more amusing, and filled with chatting. Quite often the paring also extended to an evening meal, night show or visit to one of the many cinemas. By the end of the first week, they realised that they would have to extend their accommodation booking, to fit in with this busy and enjoyable social life, and live sport watching.

After a month or so they needed a breather, and as they both wished to visit Scotland, Ireland and Wales, they hired a car and set-off for their first choice. Studying the map, they could see that careering-up the M1 and taking the shortest route, it would get them to Scotland in one day, but both believed that much would be missed.

Anton raised the fact and said, "You know we would miss so much beautiful country if we go that way: instead let's veer more to the West and travel up through those Counties." They passed through a great number of interesting towns, villages and varied beautiful countryside, chatting to one another continuously.

Eventually Mukwe exclaimed, "Yes! What a good decision! Apart from the vivid green fields and all the intersecting hedges, just take a look at these beautiful wooded hills on each side, and up ahead I can see that they are getting even higher in the sky."

Anton responded, "Agreed, and unlike Africa there just seem to be so many different flowering shrubs mixed into the forest, and an extraordinary amount of bird life. What's more, we havn't even caught sight of the first lake, yet!"

That took many hours of enjoyable travel and suddenly after rounding a spur of a hill it all opened up below them, and winding away into the hills was Lake Windermere. To them it was like a picture, with the waters in the foreground;

the Cumbrian mountains at the back. The 'whole' somehow framed by an impressive spring sky full of chasing clouds, all travelling eastwards. They drove on down into Kendall and made straight for the lake edge 'Parking'. It wasn't long before they were down on the beach and whilst absorbing the grandeur of it, they met up with a group of townsfolk. In no time at all they were chatting — questions and answers — and then introductions all round. The townsfolk were amazed and impressed that they were from Central Africa.

One of the ladies said, "We know a family in your country and communicate with them two or three times a year."

Anton was quick to add, "and we know folk here, in both Manchester and Newcastle who have returned from our Country."

The discussion continued and the inhabitants loved the fact that both Mukwe and Anton obviously found the town and countryside/lakeside so beautiful. Mukwe couldn't help but say, "It's a pity that we can't get an aerial view of this lake?"

Quick as a flash one of the men took this up, pointing to the North and saying, "You could if you climbed Scafell Pike — there. Well at least you would get a magnificent view from up high, of both Windermere and Conniston Water."

Mukwe's reply was, "That would be great and we would love to do some climbing, but is there a bus or a tour that could get us there and back?"

"Not really, said the 'gent', but there is a daily ferry

coming back here from Grasmere, under Scafell Pike. In the meantime park your car at the back of our place, and we will all drive you over there."

This the kind folk did, and the next thing that Anton and Mukwe were viewing was the very long ascent of Scafell Pike. They had good attire — plus boots — so headed up the trail in a high state of excitement. The climb proved far more difficult than they expected with the final stage being fairly sheer — from rock to rock and even up some chimney type crevasses. Eventually they made it out onto the crest and were dumbfounded at the view.

All aspects of it were put into a shadowy perspective by the receding sun, heading towards the West. There were beautiful shaded hills of all shapes and sizes for three sixty degrees, but it was the sight of the two parallel lakes winding through the valleys that thrilled them to the core. They were covered by successive dark shadows and shining bands, like the silky symmetry of a Zebras' stripes, caused by the setting sun.

Clearly the climb down to Grasmere was easier but required a high degree of care, and they made it in time to catch the last ferry heading south to Kendall, where they were re-united with the townsfolk. These kind and generous people invited them to stay over with them, for an extra day of fun and discourse.

Difficult to leave after only a few days, but they weren't yet in Scotland.

As they crossed into Scotland, they marvelled at the Roman Wall and its incredible age and were soon approaching Glasgow. Anton particularly wanted to visit the Ship Building Yards, because one of the large industries in their home town, back in Africa, was owned by a Glasgow Ship Building Company. Again, a very worthwhile visit, and they were taken on a conducted tour, which included short films on the building of the QE1.

From there they continued towards the West coast revelling in sights of the first few Islands out to sea, and of the rising Ben Nevis central mountain range. On their second evening up this route they arrived at a Pub in Oban, and decided that it looked a good prospect for their evening meal. It was too early to eat so they joined the locals in the bar where they were greeted with much enthusiasm and were soon to learn not to join locals in the ritual of 'chasers'.

Both of them had a large beer in front of them, but were each presented with a large whisky, as well. The ritual commenced, and both Anton and Mukwe, took a sip of whisky each, and then did a massive chase of beer. There was a shout of, "No no!" "In this pub, a 'chase' is a sip of Beer — followed by the whole of your glass of Whisky!" Well, by the time that sequence was complete both of them were 'out-of-their-minds' and the entire pub, were convulsed with mirth. But the residents did have the decency to escort Anton and Mukwe to their dinner table and join them, with their own meal orders.

While everyone was getting over the 'chase' sequence, the 'villains' introduced themselves. One of them by the name of Vince then asked, "Obviously you chaps are not from the British Isles — where are you from?"

Anton replied, "I'm Anton and this is Mukwe, and we are both from Central Africa, and we are on an extended overseas holiday. This is purely a round tour of Scotland to take in as many of the famous sights, as possible. So far we have seen the Roman Wall, Glasgow and its docks and ship-building, and some beautiful island views up your west coast."

Mukwe quickly added, "And believe me we won't forget this Pub in a hurry!"

That caused some mirth again, and one of Vince's friends, Kel said, "Vince and I are Oceanographic Engineers and are also on our way northwards to undertake a job for the Historic Buildings Trust people." This created much discussion within the whole group while they were eating, and it transpired that many of their assignments involved deep-sea diving.

Anton quickly intervened, "Jesus! I've often thought about being able to do that, and about the depth that one could go, and how long one could stay underwater."

"Well, we could probably organize it — if it were possible to meet you guys again while you travel round on this trip." said Vince. "Do you intend to keep going northwards? Our job is on Loch Leven Castle, not far from here — up towards

Ben Nevis. It was the place that Mary Queen of the Scots was imprisoned by the British, under Queen Elizabeth the First."

All was arranged, and that evening Anton and Mukwe travelled a short way up towards the mountains; opened a farm gate and pitched their tent just inside, closing the gate behind them. Pass-out! And they were asleep — only to be awakened, in the early hours by 'crunch', 'crunch,' all around the tent. They were somewhat alarmed at being surrounded in this 'Genteel Isle' but did venture to peep outside, to discover that they were in the middle of a large herd of Highland Cattle. Maybe the 'beasts' also wanted some of that whisky!

No damage done and they continued up the road which ran alongside Loch Linnhe to Ballachulish, where they met-up again with Vince and Kel. After a 'very much needed Coffee they were taken down to a quay on Linnhe.

Here Anton underwent in-depth instruction on deep-sea diving. Mukwe declined saying, "I'll concentrate on improving my footwork in soccer, but thanks!" Once Anton had perfected and completed his instruction on the diving — at a very basic level, he was able to go down into the lake with Vince and achieve his life-long ambition of diving in the deep.

Afterwards Mukwe and Anton stood the two Engineers to a very pleasant lunch, at which many aspects were discussed to bring Mukwe well into the whole process.

Having made their exit after much handshaking and compliments, they progressed towards the far North of Scotland on the precipitous and winding highway. The many small and larger islands impressed them — with their pounding, rough seas and rugged cliffs, and the vivid green pastures and occasional farm buildings. Mukwe couldn't help but comment, "Jeez!, what a different agricultural existence these islands have, compared to what we are used to in Southern Africa". All-in-all they loved their Scotland journey but they were disappointed not to see the Loch Ness monster!!

Edinburgh played up to its wonderful name, because they had booked to attend the Military Tattoo before they left for their trip. No one could wish for a more spectacular Show. Further exploring of the city would have to wait for another time.

On their return route, they stopped off in Newcastle to visit with the people who had lived in Aberfoyle, immediately after the war. Fortunately the folk had spare accommodation, and they spent a wonderful reminiscing dinner, and visit to a Pub with them. Next day it was back to London through the scenic and colourful — though flat — Eastern Counties. It was good to be back at their London 'digs'; the companionship of male and female company, and getting back into 'the' routine that they had left behind.

Planning the future trips was much harder, because each felt that Australia was beginning to summon. They decided to delay an intended trip to Ireland, and knew that in the future they must return, to get that properly squared away.

Soon after their return from the Scottish trip they took the opportunity to make many phone calls back to their Home Country. Each of them caught up with their Parents in Aberfoyle, and gave them 'trimmed' accounts of where they had been, and what they had been up to: likewise with Jacky and Mel. Clearly they were all very pleased to hear that they were safe and well, in England. Once they got onto the Capital, for Peter, Carry and Colin they were a bit more divulging, but could still say nothing about the dramatic events that occurred in Antwerp. They did however mention that they would be making a first approach to the Australian Embassy.

While speaking to Peter, Mukwe asked, "Would you be interested in coming out to Australia and joining us?" Although interested, he reminded them that he was now seriously involved with his girlfriend, and that he would most certainly not leave her. He did however ask them to please always keep in touch. When that phone call was finished, Anton phoned Kim and Trevor to say hi! and to ask whether they had progressed their intentions to migrate to Australia. They hadn't yet, but after a long chat, also asked him to please keep in touch.

First visits were made to the Australian Embassy to obtain all the necessary Application and other forms, but otherwise life went on normally. They had increased the number of

Soccer matches that they went to watch, accompanied on many occasions by girls, and possibly other guys. A post-match routine that became very popular for all of them, was to go into a nearby Pub for a 'toot' and dinner. Many of these visits lasted quite long into the night, with hilarious fun being enjoyed by all.

Interestingly on one such occasion, they witnessed a 'Yard-of-Ale competition between blokes at an adjoining table. Whilst watching this they heard a remark by one of their Australian companions, to the effect that he had been told that drugs were being smuggled to Australia in these flasks. Just how it was executed wasn't mentioned, but the information stuck in their minds.

Once they had completed their Visa Application and other forms, they returned to the Embassy to hand them in, and to make appointments with the relevant Officers. These were fixed for the beginning of the following week, and in the meantime they had to make sure that they had all their own documents, to bring with them. Each of their meetings went well, and they were advised that it would take about a month for them to be processed. At the end of that week however, a more senior Officer phoned them to ask if they could possibly come in that same day: and the tone of his voice indicated some urgency.

On being ushered up an extra floor he introduced himself as Dale and ushered them into his office where after they were seated, he added, "The Security Officials in the next tier, have requested this extra visit." He then phoned them and they asked that Anton and Mukwe be taken up to the next floor. Before taking them up Dale advised, "The time delay for your visas, will probably be much shorter."

One of these more senior officials received them; thanked them for making the extra visit and asked them to be seated. They appeared to be in a general meeting room and were wondering what in the hell this was all about. When he opened the meeting by asking, "Do you guys remember meeting a particular gentleman, in Antwerp, some months ago?" adding, "he is an Australian Diamond Mining CEO."

Anton replied, "Yes we do remember him, but what connection does that have with us?"

The Official added, "This particular Mining Executive visited this Embassy and gave your two names — as being potential Visa applicants. They looked at one another, and both felt the same silent response — "So What!"

The Official was somewhat amused, and stated, "There is 'some' strong interest in you two, and I would appreciate it if you would come-up with me to see one of the Consul's of the Embassy." With some concern and their minds whirring, they agreed and were escorted into the consular area which was very much more resplendent and business-like. They were again welcomed, and the Consul asked them whether they had been brought up to date on why Embassy would like to talk with them. Before they could say that they hadn't, their escorting officer informed the Consul that he had mentioned the Diamond CEO, and merely told them that they were of interest.

At this point, Anton and Mukwe realised that their part in the 'Trap' was probably going to be mentioned, and sure enough it was. The Consul said "Your part in shutting down a serious diamond smuggling operation, with Interpol and the Diamond Investigative Unit, was mentioned by Mr "X". He, as you probably know, is the CEO of one of Australia's Diamond Mines. He made it eminently clear, that each of your names should go no further than this office, and my Officer who brought you up here. We would also like to express our thanks for your efforts."

"However, without 'beating about the bush,' we wonder whether we can talk to you about something similar, where again you would be equally protected — by our Police and Interpol?" Both indicated that they were prepared to listen at this stage.

The Consul then impressed upon them, "Neither of you can mention one word of what is about to be discussed, for that will be a chargeable offence." They each gave that assurance, and he continued by saying, "Australia is experiencing serious and rampant, illicit drug importation into the country. We know that every State is affected, but the Eastern States of Queensland, New South Wales and Victoria are bearing the brunt. In the same way that you guys did, with the diamonds, we would like to set a trap, using the most sophisticated means possible. Would you two consider being an integral part of it?"

By this time both Anton and Mukwe were vitally interested, and replied in unison "Yes we are interested." They also related the instance in the pub, where they had overheard a reference to drugs being illicitly exported in Yard-o-Ale flasks. The Officers present were surprised and elated, and the Consul asked, "What pub was this?"

Mukwe replied, "The one in the Stenhouse Hotel, down in South East London — over the Tower Bridge."

"Great! That is exactly the co-operation we are hoping to secure with all involved, when we get going. Thanks for that extra bit of vital 'info'. Now, that is as far as we can proceed today: please keep this absolutely secret, and we will get back in touch with you as investigative progress is made."

The consular official who had brought them in, saw them to the door and asked, "Please phone me once a week, on a different day, and from a different phone." He gave them each a business card.

Their life and routine carried on much as before, even after the first couple of calls back to the Embassy. On the second occasion, their contact Officer was able to advise them that their Visas had been approved, and could be picked up at any time. They asked whether they could call in the following week, instead of making the arranged phone call. He agreed and this gave them the opportunity to make a quick, planned visit to the Western Counties and Wales.

The route that they had planned was out through Oxford,

which they wanted to see and to experience: mainly because of the connection that Cecil John Rhodes had with that University. Obviously, they were most impressed, and a sense of regret flashed through Anton's mind, that he hadn't made it to this famous institution. Wishful thinking!!

Continuing North West through beautiful rural country, they made it to Cirencester, which Agricultural College Mukwe was anxious to behold. With time on their hands, they actually went in, and were given a short tour of the wonderful old buildings and the faculties, by one of the Deans. When he heard that Mukwe was a Bachelor of Agriculture of a Southern African University, he asked, "Would you be prepared to talk to our students? There are many in the Conference Centre at the moment, being brought up to speed on some newly developed crop-spray variants."

Mukwe agreed and they all made their way to the Centre mentioned and initially seated themselves high-up at the back. He had mentioned to the Dean that he would like to hear the Lecture right through. Once it was complete and the Presenter had received and answered all questions, the Dean rose and requested that his guest Mukwe Filagwa be allowed to address the students. All three of them walked down to the front, where Mukwe was introduced to the presenter, who reiterated that he address the audience directly.

Mukwe went up to the podium and commenced, "First of all Sir I would like to compliment you on your lecture. It covers practice that we follow in Central Africa, and I had heard that there were advancements in the pipeline. To all of you students, congratulations on electing Agriculture for your studies: Utilising my Degree from Central Africa. I am employed there as Senior Conservation Officer over-seeing Crop Production and Quality Control. As you are probably aware, we produce a vast array of crops — principally from the Capital southwards. Virginia Tobacco is produced in the North, and forms a great proportion of the country's exports. In my area I oversee Maize, Winter Wheat and Barley — as purely seasonal crops, and Sugar which is totally irrigated. Also, a new and rising export crop — Flowers for florists which, interestingly are exported by Air. I think that is all I need to say. Any questions?" He answered all their questions, then he and Anton were invited to a meal with the Dean and Lecturers, where both were able to sincerely compliment the Cirencester establishment.

Next day after spending a night in the town, Mukwe returned to London as he had been in consultation with the IT Department, of The Institute of Technology, who had advised that Mukwe's principal Lecturer and co-inventor was in town. The Institute were geared up to assist in researching their "chip" technology, to the next level.

So, for Anton it was North from there, because the next English feature that he wished to experience was the Cotswolds. He was not disappointed, for whilst the English countryside had been lush and beautiful this far, with its wide green valleys; streams abounded by willows and crop verdant lands, it had suddenly become more hilly and more forested. Anton caught himself identifying and reciting the abundant examples of large stunning trees, "Elm, Oak, Larch and what could that one over there be? Walnut? Yes!" He found his whole being immersed in it, and was almost relieved when he drove into the outskirts of Gloucester.

He decided to take a break for his first night away, but only after going down to the river with a town's person whom he met. They were there to witness the Severn 'bore', which he was advised was imminently due to reach these higher reaches of the river valley. Viewed from 'on high', one could witness the powerful white rush forcing its way up the river, like a waterfall in reverse. Then slowly over the next critical hour it slowed, subsided and went the other way with the flooded river now taking its revenge. Next day he continued South down to the river estuary, and the massive bridge across to Newport. He had arrived in Wales, and spent a long day 'discovering, both Newport and Cardiff, before heading North.

Ultimately, he wanted a hiking holiday around Mt Snowden, with the aim of reaching its summit, but had planned to go via the infamous 'Offa's Banks' on the way. Early Welsh/English history spoke volumes to Anton's ears. Although the 'moat' effect and the embankment raised by the early diggers from the soil, sand and rocks, dug out by them had been lessened over the centuries, they were still clearly visible winding their way northwards for over one-hundred kilometres. Anton felt that this historical feature summed-up the Celtic character, and fulfilled what these ancient Monarchs would do to prevent attacks from over the dyke.

The hiking tour in the Cumbrian Mountains which finished in the far North West of Wales did not disappoint, for the district just changed completely: the gently waving lowlands purposefully rose into dominant peaks — almost as if the sea had reached a stormy surge. Mt Snowden stood up proudly and said, "I dare you."

With such a challenge Anton and the other members of the hiking/scaling party had to set-foot! It was an invigorating and pretty difficult climb, but they made it, relishing in scenery that they had never seen before. Not since travelling down the East coast of Scotland and England had Anton relished a view the sea, but spread out below in magnificent glittering-blue was part of the Atlantic Ocean, and the immense inlet leading to Liverpool. Once over the side and down, Anton took leave of the party and headed back to civilization. He was able to return on a circular route which took him East to Liverpool, then Manchester and finally down the Motorway, back to London. Sunday night, and he had made it!

Having joined up with Mukwe again, they had heaps to talk about, and Mukwe was really disappointed that he had not completed the trip with Anton, but again this gave strength to their resolve, to return again. However, he had exciting news for Anton, because his four days with the

'Boffins' at the Institute had secured an improvement of communication between the 'Chips'. "The Chips will now be able to communicate ten kilometres plus, because the same sized mini-band projector, is now more powerful ".

"Fantastic! said Anton, I'm sure there will be occasions in the future where we find ourselves in such a juxta-position."

Having compared notes thus, they got onto the subject of the next day, which was their scheduled — and physical presence — to the Australian Embassy.

# CHAPTER 22

On arrival at the secure side entrance, they asked to be able to see Dale, their contact Officer but were advised that they would have to wait some time. They therefore made their way to the Post Office to post letters home that they had written the previous evening, and to make some overdue phone calls.

After a well-earned coffee, they returned to the Embassy, and were soon shown into Dale's Office. He had collected their visas and he handed them over, for which they were most grateful.

He then explained saying, "The Australian Federal Police, Scotland Yard and Interpol have made some significant strides in identifying and watching suspected drug smuggling groups. These entities are not suspicious of the fact that they are under surveillance, and appear to be building towards a large operation. It is not yet known whether this 'Op' is aimed at Australia, the far East or possibly America. As soon as that bridge is reached and if Australia is the destination, the Consul will request you to come in and join the large investigative team."

Anton took the opportunity to quiz him, by asking, "Sir, if the team consider that we would be an operational part of the 'trap', of which Force would we be a part, and can we expect that our airfares will be paid?"

Dale was in a position to answer the query saying, "You would be employed by the Australian Federal Police, and yes, the fares would be taken care of."

He accompanied them to the exit and thanked them for coming; adding, "It looks like my next call to you guys, might be 'the one'." While they were making their way through London's streets to the underground station, they chatted about what was transpiring, and both felt more than a little concerned. Anton wrapped up the conversation by asking Mukwe, "What do you think Muk? Are we doing the right thing, for each of us?"

The reply was "Yes, I think we are. We have given it due and full consideration, and someone has to take the part."

"One thing's for sure concluded Anton, the Police and Interpol back-up is out of this world, and one couldn't wish for better protection.

So, another period of low-level fun and frolicking; going to a big soccer match and the post 'dining out party', as well as attending a good musical with a couple of girls. Then at the unexpected time of 5 pm one evening, they were requested to attend at the Embassy. When they arrived they were introduced to a group of plain-clothes policemen, headed by an Inspector with the name of Donald, and were whisked away in two cars, one in each.

En-route they were advised that they were going to a Fair Ground. On arrival Donald spoke over the inter-car radio, stating, "We reckon that some members of a Smuggling gang will be meeting here casually, to arrange an 'Export'. We hope that by mingling with the crowd, some of the eight team members present might hear something really useful. Should that be the case, that person must unobtrusively call on a couple of others in the team. At all times you must keep at least one, and if possible two members of your team, in view throughout the night."

Both Anton and Mukwe realised that apart from the seriousness of the mission for all, they were clearly being tested. They each silently vowed that they would pass — hopefully with flying colours.

They had parked in the outer ring — from the fair, but before taking separate routes into the grounds, Anton and Mukwe had a few seconds to converse. Anton whispered to Mukwe, "Have your chip tuned and I will also, so that we can communicate if need be." Mukwe raised his hand in affirmation

the Festival was *spectacularly bright* and *motion-filled*. There were motors driving vertical cars as well as others whipping them around at forty five degrees, and in the background could be seen a small train traversing a high and low 'witches' hump-back track. The lights blinded one in yellow, orange and red, exposing hundreds of children and young people swinging-it to loud music. There were also various interesting 'sales' tables and ground-level activities being carried out,

The two separate teams then entered — one heading left, and one right, with a reminder/order from Donald to reach a point of keeping at least one other team member in sight. Each team crossed over the other once, and some fifteen minutes later, Mukwe noticed a side entrance with a few exhibition tables and other goings-on, so decided to slip down this 'avenue' for a quick look and listen.

He did see some rough looking characters, and made his way, casually, like he was going to pass them: it was while he was doing this that he heard the words, "No, this lot is going to Thailand."

The reply was, "Surely they've got enough of this gunck, already."

Mukwe exited quickly, then ran around the outside, to again join up with his team, but also gave his 'chip' two pulses of red. Anton instantly picked these up, and acknowledged with one pulse in red. He made his way to Chief Donald, and suggested that he should go across to the other team, as they had noticed some small 'bite' of info.

Anton got a bit of a queer look, but the man hastened off to chat to his 2IC. Fortunately, Mukwe had already joined up again and explained to the Officer what he had experienced. When the two Officers were together, they asked Mukwe where he heard these words, and for a description of the men. Chief Donald then hastened-off to take a furtive look at these 'Gents'! He was back after a couple of minutes, and acknowledged that they fitted a description of one of the suspected gangs that Scotland Yard and Interpol, had been watching. He called off the 'listen-and-look" operation at that stage, so that he could report back to the full Drugs Team.

The two teams split-up again and made their way back to the cars, and Anton's 'Bossman' queried how he had picked this info up so quickly. Anton answered by saying "Mukwe and I can sense what one another are up to, provided that we are not too far from each other."

Chief Donald said 'Bullshit! But we can sort that out in the future: in the meantime, well done."

They were dropped off separately, at opposing ends of the road leading to their "digs", and advised that they would be contacted again, in the not-too-distant future. Mukwe waited for Anton, and after five minutes or so they caught up with one another. While walking back to their lodgings they discussed the foray to the Fair, and the fact that the Leader felt that it was successful. Mukwe remarked "We could do that sort of thing on our own, you know?"

Anton replied, "Yea! your dead right, but we would probably need to employ some of our camouflage techniques

— beard, moustache etcetera, and try out some scruffy pubs."

"Hey! What about some classy ones, as well — like in the Soho district, especially if they have a billiards and snooker 'Games' room as well?"

"Terrific idea, but not tonight: I'm 'shot' and need a bloody good meal."

The next day when alone, they talked a bit more about twice weekly "Pub Crawls", as they termed them. On their first outing all they did to distract any attention, was to wear their disreputable old clothes, which had last seen the light of day in the Okavango. Although they certainly didn't hear, or witness anything leading, both felt that the characters in the pub were sufficiently 'lowlife,' to have made this initial sortie worthwhile.

The second time was to a different location, and Anton wore a black cap and darkened his eyebrows, whilst Mukwe wore a soccer T shirt and scarf. Again, it was interesting, and while playing snooker they were able to prove to themselves that they could hear what the players, on adjacent tables, were talking about.

In the meantime, Scotland Yard and Interpol had continued their investigation. They had also put out routine alerts to the police at London's two Airports, as well as Sea Ports in England, Europe, America, Venezuela and Colombia, re traffic to Thailand. The Police in that country were also warned to be on full alert, re both Air and Sea Imports.

Anton and Mukwe were brought up to date on this at their

next scheduled meeting at the Australian Embassy. They were also told that the Team had received leaked knowledge from an 'informer', of a cache of drugs that a gang wanted to get to their cohorts in Australia. At this early stage, the informer believed that the intention was to 'Export' it partly by Boat, and partly by Air: but that the investigation was still ongoing.

The twosome were also requested to return the next day for a briefing by a more Senior member. To their pleasant surprise, they were also handed envelopes containing their first pay — for the Fairground patrol.

On their return the next day they formed part of the usual team of eight, plus the two Embassy Officers, and an extra two from Scotland Yard's Drug Investigation Unit. The meeting gave immediate and deep focus, to a growing, and serious drugs movement to Australia. No one was permitted to make notes, as the mission had to be considered totally secret.

At the end of the presentation the two Senior Scotland Yard Officers got together with the two Team Leaders; the Australian Federal Police Officers, and also requested Anton and Mukwe to join them. Their intent was not only to meet this operational team, but also to ascertain if A&M were prepared to become physically involved, i.e to act as 'Carriers'.

Both Anton and Mukwe looked across at the AFP Officers who nodded their heads. So, they both indicated that they would be, provided that they were covered at all times. One of the Scotland Yard Officers gave that assurance saying, "The pick-up of the drugs here in England will be covered by us, Scotland Yard, but from the time that they are landed in Australia that duty will be covered by the Australian Federal Police."

Anton addressed the Senior Officers, and said, "Mukwe and I frequent many little pubs around the city — mainly to play snooker. Wouldn't it be a good idea for us to go to the one, where you suspect this gang are looking for carriers? As I, and I believe Mukwe as well, reckon that it could make the ultimate hand over much easier."

The Officer addressed looked at his partner; mulled it over in his head and replied, "Is there any chance that you two may already be under watch, from gangs such as the one that we are targeting?"

Both replied "No!" Anton signalled to Mukwe to carry on, who continued, "We have not been up to any dubious activities: mainly partying with friends, playing and watching sport, and closer to this type of thing, playing snooker — all over the place." Anton quickly added that since their first approach to the Australian Embassy, they had been admitted and had exited through side and back doors — different to any members of the Drugs Team.

The two Senior Officers had a quick exchange, and agreed. The one who had been conducting the meeting said, "Okay, but we will have plain clothes Team members watching the venue, whilst you are there this time, as well as when we send you in for the pick-up." Anton and Mukwe thanked them, and felt more secure.

So, the next evening they prepared themselves as very ordinary individuals, and visited the particular Club which had been identified to them. They took a table near the back, where there were a couple of openings leading inside. Anton went and bought beers for them and while away on this, Mukwe took out a map of Australia. During the course of deep conversation lasting many minutes, and many swallows of beer, a few odd 'heavies' and others had made an appearance. At this stage Anton and Mukwe opened the map and got really involved in studying, and discussing it.

Sydney was of most interest to them, but they also viewed other options after leaving the Airport. When they had finished their beers they moved to the snooker room. Anton said, "Good there are three tables — one of which is spare. Pretty high-class too, and gee! the lighting in here is bright compared with the Pub below."

They then got going on a loud and highly competitive game. It seemed to them, that a few of the same faces appeared from time to time. Once their game ended they left the venue, without an actual approach having been made. Again they left the area in a taxi and took a circuitous route back to the vicinity of their 'Digs'.

The next day they phoned the Scotland Yard Officer-in-Charge to report on the night's activities. He was encouraged, and advised that the Plan was effectively in progress, and to make their unobtrusive way to the Embassy the following day.

This they did, and the Meeting comprised both Operational Teams of four; the two Embassy Officers; Anton and Mukwe and the two Scotland Yard Officers. The whole plan was outlined, as well as the method of operation. Anton and Mukwe were handed cash by the Senior Embassy Officer and told to go and purchase their tickets from British Airways, which had already been booked. He then added, "If it becomes necessary to amend the flight 'date', that issue will be taken care of, and you two will need to check in with Embassy, every day — from a different phone box." He then reassured Anton and Mukwe that they would be covered for the entire duration of the Plan, both in England and in Australia. He also asked the Interpol Officer to rise, so that he could show Anton and Mukwe a small indistinctive patch that all the covering team members would be wearing. They observed this very carefully. That was the extent of it for them, and they were advised that the Embassy would call them, for the evening that it was to take place. Also, that a 'taxi' would pick them up and take them to the club. They exited then, and went to purchase the tickets.

# CHAPTER 23

They were contacted the next day by their team leader and told that the taxi would pick them up at 5.00pm, so that they could execute their first planned visit to the club: This was done, and they were taken to the Club where they were to sit at the same table as before, and display the same routine as before.

They bought their beers and sat down at 'their' table as soon as it was vacant. Part way through their beer and conversation, a man came out of the rear section of the main room, and approached the table, saying "Glad to see you back — hope you enjoy your time, as much as your last visit." Without taking too much notice, they thanked him and assured him that they would. He followed up by remarking, "When I walked past last time, I noticed that you were studying a map of Australia. Are you returning there, or making a visit?"

Anton and Mukwe were pretty convinced that he hadn't walked past, but Anton replied, "Oh! Yes, we were studying it, mainly to see where Sydney was, and how close the main cities are situated. We have booked our fares, and are going out on a Back-Packer visit."

The gent replied, "Very interesting — hope you enjoy your trip." He then walked across behind the bar and out to the back at the far end. When they had finished their beers, they went up to the Games room again, and started to play snooker. Understandably it was an exciting game; made more so, when the same man as before, plus three 'heavies' joined them, and set-up to play a foursome at the next table.

They hadn't been going for long when one of the heavies said, "We've got some 'sniffs' here, if you would like to partake?"

Mukwe very quickly replied "We don't do drugs thanks, but by all means carry on — we've no hang-ups."

The original man then approached the table, introduced himself as Murray and stuck out his hand. Anton and Mukwe each shook the extended hand and gave their names. He then continued by saying, "Look, we have something that we need to get to Sydney, and would be prepared to pay for the service. Would you be interested in taking it?"

Anton replied with, "Taking some stuff is not a problem, but because of the high-powered-screening that takes place, it depends what it is. One also has to realise that baggage is screened at both ends."

Murray's response was "You won't have to worry about that, because this stuff is packed extremely carefully and will not be detected — provided that we handle the packing."

"Well if that is the case, said Anton, we should be okay. Where do we take it to, and how much do we earn? Muk, you agree don't you?" To which the latter, nodded.

They were promised 500 pounds each, and asked to bring their rucksacks down the following day. They called for an ordinary taxi then, and took a "Z" shaped route back to their Digs, getting out well short, and finding their way through a narrow alley to their street — no one following, or waiting at the end. As soon as they entered the room, they closed the curtains.

Team Member Lachlan made his way to their room about an hour later, and they gave the hook-line-and-sinker of what would take place the following day. Whilst enjoying a 'cuppa coffee' he asked, "Are you guys still feeling committed to this 'carrying'?"

Mukwe replied, "Yes! We have gone into it deeply, and we will proceed with it."

Getting-up to leave he said, "Okay then, when you actually exit their pub tomorrow give me either a thumbs 'Up' or 'Down', re its starting."

"Will do, said Anton, and remember that we depart for Australia the day after that, and that we will probably be followed by the gang, to ensure that all goes according to their schedule!" The next day they were up early to complete their initial packing, and to get ready to go across to the Club. They also took the opportunity to phone home, and advise everyone that they were on their way to Australia, the following day. Next communications would be from there.

Allowing for the time to reach the club, they set-off by taxi and were wheeling their suitcases in, at the appointed time. They were met by the same members of the gang, who had arranged everything the previous day, but were diverted to the back rooms, from the entrance hall. In a very secretive room the contraband was very carefully inserted amongst all their gear, with small square sheets of something that confused the screening process. The cases were then closed, and everyone looked across at the two, in an aggressive manner. Murray handed each an envelope containing (apparently) the five hundred pounds, and said, "That is the agreed payment, and you will not talk to anybody about this deal, otherwise the consequences will be very serious." They were told to come via the Club the following day, to pick-up their suitcases, at which time they would be given the delivery address in Sydney.

Anton appealed — pointing at the cases, "Look, me and Mukwe still have a few things to pack in our cases."

"No way! You can go out and buy a couple of cabin bags for that job." A time was set for pick-up and they were told to go, and to watch themselves. En-route to the other side of the road Anton gave a secretive 'thumbs up', then he and Mukwe walked to the shops close by to buy a cabin bag each. Back at their Digs and after the evening meal, they settled their accommodation debt, and were ready to head back to the club next morning.

Their 'taxi' arrived; they picked-up the cases from the Club, and under strict scrutiny were handed cards with the Sydney delivery address. From there they travelled out to Heathrow to catch their flight. Whilst removing their cases etcetera, the driver advised them quietly that the Airport was set-up for an uninterrupted departure.

In they went, and sure enough their cases were cleared through the 'Booking-In' area, and they proceeded through the Security Surveillance. Mukwe was the first to notice a suspicious looking guy in the standing crowd, and quietly whispered same to Anton. Soon after that they also noted a couple of their Team members, in plain clothes. Pretty 'hairy' stuff and they couldn't help conjecturing about the next 24 — 36 hours.

There were no hitches however, and they boarded without any problems. Their rationale on the direct flight was to rest and enjoy, and 'bugger' if there was a gang member on the flight, or not. Maybe one of the passengers was from their team, anyway. Both of them thoroughly enjoyed the meals and the fact that they could watch full length films on the aircraft's built–in TV service. Also being able to listen to whatever music they wanted — for as long as they wanted — appealed to them.

Landing in Sydney certainly gave them more cause

for concern, for they had no idea what to expect. It was obvious where all the exiting passengers were headed and they entered a very large hall. There were many different queues leading to the Entrance desks, and it was only after some minutes of waiting, that Anton noticed one of them was for Immigration.

He gave Mukwe a nudge, and said, "I reckon that one with the Immigration Sign is more likely for us," and they started moving across to it, only to suddenly recognise the back of the 'heavy' that they had espied in London. They daren't show recognition and just proceeded up the line. Eventually they reached the Immigration Officer behind his console, and were weary. In a business-like but friendly manner he checked each of their papers, stamped them and told them to proceed to Luggage Collection. Phew! Massive relief. They then descended to the ground floor, and on the way to the 'Incoming Luggage' conveyor belt, Anton caught site of a plain clothed person with the identifiable tag. "Thank God!"

To their utter amazement, their cases also passed through this check-point without hitch. The unobtrusive plain-clothes officer gave them the 'cap-lifting' signal. In moving away from the luggage conveyor Anton sidled in his direction, and without stopping whispered that there had been a 'heavy' on the plane. They didn't hurry to exit from the main Airport 'Waiting' Lounge, feeling that a slight delay would allow a surveillance team to get ready.

Once outside they waited in the Taxi queue, until one arrived. When the driver had placed their gear in the boot, they gave him one of the cards, upon which was the delivery address. His remark was, "Oh! That's not too far, as it is in one of the southern suburbs." Well short of half-an-hour and they were in the street, and asked to be dropped off four houses short of the 'Receivers' house. After he had unloaded, they paid him but asked him to wait as they would not be long. They then dithered about for a few more minutes before wheeling their bags down a fairly rough pavement to a medium sized, single-story house, and ringing the bell.

The door opened and they were asked (surreptitiously) what they wanted, and Mukwe handed over the other card saying, 'We have brought something for this address from London." They were admitted then, and taken into a brightly lit but dismally furnished and carpeted lounge/dining area. There were a few other blokes in the room and it smelt strongly of liquor. Without waiting they unlocked, and opened their cases — feeling pretty damn scared — and stepped away from them. The group immediately started going through them, and it was clearly apparent, that they knew how many packages of drugs there should be. Once the drugs were all out, the same group roughly settled the remaining contents, and closed them. "Okay! There are your bags — with all your own clobber," said one of them.

Unbelievably at this point, coffee was brought in for of them: Anton and Mukwe were the first to be offered same, and each took from the side of the tray, even though they realised that there was a chance that they were all laced! As it turned out none were, and the guy who appeared to be in charge, named Andy looked upwards and queried, "How was the Plane trip, and have you been paid for bringing the 'gear' across?".

Both replied, "Yes! We have been paid 500 pounds each."

Andy acknowledged this, and quickly 'stepped into the breach' with, "Would you like to buy some of these drugs?"

Mukwe was quick to reply, "No thanks we still have enough!".

One of the other top guys then asked what they would be doing in Australia, to which Anton replied, "Once we have had a good look at Sydney, we are going to head up to Glenn Innes, because I have Celtic ancestry up there." Quick as a flash he then said, "Right, then you can take some gear up to Tamworth, for us."

Anton tried to protest, but there was an obvious nasty turn in the room, and the same guy shot his arm forward and added, "Don't give us that shit: you will let us know when you're leaving for that place, and you will carry some stuff up for us. In fact, as soon as you're settled in the City, you will let us know where you are." While he was settling this demand with the gang, Mukwe happened to casually glance down a passage and noticed two very young girls — one of whom was crying. He was careful not to signal this.

Neither of them were prepared to argue with the guys, and

that was the end of the delivery. However, a new difficulty arose when they moved towards the front door, and the same guy asked, "Where do you think you're going?"

Anton replied, "We're leaving because our taxi is waiting."

The gang member continued, "No you are not. We will take you back to the city and drop you at Caloundra. Don't worry about the Taxi, we will pay and advise him to push-off." Anton and Mukwe were pretty disturbed at this, but agreed, and were piled into a large car in the garage with cases and bags, and driven off. Both hoped with all their might that they had been observed leaving the house, and would be discretely followed. They felt that they recognized some of the suburbs through which they were driving, and wern't surprised that they reached Caloundra within about twenty minutes.

The driver member got out, apparently to assist with the cases, and warned, "Don't you say a word about any of this, or of the London end, otherwise you will both be taken-out."

As he closed the trunk ready to get back into his car, armed police were running up from behind, and ahead, and he just made it to the door before he was surrounded by policemen who arrested him, and impounded his car. Anton and Mukwe were also roughly accosted and bundled into one of the police cars. One of the policemen climbed into the gang member's car, and then all three cars headed off towards the city Police Station. The gang member was quickly taken inside to be incarcerated.

Once he was out of sight it allowed Anton and Mukwe to claim their (clean) cases and bags, and they were then taken to a pre-booked hotel in North Sydney. After assisting with the booking-in process and before departing, the AFP Officer asked, "Our Team are meeting tomorrow at Australian Federal Police Head Quarters in the City, at 10.00am. You will both be required, with all your gear, so please be there."

The trip into the city the next morning was an astounding eye-opener. The Sydney Harbour Bridge towered over the city beyond, like a 'massif'. Both Anton and Mukwe had seen many many engineering wonders — but nothing to compare with this: as if from another world!. Likewise, the Harbour and the fact that the city stretched right down to its edge on both sides.

On entering AFP. HQ they were happy to be received by the Officer whom they had known in London (and on the aircraft), who took them through to a Meeting room, where he introduced them to the big group of attendees, involved in halting the Drug Smuggling operation. They were officially thanked — by the Officer Chairing the Meeting, who brought the Meeting up-to-date on the planned follow-through:

1. "The driver from yesterday has been arrested; the 'drug destination house' was raided immediately after you, Anton and Mukwe, were driven away. All present in the house have been arrested, and the delivered drugs seized. The house has become

a 'Crime Scene' and is still being investigated and searched, both inside, and out.

2.  The English gang member was also arrested for following Anton and Mukwe's taxi down to the 'delivery house'.

3.  In London, Scotland Yard Officers have raided the Pub, where the drugs had been loaded: arrested all staff present and also declared it a 'crime scene'."

Clearly all this information was received by Anton and Mukwe with a strong sense of relief, and they each handed over the 500 Pounds Sterling which they had been paid in London by the 'Publicans'.

Mukwe took this opportunity and said, "Whilst we were in the house where we delivered the drugs, we noticed two little girls." Further thanks were expressed, and then they were advised that they would be going to separate 'Safe Houses' under the protection of an AFP Officer and a NSW Police Officer, assigned to each. At a later date, they found out that the two NSW Officers were from different Police Stations, within the city.

Mukwe left the meeting room first with a female AFP Officer and a male Policeman; collected his gear, and was taken down to a car on the southern side of the carpark, and then departed. Not long after, the other NSW Policeman from an outer Station came into the meeting, was introduced — especially to his male AFP counterpart, and to Anton

— had his instructions checked, and the second party were ready to go. Anton picked-up his cases and bags; and they exited to a car on the northern side of the carpark and the three of them headed off to the second 'safe house'.

On arrival at the respective brick 'safe houses' formal introductions were made and the parties were assigned to different bedrooms, and the new arrivals informed that there would always be one Officer present (if not two). Also, that the houses would be double-locked, at all times. This gave the opportunity for the occupants of both houses to carry-out more personal introductions, particularly Mukwe and Anton to their respective protective Officers. The AFP Officer assigned to Mukwe, had the first name of Ashlin, and was of "Islander" descent, and the Policeman's name was Max, from Sydney City. In the case of Anton, the AFP male Officer was Bryan and the Policeman's name was John. First things first though — a cuppa coffee and a meal, and then do your own thing within the confines.

Once in their own rooms Anton and Mukwe green pulsed their 'Chips' and in Morse Code, gave one another the addresses to which they had been brought.

A couple of days went by, during which they each got to know their protective officers quite well, and all talked very guardedly about themselves. On the second day Mukwe had persuaded Ashlin to take him out in the car — in his camouflage! They went to the nearby Shopping Centre, where she purchased a few things that were needed for herself and for the house; then they had a cup of coffee.

Anton on the other hand had only got as far as talking about that possibility, and achieving agreement for the near future.

When Mukwe and Ashlin returned they found a note from Max with the time and the words "Out for a while". They hadn't been back for long and were sitting in the lounge — fortunately away from the main window and door — when they heard a powerful car driving-up. A heavy shooting raid from powerful rifles then commenced from the car, onto the front of the house,. The sound and the impact were deafening to their senses, with breaking glass and splinters flying throughout the room. Mukwe and the AFP Officer dived against the wall below the window, to avoid the shots: some of which were entering through the window and door. Neither were hit, and at the first slight break in the onslaught Ashlin immediately scrambled for her revolver and released the safety catch. While she was covering the front door she called across, "Mukwe! arm yourself with something heavy and go out to the back, to prevent anyone coming through there."

On the way Mukwe was mumbling to himself and sent Anton a double red pulse through the 'chip', and the message in Morse-code "Urgent. This address-attacked".

Ashlin called through from the front, "Who are you talking to?"

"No particular person, but I'll tell you when this settles down." replied Mukwe.

There was no human physical attack on doors or windows — probably because the attackers had been witnessed. After she heard the car race off, and was satisfied that the worst was over, Ashlin immediately phoned AFP Head Quarters and reported the attack. Surprisingly she was told that help was already on its way, as her equivalent Officer at the other 'safe house' had already phoned in the SOS for a response to 'her safe-house'. When Mukwe came through from the back, she asked the same question again, and he said, "I wasn't talking, I was getting a message through To Anton."

"Oh! For your information help is on its way, but I can't understand how it was so quick. How could you get a message through to your mate?"

For the first time since the 'Chips' were installed and because he trusted Ashlin so completely- in fact he now realised that he was falling in love with her — he was prepared to explain in full, provided that she told no one. "Well it's like this, you see! I have this thing in my forearm, and he extended his arm to show... and so has Anton. We call them 'Chips' and they were developed in an IT environment, while I was doing my Degree. They have two functions — one quicker than the other — A green glow for "All's Well" and a red glow for "Emergency". The slightly slower function enables us to pass Information, using Morse Code."

"What! You must be having-me-on Mukwe?" said Ashlin, looking somewhat mystified, though suddenly realising that the story must be true.

Mukwe countered that by saying, "When we can all get down to the beach, or out on a picnic somewhere, Anton and I will demonstrate its capability to you."

While one of them still patrolled the inside of house the other cleaned-up broken glass and wooden fragments from doors and windows, and prepared a snack and a cup of coffee for each.

While they were consuming these Anton and his two protective officers arrived, at some speed! They rushed inside in a real state having witnessed the damage outside' and sought assurance that both were unharmed. Conversation soon got down to the subject of the secret transmission at Anton's 'safe house', but not before John, the NSW Policeman, asked, "Where's the Police Officer from the city?". On being told that he had left — leaving a note — and was not yet back, he was highly critical.

Bryan the AFP Officer then interrupted, "Did you hear what Anton did?"

Before he could continue however, Ashlin intervened saying, "Did you hear what Mukwe did?!" They concluded by having a good laugh, and looking forward to the demo.

Soon after that a Head Quarters Team arrived, with crime scene Investigators, and only later did Max return. Ashlin and Mukwe were questioned at length, and the investigation proceeded quickly and efficiently, both inside and out in the front yard. Max was out there with them, when Ashlin sought discreet time with the Senior Team Officer, and expressed her suspicions regarding Max's absence. He thanked her and made a careful note.

The Senior AFP Officer then sought out the NSW Police Lieutenant, to co-ordinate the intelligence so far gathered, and one of the first things agreed upon was to assign new 'safe houses' for each of Anton and Mukwe.

As soon as Ashlin was informed of this, she secretly contacted her Boss, and said, "Please Sir will you consider Adelaide in regard to these new 'safe houses', as one of my training partners, Anne, was transferred there. I also feel strongly, that not only other sections of the Drug Syndicate in this city, but probably also one of the Motor Cycle gangs, have become involved." He agreed and assured her that he would look into that option, as well as giving it urgent priority.

In the meantime, for the next few days, would she and Mukwe mind joining the other two — Bryan and Anton — at their 'safe house'. She accepted that and called to Mukwe to go and pack-up again, which she also did, as soon as she was excused.

Not long after that the AFP Team left the crime scene, together with the two protective mini-teams, back to Head Quarters. John was asked, and accepted that he would be the only policeman guarding Anton and Mukwe, with the two AFP Officers. It was arranged that they would leave independently, and in different directions — with Anton and Mukwe hidden below window level — to return to the other 'safe house'. On the assumption that it was going to be short stay, Anton and Mukwe went into one room; Bryan and John into a second, and Ashlin into the third bedroom.

A quiet couple of days followed, with only two telephone contacts with AFP HQ. In the second one, the senior AFP Officer informed Ashlin, "The Adelaide option is coming together, and apart from talking to the South Australian 'Chief', I have also spoken briefly to Officer Anne". Ashlin was rapt and told the others, advising that it was not yet finalized.

The other scene that occurred was a minor — distance wise — demo between Mukwe and Anton, using their 'chips'. When they explained that they had 'pulsed' the seriousness of the attack on the other house, using morse code, the Officers were astounded.

# CHAPTER 24

O n Monday of the following week Ashlin and John, the NSW Police Officer, were summoned to AFP HQ, where Ashlin was informed that the Adelaide 'safe house' option had been arranged. John was thanked profoundly for his attention to the protective task over these two 'Immigrants'. A commendation had been made for him. He was asked to return to the Sydney Police Head Quarters after the second twosome left, where they would be expecting him.

He thanked all; particularly shaking Ashlin's hand, then returned to where Bryan and Anton were waiting for the outcome. They were apologetic for the fact that he would be parted from the group, but effusive over the fact that he would be receiving a commendation. Anton expressed with great feeling, "Congratulations John on the commendation and thanks so much for keeping a watchful eye and presence over me."

Ashlin was then given the precise plan for the move to Adelaide: again, Anton and Mukwe would be separated until they reached Adelaide, because they would be taking separate routes and leaving at separate times. Bryan would take Anton and travel via Broken Hill, while Mukwe would travel with Ashlin, down to Wagga Wagga and then West across to South Australia.

Before leaving, the Senior Officer conducting the meeting advised, "Ashlin you need to know that Max, the NSW Policeman who was with you and Mukwe, has been suspended pending an investigation, and is under close observation. The reason for the continued, extreme security is that we can confirm that one of the Motor Cycle Gangs has been drawn into the fray; possibly because they are one of the principal receivers of the drugs, and of firearms from the 'larger' Drug Syndicate. The AFP and the NSW Police are still investigating the 'shooting-up' of the 'safe house', but we feel that good progress is being made. So, both your teams must exercise total alertness."

Ashlin thanked all of the Australian Federal Police Team, for herself, and on behalf of Bryan, and left to return to the 'safe house'. There was great excitement in the house, while packing commenced for their respective journey's starting the next day.

Ashlin and Mukwe left just before dawn the following morning, making for the Hume Freeway in a southerly direction. In private discussion Bryan and Anton had decided to delay their departure an extra day, as Bryan believed that they could make better time. It had been made clear to both teams, that Officer Anne was their contact person at the AFP South Australian HQ, in Adelaide. Each of Mukwe and Anton were to lie out of sight, below window level until they had cleared Sydney.

Mukwe was just beginning to get a feel for this Australian landscape with its distinctive gumtrees and wide-open paddocks, when Ashlin exclaimed, "Mukwe, to hell with going the boring middle route across to Adelaide, I'm going to take you virtually down to Melbourne and then across on the spectacular Great Ocean Road to South Australia."

"That sounds much further, said Mukwe, but wont we be much later arriving than Anton and Bryan?"

"No we wont. I overheard them planning their trip and they are only leaving Sydney tomorrow, to go via Broken Hill. We'll still be much the same distance from destination, as they are."

"I'm all for it, and could handle a famous tourist route: Aren't the Twelve Apostles down that way?" For Mukwe this had further significance, as it gave him more alone time with this girl, whom he now realised that he had fallen 'head-over-heels' in love with.

"Yes! replied Ashlin, and The Otway Mountains and Blue Lake, just over the border at Mt Gambier."

She was an excellent driver, and they made good time down the Freeway. They passed through a few small towns that were obviously supporting agriculture, as the terrain on both sides was obviously farmland. On heading into the lower Blue Mountains they discussed the beauty of the close and far mountainous views, and how many of the views had been captured in Australian 'country art'.

When they descended down through Gundagai, passing the 'Dog and the Tuckerbox' and over the Murrumbidgee River bridge in the wide valley, Mukwe couldn't help exclaiming, "Now this is what I call a river!"

"Wait till you see the Murray, a bit further on", countered Ashlin. Predictably he did rave on that as well, while they crossed into Victoria. As they progressed down the Freeway to Melbourne, absorbing the changing scenery and chatting all the way, Mukwe suddenly realised that Ashlin had slid her hand across and was holding his. He experienced a sense of unutterable pleasure, and smiling at her, knew that this was 'it' — the future. On reaching Melbourne they took the Western Ring Road, crossed the river and headed down to the South coast, past Geelong.

They booked into an hotel; cleaned up and went through to the Dining Hall and whilst they were eating and chatting Mukwe suddenly said, "Ashlin will you be my Girl?"

"Yes! She said, I would love to be." The companionship of sharing a room that night was an endearing experience for both of them. During that evening Ashlin phoned Anne to advise her of their delay and explained their new direction of approach. Much chitter-chatter followed, and the next thing was that Anne would take half a day's leave and fly down to Mt Gambier to meet them. Great excitement!

Leaving early the next day, they could soon appreciate the Otways. Mukwe's delighted remarks were, "This road is actually cut out of the mountains — they start here right at the waters edge." Ashlin agreed and was equally impressed with them.

Next was the spectacle of the Twelve Apostles, which suddenly- around a corner — leapt out of the sea at them. She couldn't contain herself exclaiming "Wow! I had no idea that they were all so beautiful: it doesn't matter whether one is looking at the big ones, or the small ones." Pointing virtually along the bonnet of the car she continued, "Right up towards the western end — that one fairly close to the cliff face — apparently used to be joined to the cliff. Unfortunately it was blown down/washed away in a massive storm, not long ago."

Mukwe was also beside himself in wonder at them replying, "Bouy! Are you right, and the blue background of the sea with its crashing white waves against the Apostles, is also to die for!" Here they paused for a cup of coffee so that they could hold hands, talk and take more of it in, then on towards the border. They pushed through this section as it was mainly rural, and Ashlin was becoming more and more excited at the impending reunion.

This first meeting for ages between Ashlin and Anne, was an extremely happy event. Mukwe was introduced and they enjoyed coffee and each other's company, before heading off on the long final leg to Adelaide. It was however, an exciting journey through dense forest to start with and then vast areas of superb cropping land: mostly Wheat and Barley. The Adelaide Hills provided the final impressive backdrop. With Mukwe safely below window level they drove directly to Anne's flat where he was secretly shown in, followed by gear that they would need for the night.

Next morning, using the same tactics they drove to the AFP South Australian HQ and retired to Anne's office. After preliminary introductions, including to the Chief, they spent the rest of the day waiting for the other team. Post afternoon coffee, Ashlin felt that it was time to try and contact Bryan and Anton, to which suggestion Anne looked a bit confused and said, "And how do you propose to do that Ashlin?"

"Oh! I forgot to tell you Anne, we do have the means......."

"What means? I didn't see any 'two-way' radio in your car, nor do I see any on you guys now."

\*\*\*

In the meantime, Bryan and Anton left Sydney a full twenty-four hours later and headed up into the Blue Mountains through Katoomba, and out onto the Mitchell Highway driving due West. All through the morning Bryan was driving up through Bathurst, Orange and on to Dubbo, and they were talking about the towns, the flat Australian land-scape as well as everything else that 'opened or shut'.

They stopped for Lunch in Dubbo, where Anton opened and started studying the map of the continued route of the Mitchell Highway, while they were waiting for their meal. Suddenly Anton queried of Bryan, "This White Cliffs to the north of the highway, after we cross the Darling River at Wilcannia — isn't it well known for its opals?"

"Yes it is," replied Bryan. "do you want to do that circuit into Broken Hill?" The reply was in the affirmative, and that was the course they took through the afternoon. There was a very pleasant little shop there, and Anton made *three precious little* purchases before they continued on to Broken Hill for the night.

After an early morning walk around this famous mining town, during which they discussed its location and fame, they had a late breakfast and headed onto the road. A short way out of town was the border crossing and then it turned virtually due South, and the days driving took them out into semi-desert flats. Anton exclaimed, "We are passing through a moonscape of saltbush here, and it just seems to go on forever in every direction. It reminds me of the Karroo in South Africa."

Bryan interjected saying, "That maybe so, and I agree that it is barren and featureless but not far down the road, on the East side is one of the most productive Sheep Stations in Australia." Anton would never have believed it and was pleased that sheep could be ranched in such featureless and very dry conditions.

When they eventually drove into Burra and stopped for lunch. Bryan continued saying, "This little town has some sad, but followed by some good history. The original miners here, came up from the coast with their families and over the years were forced to dig into the banks of the Burra creek, to house their families. For many years it worked and more dwellings were dug. Then at a particular stage Broken Hill beckoned and the miners left in their droves — leaving their families behind. Unfortunately, a massive storm occurred which flooded the river and many of the dwellings in the bank of the river. It was a South Australian disaster but resulting from it, the Government decreed in an 'Australian First', that proper Mining Accommodation had to be built to support such ventures in the future."

After their meal their journey entered an extensive zone of quality agricultural land, and to the south of it — Civilization! As they were entering the outer suburbs of Adelaide — Anton suddenly said, "I'm getting a message from Mukwe: drive on, I'll attend to it" — he pressed his flap to give a green pulse, followed in morse code by...

\*\*\*

Ashlin leant across to Mukwe and said, "Muk, now is as good a time as any to give Anne a demo, especially as she is going to be the other AFP Protective Officer here in Adelaide."

Mukwe stepped across towards Anne, and indicated the skin flap on his arm, and said "there is a 'Chip' embedded under the skin and muscle of my arm. Anton has the same in his arm, and we can communicate with one another".

Anne retorted "I don't believe it. Show me".

So, with his arm open to the two girls Mukwe said, "I'm going to give it one gentle press and it will bring-up the green pulse". This was followed seconds later by another green pulse — then — in morse code pulses: "Hi! Where 'u'?" "That's Anton's reply. I'll tell him now where we are, and ask where they are — in green pulses — also in morse code: "In Adel'. Where u2?" Further green pulses from the 'chip 'on Mukwe's arm, and he read the reply out to the girls, as he received it, "Just past Gawl; heading Eliz". A final 'press/pulse' from Mukwe, with "Thanks, 'c u'".

When Mukwe had conveyed all of this to the two girl officers, Ashlin was as proud as punch — which deepened Mukwe's love for her, whilst Anne was blown away at the prospects of this, and said, "No wonder you and your Mate were not scared of taking on this drug courier thing, that Ashlin has told me about."

While they were waiting, Anne told Ashlin and Mukwe that the South Australian 'safe house' was tucked away in North Adelaide, about four kilometres from the City, and that she would be taking over from Bryan as other AFP

Officer. There would also be a South Australian Policeman, guarding the house and all of them. Soon after that Bryan and Anton arrived, and were shown into the Office. Ashlin carried out all the introductions, "Bryan, this is Anne the South Australian AFP Officer who will take over from you. Thank you very much for your part in the protection plan to date." After that they settled down; talked about their respective trips, and had coffee.

Ashlin asked Bryan to accompany her to meet her Boss — the Head of AFP in South Australia. This left the other three together, and Anne took the opportunity to engage in conversation with Mukwe and Anton. Very pleasant for both, and in Anton's case, it entered his mind that this was a girl that he would like to have much more to do with. It appeared that she was likewise impressed. She concluded by complimenting him, "That 'Chip' thing that each of you possess is incredible, and it will give Ashlin and I a strong sense of security."

When Ashlin and Bryan returned, they all went off to lunch at the in-house 'Café', and Bryan advised that he would be flying back to Sydney, on the morrow, and thanked all of them, for the excellent company and the good training it had afforded him. The Senior AFP SA Officer had phoned his equal in NSW, and commended Bryan. During the afternoon they all drove out to the new 'safe house', with Anton and Mukwe hidden below seat-level. What's more, they took a very unusual route to attain their goal. A quick exit into the house, with the officers bringing all the cases, bags, boxes etcetera, inside. Anton and Mukwe were assigned one bedroom; the two AFP Officers, a second, And Bryan was given a bed for the night , in the third. This would later be the SA Policeman's room.

All of them accompanied Bryan to the Airport the following morning, except that Anton and Mukwe stayed in the car once they reached it. Before he got out of the car however, they sent him off with strong handshakes, and he responded saying, "I wish you all 'the very best', and a rapid end to this whole drug fiasco."

Anton followed up, "Hang-on! Just before you leave, here is a little memento from White Cliffs, which — and watch my lips — you bought; all the best to you as well, and we look forward to seeing you again." With that Ashlin and Anne accompanied him into the Airport and saw him off on his return to Sydney.

When the girls returned Ashlin tapped Mukwe on the shoulder and said, 'Come on Mukwe you can be in the front with me." That being the situation Anne climbed in the back beside Anton and although he didn't show it...a keen pulse of excitement shot through him. Ashlin then drove them through the city down to Glenelg beach, so that their 'wards' could see the great prospect that South Australia offered! They would not permit Anton and Mukwe out of the car however, and they all spent the time chatting. Anne was particularly interested in finding out more about them asking, "Hey! you guys, I know nothing about you. Where are you from; what do you do and how come you're in this position, with us looking after you?" They filled her in with all the basics, adding that the Australian Embassy had asked them for their assistance on the drug movement thing to Australia. "Throw me another one!, Anne replied, That's about the best precis I've ever heard. Ashlin has Mukwe told you any more than that brief?"

She added, "A little bit more I suppose" ... with some giggles from she and Mukwe.

Anton jumped in at this point and said, "Anne I promise you that I will give you the full account later, but I feel that there is much more to come."

There were many other good times, during this period in Adelaide, but to be on the safe side they each travelled with their appointed AFP Officer. Although Mukwe and Ashlin had definitely became Boyfriend / Girlfriend she had the duty of being constantly alert, so they weren't able to spends nights together. The other pair of Anton and Anne were a few weeks behind in their relationship, but at least Anton found out that she didn't have a current Man-friend, and seemed to enjoy being with him. However, she also took her duties very seriously, and nothing was left to chance.

One 'jaw-dropping' event did occur in Adelaide when the Girls had suggested to their two wards to put on some unusual jackets and hats, so they could take them down into the City and show the 'business district' to them. They were all on their way there when they noticed a 'bogan' looking character clearly looking for a car to steal. They witnessed him trying the driver's-side doors on two cars parked behind one-another: then missing a third, smashed open the door of a Holden and immediately disappeared below window level. "He is going to steal that car" Said Ashlin. To which Anne replied, "Yes but we can arrest him".

Without waiting, Mukwe grabbed Anton by the shoulder and said, "Come Ant!". They ran quickly to car and Anton ripped open the door fully — giving Mukwe the opportunity to give the intruder a massive push, which at the same time lifted both his legs. "Grab him by the boots and pull hard Anton — until he is on the ground", was the next shouted instruction from Mukwe. Once he was on the ground, both dropped on top of him to prevent him escaping. At that point the two AFP Officers arrived, and Anne instructed the offender, "You are under Arrest". The final 'cog on the gear' was that an on-looker who had witnessed it all, came up and advised that she had called the Police.

With the exception of the above event they were only permitted to go out to sports fixtures — still camouflaged — and then the four of them could not sit together. Tough!, But they did visit the Port, Mount Lofty, the Barossa Valley and Victor Harbour, but only got out of the car once the girls were certain that they had not been followed.

It was at Victor Harbour, when they had gone their separate ways and the Anne/Anton 'team' were crossing to the Penguin Island, that from a position close beside him she asked, "Do you still have a lady friend back in Aberfoyle?"

"No! I don't. But going back some, a girl by the name of Kim and myself were pretty close — but never committed — because she knew that I wanted to travel. She worked for the Immigration Department in the country, and not long after things went totally 'pear-shaped' she was transferred to the Capital. Thereafter our close relationship slowly dwindled. So, I'm as free as a Kite"

"Do you write to her or phone her?"

"Again, the answer is no. She is now engaged to a bloke that we have all met, and we are good friends with them. As is Peter, our Number 3. But funny that you should pursue this, because Kim and my cousin Kathy helped myself and Peter out of an impossible situation".

Oh! What was that?" asked Anne

"They engineered new identities for both of us — including all paperwork — but that must be a secret between us?'

Sure, I quite understand, but I'm glad that all of that is behind you. We can start on a fresh page".

Quick as a flash Anton added, "I hope that that page is going to be colourful, fast moving and never-ending."

Anne laughed, put her arm through Anton's and exclaimed, "So do I, with Bells on!"... And so they literally danced through the afternoon enjoying the tour. At one point when they were both kneeling down to closely inspect a nest with a baby penguin in it, they suddenly realised that their heads were together. In slowing turning their faces together they each fell into a deep, exquisite and lasting kiss, with arms ending-up round one-another.

Memories of the penguins; the hiking trail that they had taken and the impressive view of Kangaroo Island, persuaded them that this was a destination for them all to visit later.

Some three weeks into their South Australian sojourn, they were advised that the AFP Chief Officer was coming through to SA, and that they would all be required to meet him at the SA Headquarters. They travelled in separately, with Anton and Mukwe again hidden from view. Some of the news — via his reports — was good.

For example, the clean-up and arrests in both London and Sydney had been very effective. However, once the container of cleverly hidden Cocaine worth some $50million, had been seized in Sydney Harbour, the International Drug Lords had 'gone viral'. The Chief closed off by saying, "Note with full attention — it is however, accepted that Motor Cycle Gangs, or at least one such 'outfit', have been alerted to keep a lookout for the 'carriers' — Australia wide." An item of really good news was that the two little girls who were captive in the Sydney 'delivery house', had not only been rescued but were under auspicious State Care.

# CHAPTER 25

H is main message however, was that there needed to be a further move into an other State; either WA or preferably the Northern Territory. Both Ashlin and Anne were aghast at this, and Anne stood and suggested, "Roxby Downs will be a good option because it is way off the beaten track in South Australia, and the AFP are represented there."

The Federal Chief and the SA Senior Officer both agreed with this, and the latter went off to phone through this possibility and seek approval from the Officer stationed there. He returned to advise that it was 'on'. The AFP Chief took over and ordered, "Officers Anne and Ashlin this must be done right away, but you will need to move a day apart and report to the Olympic Dam Officer, as and when you have arrive there." This concluded the Meeting and the attendees returned to their appointed offices.

After the lunch break the AFP girls approached the Senior SA, AFP Officer and requested changes to their vehicles in the form of Four-Wheel Drive SUV's, and additional firearms — preferably 'automatics'. There was much consultation — particularly with the Armoury Officer, after which he addressed them, "We have agreed with your requests as there is a strong possibility you may need them. Also, I would like to thank you both for your dedication and — looking across towards Anton and Mukwe — I commend you two for 'hanging-in." He also paid them their agreed 'stipend' which made them even happier. Less need to live off the housekeeping awarded to Ashlin and Anne.

So once again back to the 'safe house' to pack-up, and for Ashlin and Mukwe to thank their Police guard. They travelled down to HQ accommodation that same evening, and left for Roxby Downs at 4.00am the next morning. Their reason for leaving in darkness, was that the Team in Adelaide sought to be particularly cautious: there were suspicions that the 'Bikies' had also commandeered a helicopter. Their trip of just over six hundred kilometres was hassle free, and they felt that they had arrived without being observed. Again, they moved to the first of two 'safe houses' and were assigned a South Australian Police guard.

Still in the 'safe house' in North Adelaide, Anne, Anton and their guard spent a day indoors — to reduce the risk of being observed — playing cards, chatting and watching this new thing TV. During the day Anne confided in Anton,

"I have a strange feeling that 'all is not well in the State of Denmark', with regard to Ashlin and I covering you two."

"Can you put your finger on why you are feeling that way," Anton asked.

"Look, we have been trained and have learnt that the whole 'Bikie Gang' and Drug Lord network, pay literally hundreds of informers all over the country for possible leaks that might have the slightest connection to 'actions' that they are planning". The three of them discussed the situation, and the Policeman likewise felt uneasy. So they decided to take turns guarding the house, whilst being fully armed and prepared.

Anne's ears must have been ringing when she had discussed it during the day, for the world seemed to explode at about 10.00pm that night. Again, high powered 'repeater' weapons were used, for what seemed like five minutes. If it had not been for the fact that all three occupants were in separate rooms — two of them at the back of the house, and the fact that Anne started to fire back towards the road, any one of them could have been killed or severely injured. This action on her part, then assisted by Anton and the Police guard could also have prevented a physical attack on the house. The lounge and dining areas presented a bomb scene, but the policeman did manage to get a 000 call through, after which Anne alerted AFP HQ, and they had a Team on the way, within minutes. The three occupants felt very glad that they were only minutes from the city, otherwise the attack could have lasted longer.

The Police were also on the scene very quickly, and the two Teams worked very effectively to collect all the information, that they could. One Officer by the name of James said, " On my way here I noted a vehicle speeding — almost out of control — in the other direction, approximately three kilometres from here. I was able to note its registration and have already reported it."

This action was professionally acknowledged, and the other team member responded by saying, "That should get the Investigation Office onto it pretty quickly."

Anne and Anton were asked to pack quickly and were taken back to AFP Head Quarters, to see out the rest of the night. Before going to their rooms there, they discussed the impending move to Olympic Dam, and how to achieve it without their exit from Adelaide being discovered. Also, in view of the deteriorating situation Anne confirmed, "I'm going to follow Ashlin's lead and, in addition to the issue of an SUV vehicle, I will be asking for an automatic weapon, as well as my revolver."

"Yes, and will you also please support me in asking for a long-barrelled rifle. I will be able to prove my proficiency with it."

When HQ opened, they were ready to consult with the relevant Officer handling movements out of the city. Upon putting their requests, he readily ticked off against the change of vehicle and Anne's automatic, but raised his eyebrows to the long-barrelled rifle concept. When asked why, Anne replied saying, "Both our Teams have been attacked, and there is a very real threat of being followed and engaged by guns."

He acknowledged that: turned to Anton and said "How do we know that you can use this rifle?"

"Because I have done National Service in the army, and besides, I am a Range Shooter."

"We'll have to check that first, and the Head of this Office will want to be in attendance as well." Anton accepted that, and the Officer phoned through to the "Chief's' Office. It was arranged for the lunch break.

At the appointed time, the two Senior Officers; Anne and Anton and a few other 'lunch goers', trooped down to the internal range. Anton was handed a rifle and he immediately asked "Is this loaded?" He was told that it was, and he continued by saying, "Good! the safety catch is on." He then checked the magazine and slid it firmly back into its recess. Finally, he stepped-up to the firing-point and said, "That target appears to me, to be at 80metres: I am going to aim low, because it is a long-range rifle." He clicked the 'safety' off again, then taking aim, fired five quickly repeated shots. At the end of these he clicked the 'safety' on again.

Although he had not hit the Bulls Eye, and was slightly above, he had achieved a grouping of about 4cm across, at Twelve Noon! The two Officers commended the achievement, and the Chief said, "It's yours for the duration." Quite secretly, and in the background, Anne was enthralled.

Once they had received everything Anne and Anton bunkered down separately until darkness, then after having had a meal they proceeded down to the Parking and climbed into the Toyota Pajero, allocated to them. The plan agreed with the Movements Officer was to drive right through the night, and hopefully, achieve Olympic Dam by mid morning of the following day: the difference being that they would take the 'little used' Easterly route, through Clare, Hawker, Maree and onto the Oodnadatta Track. Then come down to 'the Mine' from the North.

They headed North out of Adelaide to pick-up the Sturt Highway and continued on that until they were past Gawler, then they turned left onto the Clare/Hawker route. This seemed the appropriate moment for Anton to say, "We will need to split the driving on this trip: do you want to change over from driving now and have a 'kip', or should I start off with a sleep?" "Why don't you sleep first and I'll hand over to you at Hawker." Said Anne. "Okay!" With that Anton flattened out the front passenger seat and stretched back full length — putting his hand under her left leg. Both were comfortable and she made good time.

She woke him at Hawker after traversing the heavily forested area parallel with the rear of the coastal mountain range. They refilled with diesel; then he climbed into the driver's seat and Anne re-lifted the front passenger seat before climbing in; a move which surprised Anton but he did not question it. Anne got out her small cushion — put it between the front seats and said' "You wont mind, will you, if I stretch across and use your lap as my pillow?"

"Go-for-it my Sweet; can't think of anything better."

All went according to plan through this lower desert area and after they had caught up with Ashlin and Mukwe by phone, they all felt pretty satisfied that they had 'covered their tracks'. Anne and Anton moved into the second 'safe house', and another SA Policeman, Mike, was appointed to guard them.

Over the next month, they kept in regular touch with the AFP Officer stationed in Roxby Downs, but always using different phones, and at different times. Towards the end of that time, and with the approval of their Police Guards, they started to visit one another and whilst preparing lunch — separately from the group — on one of the first occasions, Ashlin hesitatingly said, "You've probably noticed Anne, that Mukwe and I are very close and unashamedly in love with one another: were you aware that Anton is a lot more than 'just fond of you'?"

"Yes! I am, and I feel exactly the same towards him. We are now serious Girl Friend / Boy Friend and just love to be together. He is just Terrific!"

Ashlin retorted, "Super! What a foursome we are: here grab a 'toot', and lets drink to this whole thing settling down completely". This they did, together, then went out to join the Boys.

On a later visit when all four were together in the lounge

of Anne's Safe House, with a map of the area open on the table, Anne expressed their visions, "Ashlin, what are your thoughts on a bit of an escape — by way of a mini holiday?"

"My thoughts match yours exactly but I suppose the two guys could be a bit 'backward' on it!!"

"What! said Mukwe, unless you two put some pedal to the gas, Anton and I might go alone. What do you reckon, Anton?"

"Yeh! I've been looking for a Five Star condominium, but outside of Adelaide they are pretty rare ...!!" There was much mirth over all this wrangling, and the girls undertook to put the question of such a Team test to the Olympic Dam Chief Officer.

Before proceeding with that Anne said, "Anton, Mukwe the place to go is unquestionably Arkaroola Resort." Pointing to an area on the map she added, "Here it is, right in the middle of the Flinders and the Gammon Ranges, and it is famous for its scenery and geological and astronomical history."

The Chief Officer and the SA Policemen approved of the trip, but advised extreme caution. The Officer would call for aerial cover, and also asked *them* to keep a close watch on the sky, as well as maintaining their usual low-profile image.

The trip was one of some six-to-seven hundred kilometres of main roads, side roads, highway tracks and 'low-way' tracks, plus about one kilometre of sealed road, mostly traversing low flat desert country with scanty scrub, cacti and spinifex. The lack of 'eye-catching' scenery gave them all, ample opportunity to talk about their earlier lives.

Ashlin asked, " Mukwe and Anton when did you guys first meet, and where was it in Africa?"

"When we were about four or five, and it was in the small Central African town of Aberfoyle."

"Gee! You were young hey — what did you do with your days; what did you get up to?"

Anton answered saying, "Apart from going to different schools, because there was still segregation then, we would spend a lot of time exploring around our town on our bikes and then our horses."

Anne intervened then saying, "Anton you mentioned that when you both finished school you each did Diploma type courses and were working in offices relative to your studies?"

"Yes, I was working in an Accountant's Office and Mukwe with the Government Agricultural Department."

Mukwe added, "We each had to take a year off to do National Service in the Army: that was pretty full-on and hectic."

"Then things went all wrong for you guys, in some way didn't it?"

"Sure thing! for Anton and his dog, Monty. I joined him and another mutual friend later."

Anne was intrigued and asked, "How did they go wrong Anton, if that's not exposing your private life?"

"No, It's okay! We have all known one another for quite

some time now, so you're entitled to know — but it is a secret between the four of us. There was a serious threat of Rabies in the country at the time, and dogs were supposed to have been tied up. Monty wasn't because he was at my feet, whilst I was studying. The Police were informed by some scumbag and came round to shoot the dog. I got in the way and he shot me instead. I do remember him panicking; jumping in his Jeep and racing back the ten kilometres to the Police Station, where he was thumped by a superior officer, I presume. They then twisted the episode, to a prosecution case that he had shot me in self-defence, when I had allegedly assaulted him. Crazy stuff".

The two girls were appalled and Anne asked, "Where did he shoot you?"

"High up in the left thigh — just here, replied Anton, pointing to it. I bandaged it as best I could, then phoned Mukwe to come and fetch us. I left the house at speed on my bike with Monty, and used a circuitous route to a bush rendezvous that we both knew. They did come back in force, but would never have been able to track us to that spot."

Mukwe entered the conversation, "Unfortunately when I got to the appointed spot he was in a bit of a bad way, so after re-bandaging I got him to a small country hospital, and took Monty home with me — and kept him tied-up!"

"The Doctor and Nurses there, fixed me up and I was able to catch-up on some sleep but the Police came and fetched me from there, and jailed me until my court case."

"How long was that for?" asked Anne.

"Three weeks, and it was in the jail that I met Peter again. We had known one another through school days. And that was so fortunate, because he escaped first — at night — and it was he who opened the window of the Courthouse on that epic day."

Ashlin immediately interrupted and said, "You mentioned to Anne that you defended yourself in Court. Wouldn't it have been better to have had a lawyer?"

"No! Definitely not. For two reasons:-. One, that it was such a simple case. Apart from the fact that I hadn't tied-up Monty, no crime had been committed. The shooting of me was an accident. The policeman's Superiors had concocted this ridiculous prosecution of assault. Two, a Defence Lawyer would have lost because I could see that the Jury were petrified of the Senior Police and the Magistrate."

"How horrible, and so how did you escape?" Asked Anne.

"Through the window that Peter had opened, replied Anton. I knew from having lived in the town all my life, that I could get to the cover of the first house garden within thirty seconds. None of the police perceived that. I made it, with only one chaser seeing me, and I soon lost him. No one has ever seen me since!! I made my diverse way to meet up with Peter and we then used the Aberfoyle River to escape the town and ultimately join-up with Mukwe and Monty, at the confluence with the next River."

Mukwe enlarged on that saying, "The confluence of the

two rivers breaks through a high ridge line, and on the other side of that the country was absolutely wild. That's where we were able to set-up our 'Hideaway' in a large cave, such that we weren't even visible from the sky."

The two girls were fascinated at the differences in their respective growing-up experiences, and the different culture in Central Africa. They were also astounded at what had happened to Anton, and the change in direction that was initiated by the event. They loved the constant references to Monty, and nearly cried when Mukwe related the attack on the ranch house and the fact that he was mortally wounded. The two guys then got all that they could from the girls, on their early lives; schooling, and training for the AFP.

Anton opened this aspect saying, "Girls, I arrived on the scene here in South Australia somewhat later than Muk, and have no idea of where either of you grew-up; of your schooling, or of your later years. I don't know whether Muk knows, but I would be very interested to know?"

Mukwe very quickly added, "You have only told me very little Ashlin, so I would also love to hear a bit more."

"I am an islander girl, from way out Tonga way in the South Pacific. My early schooling was there and we loved the open-air life, spending most of our time on the beaches or in the water. It was mainly the men and boys who did the fishing, but we liked to watch them, and became quite good cooks of fish, under our Mother's tuition. Yours was pretty different though, wasn't it, Anne?"

"Yes! Very different said Anne. I was born in India where my Dad was fairly senior in one of the large Steel Foundries, near Calcutta. I can't remember anything about it as we left to return to the UK at the end of the war, when I was only two. The family moved again, within three years and came to Australia, where he worked at the Port Kembla Steel Works. All my schooling was in Wollongong and after a gap year taking my parents back to Scotland, I returned and started my training in Canberra, with the AFP."

Mukwe asked, "When did you come across to Australia Ashlin?"

She replied, "Tonga had a bit of a bad time, and my Dad needed to come across and get a better job here. It was just about when I was entering my second year of High School, so we all came with him and I finished school in Queensland. After that I joined Anne in Canberra."

At their final stop before reaching Arkaroola Anton and Mukwe had a short and secret 'hanna hanna' and agreed on a little dual-presentation to Anne and Ashlin. Anton walked across to the car, opened the door and while he was searching his pack the two girls got up with Anne announcing, "Right Guys! Last stage to go."

Mukwe quickly intervened and said, "We're not ready yet." Before the girls could argue the point Anton came back and handed Mukwe a small parcel — retaining a similar one for himself. They then presented the small gifts to each of their Girlfriends: great pleasure and excitement when they opened up the White Cliffs opals.

Over the course of this break, all of Anton's and Mukwe's later experiences came to the fore, and the girls finally found out how and why they were involved in both the diamond smuggling, and how that led to the drug smuggling involvement.

During the whole of this, they all had a wonderful time making sure that they viewed every well-known site. The high desert mountain ranges leapt out of the deep forested valleys showing steep stone cliffs of smooth granite, or an incredible jumble of rounded rocks. They were also fortunate enough to frequently see Mobs of small Mountain Wallabies.

Only one 'slightly' strange incident occured, when Mukwe got a strong impression that they were being observed by a seedy looking character. However, he soon disappeared and all seemed to be back on course. The incredibly steep 4WD track up to the summit of a conical hill in the North Flinders Range, and the fantastic and distant view of Lake Frome, was the highlight.

They also loved the 'beaut' Motel, at which they stayed. For the first time, Mukwe and Ashlin stayed in one of the rooms, while Anton and Anne stayed in another. On a number of occasions there were distinct delays in the mornings, before the two teams got together — with sly smiles between them: each couple was definitely becoming 'an Item'!

Before returning, they phoned through to advise the timing, and were again warned to be on an especial lookout for strange behaviour from any vehicle. This immediately brought back memories to Anton and Mukwe, of the strange 'intruder' of some days before. The Chief would also put a helicopter into the air, after a couple of hours of their travel time.

All went well until they turned off the Coober Pedy link road and started to travel South towards Olympic Dam. Anne and Anton were sitting in the back of the vehicle and while checking through the back window for sight of the helicopter, Anton noticed a Harley Davidson motor cycle coming up from way behind at speed, with two men dressed in complete black, upon the bike.

Instinctively he shouted forward, "Motor cyclists in black coming up Ashlin; when I say 'Brake', don't argue; brake very hard and straight". Sure enough, as the motor cycle approached the rear of their SUV, the passenger in black, drew his revolver. As it reached the rear window, Anton shouted "Brake!" There was a loud screech from the tyres, and two, even louder blasts from the revolver, aimed at the driver, but because the shooter hadn't anticipated the hard braking, the shots went over the bonnet of their vehicle. The shooter tried one more shot but that also missed.

The motor cycle raced away, but not before Ashlin

shouted to Mukwe, "Take a shot at them." He was able to lean out with the automatic, and chase them with a series of rapid shots. That made the motor cycle go even faster. The foursome hoped that the helicopter may have witnessed, what had happened. They continued their journey with extreme care, in case of an ambush, but got to AFP HQ without further mishap.

Whilst still travelling, two-way radio contact was made with the helicopter, and although it had not witnessed the attempted attack on their vehicle, the crew had noticed a motor cycle, with two persons in black, far exceeding the speed limit. For that reason, it had been photographed and HQ would just have to wait, to see if the registration number could be checked out.

Anne took the opportunity to speak with the helicopter crew, "Please check each road travelling south from Arkaroola for a possible motor-cycle crew in black".

The incident was reported to Adelaide, and they in turn passed the news on to AFP Canberra. The Roxby Downs Officer got the foursome to attend a meeting right away, such that they could all discuss the next moves for each Team. It was patently clear that the Olympic Dam area was not a safe option, any longer.

While they were considering options a phone call came through from Canberra, which effectively delivered some good news, as well as some bad news. The good news was that the FBI in America had also been very busy, and had made multiple high-ranking Drug Lord' arrests, which it was felt, would force the sector into deep hiding. Scotland Yard in England, had also continued their investigations in the UK with promising success. The bad news was that all the 'gangs' already on the move, in Australia, would not yet have heard about this international news. Therefore, Canberra also wanted the Teams to move on, and that they must have a policeman with each of the teams.

That settled it, to the disappointment of both Ashlin, and Anne — where would they go, to be safe? The two teams were each taken back to their respective 'safe houses', where they, and their Police guards were told to re-pack everything, and return to the Base at Roxby Downs.

While packing, the girls got everyone together so that they could confer on the situation. That they would move separately was a 'taken' fact, but it was imperative that each Team covered the other. To this end, Ashlin and Anne wanted to know for sure, what range their 'boyfriends Chips' would cover, and be interpreted perfectly. Mukwe said, "to-date we have been successful up to ten kilometres, as 'the crow flies."

The two policemen looked at one another in an enquiring way, and the one asked "What is this about chips?"

A compact but good explanation was given to them, and other said, "this I want to see, but it sounds fantastic."

Mukwe then made the point that the vehicles should be

fitted with Two-Way radio communication, with Base; the helicopters and the other vehicle.

Anton finalised that issue by adding, "Provided that we are all issued with a rarely used radio channel." They were all in full agreement with the suggestions.

# CHAPTER 26

**W**hen they all, separately, got back to the Base in Rox-by Downs these requests were put to the AFP Offi-cer, and he was able to smile, turn around, and pick-up a box which he then presented saying "Your Two-Way Radio equipment, for both cars! It also struck us here, how important such contacts must be. Now, the first to leave here will be Officer Ashlin with Mukwe and Policeman Ken. The other team will follow, about half an hour behind, and attempt to keep within ten-to-twenty kilometres. Our helicopter will cover you to the border with the Northern Territory. From there an NT helicopter will take over."

"The channel that each of your cars must use is Channel 11, and you Ashlin will be called up as 11ZULU. Anne your vehicle will have the same channel, but your 'Call-Sign' will be 11YANKEE. Any questions, so far?" Because they had all discussed these safeguards already, the only question was from Ashlin:-

"What will the call signs be for the two Helicopters?"

"Ours will be 11ALFA1 and the NT one will be 11ALFA2. He continued with his instructions: Because there have been various attempts to eliminate Anton and Mukwe, and the rest of you as well, we want you to be prepared to defend yourselves by 'force of arms'. If either of your vehicles come under fire, take full cover behind it, but engage the attackers. As soon as that situation is observed from the air, and probably conveyed by your 'Inter' radio contact, the helicopter will also bring fire to bear, on the attacking vehicle. In such a situation, you will be defending your own lives. Make the defence work!"

As they were completing preparations to move and the Chief was about to contact 'Air Wing', a call came through from the Police at Port Augusta, to advise that the identified Motor Cycle was impounded, and the riders arrested. They were being taken down to Adelaide to be charged. No riders had been identified on other roads.

Loud 'back-slapping' and elation, all round.

'Ready to move' and both Teams were advised that as soon as they were out on the road, they would be able to see the helicopter flying high over them. Ashlin's Team left, travelling SW towards the Stuart Highway, followed within half-an-hour by Anne's team. Sure enough each of them picked-up the helicopter — a mere speck above them.

Each turned right onto the highway and made their way

towards first stop — Coober Pedy. No strange vehicles or helicopters were seen. They made their first stop by nightfall and were greeted and accommodated by the Police. Their own police guards took turns to guard them through the night, as well as an extra guard, stationed in the town.

To Anton and Mukwe It was a great pity that they had to leave promptly the next day, with Anton consoling, "This Coober Pedy joint has much to offer, by way of sunken Showhouses, potential trips into the Mines and of course, the wonder of their Opals."

These observations were virtually ignored because they had to cover over four hundred kilometres to the next stop, which was Kulpera Roadhouse, just inside the Northern Territory.

It was a long, straight road through semi-desert most of the way, but at least this highway was sealed! Anton said to the other two in the car, "This is like travelling over a large Billiard Table — except that 'the table' is ten kilometres in every direction! Just as well the scrub and coarse dry grasses are gentle on the eyes!!"

When drawing fuel half way up the highway, they sensed that they were being observed. Once on the highway again, Ashlin radioed through to the helicopter, "11ALFA1, 11ALFA1, this is 11ZULU, how do you read, over?" Her call was acknowledged a few seconds later –

"11ZULU, 11ALFA1, loud and clear, Over."

"11ALFA1, please keep a special lookout for a pursuing Vehicle or Motor cycle. Over and Out."

Nothing followed them, but they were nevertheless nervously suspicious: the more so, when they crossed the border into the Northern Territory, and reached the 'Road House'. Here they were met by an NT Policeman, who introduced himself, "Hi! I'm Nate of the Northern Territory Police. I'm to take over from your South Australian Guard. I've also been instructed to advise you that a Northern Territory helicopter will arrive tomorrow morning, to escort you through to Alice Springs."

Ashlin and Anne welcomed him; introduced the other members of their teams, then Ashlin said, "Great to meet you Nate, and thanks for coming down to join us. Ken and Mike your SA compatriots will also stay with us until we get to Alice Springs. You will be the third Guard for the night."

After a pleasant dinner, which included him, the foursome talked long into the night. As the foreboding increased, Anne said, "I insist that Anton and I do the first 'internal' guard of the night, until 1.00.am — to supplement your external police guards. Ashlin and Mukwe will take over from us and guard internally through to breakfast."

Next morning, while waiting for the extra helicopter to arrive, Anton piped-up, "Listen all of you. Our two vehicles will be driving much closer to each other today, so that Mukwe and I can keep in constant touch through our Chips." Everyone was reassured by this.

When the two helicopter pilots did arrive, discussion ensued on tactics for the day, which culminated in Ashlin saying, " Anne and I have been put in charge of this move by the Australian Federal Police, and if circumstances determine a change of tactics, you helicopter Pilots must accept that change — no questioning."

Anne added, "We are expecting trouble, and we do ask you Pilots to particularly keep a watch for a very low-flying plane, or helicopter."

They gave the pilots half-an-hour to get to their craft, and to take off, then Ashlin's team drove out onto the highway, heading North. Fifteen minutes later, Anne's team followed, with Anton immediately tapping Mukwe a green pulse, which was returned — by arrangement. It was only a short distance on the highway, to Erindunda, where a prominent side road turned West to Uluru and further. As Ashlin's 'team vehicle' was approaching this point, they received an urgent alert from the NT helicopter: "11ZULU, how do you hear me? Over.

Ashlin replied, "11ALFA2, loud and clear. Over."

The Pilot continued, "11ZULU, suspicious white station wagon approaching from the North. Over."

"11ALF2, thanks. We will turn left — West as if making for Uluru. Please keep on call. Over and Out."

Mukwe immediately tapped two red pulses to Anton, then in morse-code, "Utmst urg..cy, B.ng foll..wd, West to Ulu. Out." Anton acknowledged with two red pulses.

No sooner had he done this, when their helicopter called Anne, "11YANKEE. How do you hear me? Over.

Officer Anne replied, "11ALFA1, loud and clear. Over."

"11 YANKEE, the white Station Wagon has also turned West. Over."

She acknowledged and said, "11ALFA1, we are plus/minus five kilometres from the turn and will follow. Please keep in touch — Over and Out." They immediately sped-up to ensure that they maintained the ten-kilometre separation.

When Anne's team turned left on to the Uluru Road, Anton used his Chip pulsing two green to Mukwe, who acknowledged with a green pulse. Anton then pulsed using morse code, "We are now Bhind the wh SW and in radio cntct wth Heli."

All three vehicles proceeded West at some speed — this part of the highway being sealed, and very straight. Anne was travelling the fastest, in order to make sure that they remained in contact distance with Ashlin. Coming to the top of a slight rise in the road, they caught sight of the Toyota, for the first time, and she slowed down slightly as this seemed to be their optimum distance for control purposes. Anton immediately double-pulsed Mukwe in red, and coded a message to him — "Have them in sight at approx. 4 kms. Keep chk on yr rv mirror."

Very soon after that, and on a continued straight stretch of the road, the policeman in Ashlin's vehicle did catch sight of the following vehicle for the first time. He and Mukwe estimated it to be five kilometres behind. Ashlin immediately radioed the helicopter, " 11ALFA2, how do you read. Over."

"11ZULU, loud and clear. Over."

11ALFA2, We have sighted the white Station Wagon in our rear-view mirror, four or five kilometres back. Do you have anything else? Over."

"11ZULU, Yes! They are gaining on you, so speed up. However, about ten kilometres ahead and after a distinct right bend there is a turn to the left, which leads down to the Gunbarrel Highway in South Australia. On your map this about fifteen kilometres short of Curtain Springs, and is referred to as the Lassiter Highway. Our advice is to take this, and an advantage is that a few hundred metres down, you will travel into some thick bush which will give cover. Over."

Ashlin responded, "11ALFA2, Thanks we will comply. Over".

11ZULU, "We will now advise YANKEE11. Over and Out."

Anne's team acknowledged the move,

Ashlin recognized the bend and was ready for the left turn down to the Gunbarrel Highway, which she executed. Soon they were in the tree line, and out of sight. The suspect Toyota tore round the bend and carried straight on — unaware that Ashlin's SUV had turned-off.

The AFP helicopter called Ashlin, "11ZULU, how do you read. Over."

"11AIR1, Loud and clear. Over."

"11ZULU, the white Toyota Station Wagon has carried

straight on towards Curtain Springs. No! No! Cancel. Damn, they have realised something and are turning back. Proceed away at speed: we'll get back to you. Over and Out." Anne's Team were brought-up-date, and told to slow down, while the situation was evolving. She radioed that she understood, and was standing-by.

The Toyota did turn down to the right and South, as if in pursuit. This was soon verified, and with the best possible news — first to Ashlin's team and then to Anne's. The radio message from the helicopter was "11ZULU, Continue towards Amata, and keep going — we will also be covering you. YANKEE11 will also advised of this and are following within 8kms. Good news: the Alice Springs helicopter have sighted the foreign aircraft, and are forcing it down. RAAF very close, and will take that over. Over and Out."

Thus the pursuit — followed by the pursuit, continued: through Amata and on towards Kanypi.

Anne's Team discussed the impending crisis point with increasing concern and tension, as they sped along the dirt road. Before either of their vehicles either lost control, or ran out of fuel, something had to be done. Anne said, "Anton use your chip to get in touch with Mukwe."

This he did, double-pulsing Mukwe in red, then in morse code — "Ash to stp SW in brdside: All out and defnd frm Bhind. Over and Out." This was acknowledged by Mukwe in red.

Anne then signalled the helicopter, "11ALFA1, how do

you hear? Over." They accepted as 'loud and clear' and she continued, "Team 1 will be stopping and defending from behind their vehicle. Please be forceful in defence of Team 1. Over and Out."

Four or five kilometres on the western side of Amata, a seemly good defence spot loomed up, and Mukwe said, "Do it here Ashlin". She executed a rough but effective broadside to the left of the road.

They all exited the vehicle on the far side, and Ashlin loudly ordered them, "Make sure that your weapons are fully loaded and ready." They were reassured when they heard the helicopter screaming down towards them from the direction of Amata.

More or less at the same time, the white 'Gang Toyota' surged around the corner about four hundred metres away, and slid to a violent stop. Three armed men leapt out, with the leader shouting, "Now we've got ya: ya bloody bunch of 'no-hopers'." They immediately started rapid firing at Ashlin's SUV.

They returned fire, and one of the gangsters at the back shouted in pain and seemed to have been wounded. This did not stop the advance though, but rather increased the level of fire towards the SUV, with a very large man running forward. Suddenly Ashlin gasped with pain and fell backwards. Mukwe leapt up in fury and screamed at him, "You bastard". He scored a direct hit on the large man in front. The SA policeman was also being very effective and managed to wound the third attacker. Their advance started to falter. At that precise moment the AFP helicopter — having swerved to the side — also brought fire to bear on the attackers, and they retreated back to their Toyota, that was already turning to head back the way they had come.

In simultaneous moments, Mukwe dived down to take Ashlin's upper body in his arms, and to comfort her, and the policeman opened the door of their SUV and got on the radio, "11ALFA2, serious injury — please put out 000 ambulance call. Also contact YANKEE11, to advise that the Toyota is now speeding back towards them, and to execute the same broadside that we did, and to defend from behind. Please assist them as well. Over and Out."

This was done in good time, and they jumped out behind the vehicle fully armed, with Anton selecting the long-range rifle. He had noted a large stump on the other side of the road, but first said, "I'm going across there — pointing to the stump — you and Mike stay behind the SUV and defend yourselves." He then ran across to hide behind the stump.

Anne still had access to the two-way radio and received the incoming information: "11YANKEE, do you read? Over." She replied in the affirmative, and 11ALFA1 continued, The Gang Toyota is a kilometre away, and coming at speed. Engage it with full power, because Ashln has been wounded, and the occupants are heavily armed. Over."

She acknowledged, "11ALFA1, thank you. We will comply. Over and Out." She was shattered and even more determined to stop the gangsters. As the Toyota came around the bend ahead and started braking, Anton took careful aim and shot directly at the driver. The vehicle lost speed and went out of control, with Anne and her policeman continuing to shoot at it. Just before it stopped two of the occupants leaped out and started rapid firing at the SUV: one of them was the large member, who was extremely aggressive. To Anton's horror, Anne stood up in full view and mowed him down with her automatic. Between Anton and Mike, they took out the other one. Then the final act in the saga was the helicopter firing on, and shattering the Toyota. The helicopter then came into land.

During that sequence Anton had made his way back to the car, and discovered to his dismay that Anne had received a slight bullet wound above her left ear: like three inches from extinction. He took her into his arms to calm her, but she just dissolved into tears. When she got over it, she tearfully said, "I was terrified for all of us, especially you running across to take cover behind a mere stump."

"I'm also desperately worried about Ashlin, who has been wounded, and would like to get across to her as quickly as possible."

The policeman said, "Not before I clean, and put a protective patch on the wound above your ear."

Once this had been done, and the helicopter pilot and co-pilot had come across, Anne was told that she and Anton could leave, to join Ashlin and Mukwe. The policeman would help them to clean-up the gangster mess, and with them, await a large helicopter group coming down from Alice Springs. Anne took Mike's arm and said, "Thanks Mate. If it hadn't been for you, Anton and these Pilots, we could have been in real strife."

He replied saying, "What about you. That was real gutsy stuff. Congratulations and I hope that the wound heals quickly."

They left in her SUV and within fifteen minutes were at the site of the first battle. The ambulance helicopter was in the process of landing, so Anne was able to get to Ashlin and take her into her arms, and hug her tightly. Her wound was serious, but now that the ambulance had arrived she would be given the necessary paramedic treatment, that would hold her in good stead until she reached Alice Springs Hospital.

She came across to Anton, who was examining the scene and told him that she would like to go with Ashlin — basically to hold her friend's hand. He just hugged her and said "Not before you answer one very fundamental question of mine?"

Anne said "Yeah okay! What is it?"

Anton said "Will you marry me?"

She loosened herself from his clasp, stepped back, looked up at him and with a great smile said "Yes". They hugged closely and lovingly kissed one another.

With that wonderful accomplishment, Anton walked back with her to the Ambulance Helicopter, where Mukwe was helping the paramedics get Ashlin into the stretcher recess. Anne asked the pilot if she could accompany her friend, and was given permission. It was a sad, but hopefully short separation, as Mukwe and Anton watched the helicopter head North.

Apart from catching-up with Ken, who was able to say that there was nothing further to do at this site, they all chatted over what had taken place.

Mukwe said, "Ken, I would like to thank you for all you have done — above the normal 'Call of Duty'." Anton likewise thanked him, then they took the SUV 'ZULU11' back to the second attack site and the four helped one another with their part in the clean-up there. In addition to expecting the large helicopter team arrival, a tow-truck had also been ordered to tow/load the remains of the Toyota back to Adelaide, for forensic examination.

The smaller of the helicopters was available to take Anton and Mukwe through to Alice Springs, and this left just before nightfall.

# CHAPTER 27

I n the helicopter and heading North, Anton and Mukwe were behind the pilot and co-pilot who were both in deep conversation. It was an opportunity for Anton to quietly say, "Mate, I must tell you that I have become engaged to Anne and would very much like you to be my Best Man." To his alarm, Mukwe turned down the offer.

Before any protests, Mukwe quickly said, "So have Ashlin and I: my preference would be that we have a double-wedding." Hand shakes and claps on the back, which helped them to get through all their recent experiences, without a fatality, making it a very pleasant journey.

When they arrived in Alice Springs, they thanked the pilots for their part in the 'contact' and for their generosity, and made their way to the front of the Terminal. There they caught a taxi straight to the Hospital.

The important thing was to get the latest information on

Ashlin's condition, and they were directed to the surgical waiting-room. Unexpectedly, Anne was still there and they joined her. She informed them, "Ashlin is in surgery and the wound is not life threatening. However, I was very glad to have been able to accompany her on this critical trip and feel that it has helped her immeasurably, to have me with her." Both guys — but especially Mukwe — were extremely happy to hear this news. She continued, "Anton please come and sit next to me." She immediately put her arm around his shoulder.

They then brought her up to date, with Mukwe saying, "Both attack sites have been cleaned-up and the larger helicopter arrived with eight officers aboard. In addition an order has been put out for a tow-truck to take back the remains of the Toyota Station Wagon."

All of them waited the few hours into the night, until one of the surgeons came out and gave them the good news, "The surgery had been successful, and Ashlin is being moved into High Care. You will all be welcome to come back in the morning."

Three very relieved friends went out, and returned to AFP Head Quarters in the town. They were given accommodation there, with the two guys taking one room and Anne another. When everybody had left, Anne asked Mukwe to take over her room, and moved in with Anton.

The next morning before going to the hospital, they were allowed in to see the Alice Springs Chief Officer. He was not fully informed on the occurrence of the previous day in upper South Australia, but was as interested as they were, in the final outcomes of that frenetic event. He therefore placed a call to Adelaide while they were all with him, and spoke for some minutes with the Senior AFP Officer in Adelaide, then handed the phone to Anne, saying "The Chief would like to speak to you." Anne thanked him and took the phone.

The first thing that the officer wanted to know was how Ashlin was, and how she, Anne, had come through the terrible experience. She brought him up to date on their health, and he was very relieved. He then said, "Essentially three of the four gang members are dead and the fourth seriously wounded. He is under police guard in hospital, and will be heavily questioned, once he is well enough. While the sites are still under Police guard they have been cleared, and the wreck of the attack vehicle has been towed away."

Anne also requested, "Please contact SA Police HQ, and record all of our thanks in respect of Officers Ken and Mike, for their dedicated duty."

The Chief replied, "Yes I will and thanks for that, and Oh! Please tell your 'subjects' to collect their earnings, when you come down to the City."

*** 

Off to the hospital to re-unite with Ashlin, whom they were allowed to see. Although subdued, she was delighted to see them, and gave Mukwe a well-earned kiss, then asked,

"Anne how is your wound coming along?" Anne hugged her and told her that she was the important one, in the current situation. The next splendid announcement from Ashlin, while looking directly at Anne was, "I must tell you that Mukwe and I are engaged."

Anne let out a delighted laugh and said "So are Anton and I!" Everyone (except Ashlin) jumped around with sheer pleasure. After that they quietened down and just enjoyed being together again. On the subject of engagement rings, it was decided to wait until Ashlin came out of hospital, so that the girls could do some serious searching.

This suddenly brought back memories of the celebration in Antwerp, after the success of the trap, and of the Australian Diamond Mine CEO, with whom they had talked that evening. In an encouraging tone Anton said, "Take a careful look at Argyle diamonds, as they are 'dinky di' Australian."

The Hospital kept Ashlin within their confines for ten days, while her friends remained in Alice Springs to keep her company. During that period, much was discussed as to when a joint-wedding could take place; who would be Bridesmaids, and the Best Men. These issues immediately brought up questions of great distance — both East Coast of Australia, Scotland and Central Africa: all Parents; Peter and Elle plus Kim and Trevor –wherever they were in Australia. However, once the guys had worked out their finances, they realised that they could fly all the important people out to Australia.

At last they could all start to give detailed attention to every aspect of arranging a wedding: doubled-up, at that! All family members and friends of the girls had to be considered; plus their dresses, and those for their brides-maids; plus the selection of the appropriate church, and the wedding reception. On the other side, who to invite and bring out from Africa — Peter and fiancé, and Mukwe's friend from University; plus both their sets of Parents, and hopefully Colin and Carry, Jacky and Mel, plus Rick/lil and Kathy. The girls thanked Anton and Mukwe for settling on Australia, so that all the arrangements could be started.

When Ashlin was released from hospital they all returned to Adelaide, after offering their thanks to the Alice Springs Officers and Personnel, for their attention and services. Ashlin and Anne returned to work, but immediately applied for a short stint of leave to fit in with Mukwe's and Anton's plans. It might have been difficult for the Chief to grant this, except that he and many of the Officers had been invited to the wedding! From then onwards it was down to AFP work. It was extremely pertinent and interesting to both of them, to be given copies of the initial report on tackling the drug problem in Australia. This was from the date that Ashlin was appointed with the other NSW Officer and Policemen, to protect Anton and Mukwe. This document was studied by all of them, with Ashlin and Anne suggesting extra points that their Chief should consider.

Anton and Mukwe had booked flights for each couple to

Paris, and when the day arrived they headed out to Adelaide Airport for their pre-nuptial holiday. The flights were long but enjoyable and the girls were astounded that they could watch TV during the flight, or listen to their favorite music. They arrived as eager as puppies to take this historical and beautiful city, into their joint hearts. After a night of love and glorious comfort — including breakfast brought to the rooms — the two guys informed the girls that they had been planning the next stage. Anton announced, "Okay! You've each got three guesses as to where we are going first, and where we are going second?" Unsurprisingly Ashlin and Anne very quickly nailed number one, Versailles, but couldn't for the life of them, guess number two. A memorable day was spent at Versailles, both through the historic buildings, and through the acres of beautiful gardens.

When they got back to their hotel, and were enjoying the evening meal, Mukwe said, "Girls, tomorrow we will be heading off for Belgium. The girls tried to resist, saying that they hadn't seen enough of Paris yet, but he insisted. We'll come back again — no arguments."

They hired a smart Citroen and drove off, West of North towards Belgium, taking in the lovely rural scenery, towns and rivers of the Somme area. Once over the border, Anne asked, "Is the purpose of this trip, to pay homage to all the soldiers, who fell in the Ypres theatre, during the First World War?" The Boys agreed that that was part of the reason, and they were all solemn travelling through the

Villers Bretonneux area, which although it seemed to have recovered wonderfully from the desolation wrought upon it, did have numerous large Military Cemetreies.

On arrival in Antwerp they parked in the City centre. Anton then said, "We need to go into that Bank; come-on everyone."

There was some opposition, with Anne saying, "Jesus!" "Anton this is a long way to have come to an ATM."

"Rest assured, we will all be returning to Paris, and then, wherever else you want to go." Eventually they all climbed out and accompanied Anton and Mukwe into the building. They did not go to the Tellers, even though Ashlin voiced that suggestion.

Eventually a particular Service Officer was free, and the Boys walked towards her, with the Girls in-tow, and each produced a document from their respective wallets, which they handed to her. She said in French, "Please follow me to the Deposits sanctum." She took them into the deep corridors below the Bank, where she eventually stopped, handed Anton and Mukwe a key each and pointing — continued, "Those are the two safes — please return the keys to me when you come up through that exit."

The boys opened the safes and produced two neat wooden boxes, beautifully crafted and polished. Anton passed his onto Anne, and Mukwe his onto Ashlin. The Girls were highly intrigued at the gifts but were ecstatically overcome when the boxes revealed stunning Diamond Necklaces. Not only were they genuine Botswana diamonds, but each neck-lace had Seven carats of the exquisite stones. Each of the Boys then had the delightful pleasure of hanging each of the necklaces, around the neck of their 'Beloved Sweethearts'.

On the trip back to Paris, they all discussed what they would still like to explore in the city, and what entertain-ment they wouldn't miss for anything. Seven wonderful days were spent taking in all aspects and attractions of the Capital. When back in their rooms or enjoying meals or coffee, the guys were trying to gently impress upon the girls that they would like to meet their respective parents. This was difficult distance-wize as they only had a further week, so in the end it was decided that Ashlin and Mukwe would fly back to Queensland to meet her family, whilst Anne and Anton would head across the Channel to visit her parents in Scotland.

"See ya back in Adelaide!"

# EPILOGUE

The couples met up again once they were back in Adelaide, and on the Monday it was back to work for Ashlin and Anne. Outside of the AFP Offices however, planning for the Weddings started to progress apace. Anton and Mukwe had phoned Peter and Des the Uni/Soccer friend in Central Africa, to advise that they were 'Wanted Men', and to enquire when they would each be available to come out to Adelaide to fulfill their 'duties'. School holidays were coming-up back there within the next ten weeks, which gave those in Adelaide a first aiming mark. Phone calls were also made to all parents, to Colin and Carry and to Jacky and Mel, inviting all of them to the wedding. Anton had to do much chasing after Kim and Trevor, and to his delight found that they had just moved to Australia. After much searching he was able to find them, and guaranteed that he would get them to the double-wedding. When not seriously at work, both Ashlin and Anne invited their parents, and a list was made to complete the numbers that they would dearly love to see.

Everything came together miraculously, with the overseas guests arriving at different times over a period of a week, and everybody assembled in Adelaide for the day of the Weddings.

Having effectively been 'Bush' for some time, Anton and Mukwe were astounded at the beautiful dresses of the two wedding parties, and at how smart all the men looked. Their brides didn't keep them waiting too long, and were unquestionably magnificent in their wedding gowns. The wedding ceremonies would remain etched on their respective memories forever, and the reception was just as wonderful. After tossing their garters the two girls and their husbands were sent on their journey, under a 'snow storm' of confetti. Initially they only took the 'long weekend' away, then returned to spend more time with their beloved families, as well as returning to work.

Gradually everybody returned to their respective country, and normal lives, and the two married couples couldn't thank them enough for coming. Promises were made to all sets of parents, and to the 'Africa mob' that future trips to visit them were planned for the foreseeable future, which would include at least one Game Park Tour.

# ALPHABETICAL GLOSSARY

## EXPLANATIONS — FRIENDLY SLANG WORDS

| | |
|---|---|
| Bant | Shortened first name of Bantry |
| Beaut | Fantastic, enjoyable, etc |
| Bikkies | Biscuits |
| Brekkie | Breakfast |
| Bush | Rural woodland/grassland (Australian) |
| Bushie | Those who frequent the above! |
| Casevaced | Casualty evacuated |
| Chuffed | Very pleased |
| Dassies | an African version of Rock Rabbits |
| Dayskies | Day students (opposite of Boarders) |
| Dinky-di | Genuine (Australian) |
| Donga | Eroded gully |
| Dorp | Small town (in Afrikaans) |
| Esky | Portable food/drink freezer |
| Fellicky | Leather pouch to hold catapult stone |

| | |
|---|---|
| Fibs | Lies |
| Gunck | Rubbish |
| hanna hanna | Intense discussion |
| Heebee Jeebees! | Sense of confused fear |
| 'hit-it-off' | Instant enjoyment of one another's company |
| Katty | Catapult |
| Kinder | Kindergarten Class |
| Newby | First-year boarder at High School |
| nouse | Sense / enlightenment |
| Nout | Nothing achieved |
| Nyaminyani | Zambezi River God |
| Out of their minds | Approaching drunkenness |
| Over-nighter | Night camp-stop |
| Punce | Fool |
| Rinkals | Spitting Cobra |
| Sadza | Corn meal dough (African) |
| Sortee | part-of table game |
| Tackies | Cheap running shoes |
| Throw me another one | You must be joking (Australian slang) |
| Uni. | University |
| Up-the-drag | Further along the main road |
| Veld | Rural woodland/grassland (Southern Africa) |
| Ya | Yes ( Dutch & German) |

www.ingramcontent.com/pod-product-compliance
Lightning Source LLC
Chambersburg PA
CBHW020258120726
47904CB00001B/254